I0742487

Old Enough
To Know Better

One Woman's Journey To Freedom

Alfreda S. Jackson

Legacy Word Publishing, LLC

Alexandria, Virginia

Legacy Word Publishing
1767 Lakewood Ranch Blvd #182
Bradenton, Florida 34211
www.legacywordpublishing.com

Please contact publisher@legacywordpublishing.com about special discounts for bulk purchases.

Publisher's Note: This is a work of fiction based on a true story. Due to the sensitive nature of the content, many of the event details, names, characters, and places have been changed.

Old Enough To Know Better/ Alfreda S. Jackson. -- 1st ed.
ISBN - 978-1-7320592-0-7
ISBN - 978-1-7320592-1-4 (ebook)

In loving memory of my grandmother, Elmira J. Smart.

Anyone who belongs to Christ is a new person. The past is forgotten, and everything is new.

2 Corinthians 5:17

AUTHOR'S NOTE

I wrote this book for several reasons, but the main reason is that it is my testimony of what God has done in my life. I spent many years struggling to be free. My days looked normal, but the nightmares were there every night. This book evolved as that freedom became a possibility and then a reality. One of the things I discovered in the process is that I could not- not write the book. I tried.

In my family, we didn't talk about things like childhood sexual abuse, domestic violence, mental illness, and abortion. In fact, nothing was talked about, or so I thought, until one day I discovered people were telling inaccurate versions of my story in a hush-hush secret way. I didn't fault the storytellers because they were only speaking what others told them. When the truth is hidden, the pain never heals, and it gets passed on from one generation to the next. If you grow up in a small town, it's amazing how everyone seems to know more about you, your mama, and your mama's mama than you do. This book is a revelation of the truth structured as fiction.

Because I have no story apart from my family, this is not my story alone. Family members who felt that it was time for someone to speak, told me about the incidents that occurred during my childhood and ones that happened outside of my presence. I am indebted to them for their courage.

I write some hard truths, but they are written in love. I love my family, and I know they love me. With age and maturity, I've been permitted to see things through the eyes of life. So, I now know a little bit of the meaning of that old saying, "Just keep on living." I see now that our family is no different than any other family. We all have our share of closet skeletons, convicted felons, mental illness, drug addiction, prostitution, homosexuality, oak tree preachers, and successful teachers. If you don't believe me, just ask Jesus about his family tree.

As a teenager, I searched, but couldn't find any books about some of the things I was going through. I looked to the Bible for answers, but found out I was hopeless, should be stoned to death, and was destined for hell. That was before I discovered that Jesus had already provided for my salvation. Within me was a compelling force that would not let me give up. I believe it was that force that drew me, a young teenage Black girl in the late 1970s, to the big church downtown where there was a mostly all-White congregation. I didn't know it then, but they had a new pastor, who cared more about the love of Christ and a person's soul than the cultural and racial divisions of the South.

For privacy, most of the names, places, and events are fictionalized. I am thankful for the gracious generosity of the woman I met at my childhood home, who granted me the opportunity to come inside. Each room of that little house has special memories for my family and me - if only those walls could talk.

I hope you enjoy the storytelling of the story. I tried to follow the example of Jesus and other great leaders who told stories. I pray that I will grow as I seek to learn and develop the craft. In all our lives, amid the lies is the reward of truth. The truth for me is that I am fearfully and wonderfully made, uniquely created by the God of this Universe who truly loves me. This book is my testimony. And the only preached word that I cannot resist writing is for you to know that the God who created and loves me, is the same God who created and loves you too. His grace abundantly abounds, and both his love and his mercy are forever.

Alfreda S. Jackson
Virginia

Part 1

Room One

1

October 2009 | Cambleton, Florida

AS BELINDA APPROACHED the house, the first thing she noticed was the house number - thirty-eight-twenty. "That number wasn't there before," she thought. But there it was, as plain as day, proudly displaying all six inches of its ebony iron. Nailed to the side of the front porch, those numbers gave that old house its defining spot in this world, which was something Belinda wasn't sure she ever had.

The house sat back seventy-five feet from the main dirt road. The driveway was an obstacle course of potholes created by the rain that washed away the shell. Trenches formed by the tire tracks trying to avoid them lined the edges of the driveway. Belinda parked at the edge of the front yard. Slowly stretching as she stood, her legs were stiff from driving three hours straight. It was early fall, but the Florida noon-day sun does not change with the seasons. The beads of sweat on her forehead gave evidence of the 90-degree temperature, but she was not concerned with the heat from the sun or the moisture on her forehead. This piece of land was sacred ground-the place where she was born.

Belinda moved closer with her eyes fixed reverently on the house. She paused under the shade of a large oak tree, whose limbs stretched towards the house, but didn't quite reach the roof to give it shelter. There, she marveled at the sight of the house and that it was still standing after all these years. It was the same house where her grandmother Elena raised her nine children. The middle girl was Roberta, Belinda's birth mother. Although Belinda knew Roberta was her mother, her grandmother Elena raised her and would always be Mama to Belinda.

Cambleton is a small country town in the middle of the state off Highway 40. It's famous for its agriculture, citrus trees, sandy spurs that poke the bottom of your feet, and a population smaller than the family reunions. The road leading into south Cambleton, named after the town, turns from asphalt to a dirt road as soon as it crosses the railroad tracks. The town's only traffic light is at the intersection of Cambleton Road and Highway 40, on the east end of town.

The railroad tracks and skin color separated the folks in Cambleton. Poverty taught them poor was not prejudice, and hunger knows no respect of person. Black folks in Cambleton learned to survive by helping each other. Neighbors didn't mind lending each other a cup of flour or a spoonful of sugar. The adults knew the names of all the children and their parents. If a child misbehaved in front of an adult, the child's parents knew about it before that child got home.

The counter at the rear of the corner store hosted the town's post office. Before the house number was hung on the side of the front porch, everyone in Cambleton had the same generic mailing address. It was their name-General Delivery, Cambleton, Florida 33985.

Belinda debated whether to knock on the door. If someone was at home, what would they think of her unannounced appearance at their doorstep? She didn't have to wonder long. A stout dark-skinned woman in her early sixties appeared on the front porch and spoke to her through the screen door. "Can I help you?" She asked.

"Hi, my name is Belinda Williams. I know this might seem a little strange, me being here, but I used to live in this house."

The woman came outside and extended a handshake to Belinda. "My name is Inez Jenkins." Her salt and pepper hair protruded on the sides from underneath a tan cap with a bow on the front. "When I saw you standing out here, I knew you had to be part of the family that used to live here. I could tell by the way you were looking at the house."

Her smile eased Belinda's nervousness. "Yes, Ma'am. It's nice to meet you, Ms. Jenkins."

"Please, call me Inez."

"Okay, Inez," Belinda said. "I can't say that I just happened to be in the neighborhood, but it has been a long time since I was here last. Have you lived here long?"

"Well, let's see," she said, in her Jamaican accent. It's been about three years now. I bought this house in a tax deed sale and fell in love with it from the moment I saw it. They don't build them like this anymore."

"No Ma'am, they don't."

The conversation was cordial as the women became acquainted with each other. Instinctively they walked as they talked and before long, they were halfway around the house. Belinda remembered how the outside of the house stood bare, thirsty for paint, and in need of repair when she lived there. The exterior boards facing the railroad tracks popped away from the frame leaving holes once filled with rusty nails. Small insects and lizards found refuge in the old newspapers stuck inside the cracks for insulation. One year, Belinda's Aunt Maxine couldn't stand to look at their home's nakedness any longer. She single-handedly replaced the weather-faded wood and painted the house a rich color of navy blue. It stayed navy blue for as long as Belinda could remember. Over the years, people complimented the quality of the paint and how it held its color for so long. Now, the house was painted white with black trim.

When Belinda saw the torn remnants of a faded blue plastic tarp that once blanketed the roof, she thought about the rain playing the prettiest melodies as the water danced on top of what was a tin roof back then. A newer shingle roof now covered the house and its newly enclosed front porch.

"Cambleton has not had a direct hit by a hurricane since 1934. Last year's storm wasn't hurricane strength, but the sixty miles an hour winds were powerful enough for me," Inez said. "Because the storm was only a tropical depression, FEMA, that Federal government agency that helps when there's a disaster, didn't want to fix the roof. So many people protested that it caused them to change their mind. The roofing contractors estimated the damage and placed those tarps on the roofs. Thankfully, it was no worse than it was because I'm still waiting for them to come back to do the rest of the work."

"Were you at home during the storm?" Belinda asked. "I remember how frightened I used to be when the big storms came. One year, the lake behind the house overflowed, causing water to reach the height of the porch. I watched the water run swiftly under the house. I thought the house with everybody in it was going to wash away like a canoe swept down river by rapid running currents." Belinda shook her head. "It's funny how tall a porch that is less than two feet off the ground can appear to a child who's only three feet tall."

"I didn't leave when they announced the evacuation shelters," Inez said. "Stubborn, I guess. So, I laid right there in my bedroom listening to all the wind and the rain and praying mightily for the Lord to keep me safe. Other than the damage to the roof everything turned out alright. The most important thing is no one was hurt."

After touring the house on the outside, Inez invited Belinda inside to get out of the sun.

2

SINCE THERE WAS NO FOYER, once they stepped from the porch, they were inside the room.

"This here is the living room," Inez said. "And here's what's left of the original chimney over there." Inez pointed to the yellow painted bricks that ran along the center of the wall. "Of course, it's all closed now, but there it is."

Seeing the inside of the house took Belinda back forty years to when she was six years old.

"This was all one big bedroom. I separated this part to make room for a living room," Inez said. Among the furniture was a small television on a little white pedestal stand beside the chimney.

Inez stepped back so Belinda could walk past her. "Take your time and look around while I get us something to drink. How do you like your tea? Sweetened or unsweetened?"

"I'd like sweetened, please."

The portion left of the original bedroom held a full-sized bed pushed against the wall. On the opposite wall were a dresser and a recliner chair. Belinda tried to imagine the room with her grandmother's furniture.

Belinda's grandparents were Robert and Elena Stephens. Robert, known to everyone as Bobby, was a cotton picker from South Carolina. He stood 6 feet 2 inches tall and carried 210 pounds of muscle sculptured by manual labor. Bobby had a charming smile that matched his personality. Unless he was going to work, he never left home without a crease in his khakis, a starched shirt, and a wide brim hat tilted slightly.

Like other men, the Great Depression of the 1930s affected Bobby. White men took many of the jobs in the cotton fields. The cotton machines took the rest. Many Blacks migrated north. Bobby hopped on a train and headed south. He met Elena in Macon Georgia. She had long jet-black hair. Her pecan brown skin and high cheeks evidenced her Seminole Indian heritage from her grandmother's side of the family. Elena had a two-year-old daughter named Willie Mae, whose father died in a hunting accident before Willie Mae was born. That was the story that stuck anyway.

Bobby stayed in Macon long enough to convince Elena to marry him. Then he moved his new family to Florida. It wasn't easy for a Black man to travel in the South. It was even harder to raise a family. Stories told by those who succeeded attributed their success to lots of prayer and help from the good Lord above.

Unable to read or write very well, Bobby didn't have many choices for employment. Joe Turner, who ran a fruit-picking crew and owned a few houses, gave Bobby a job. So, he went from picking cotton in South Carolina to picking oranges in Florida.

Joe also rented Bobby a house down in "the bottom." An orange grove surrounded the house. No one ever said why that part of Cambleton, was called "the bottom." Folks reckoned it was because things were as worse down there as they could ever get. There was no place to go any lower than the bottom in poverty or spirit. Once there, it was hard to get out. Although times were hard, there were some bright moments. Fourteen times, God shined his light and granted Bobby and Elena the blessing of experiencing the birth of a child. However, sadness came along with joy. The sadness visited them twice when two of the children were stillborn. Later, childhood illnesses that took the lives of the poor, who couldn't afford doctors, took the lives of three more of the children. With each loss, Elena was heartbroken but accepted that it is the Lord who decides when He wants to call his angels home. We have no say in the matter. "The Lord does what the Lord sees fit." Later, she tried to instill that truth in Belinda.

The only people the family saw regularly was the work crew that came to "the bottom" to pick the oranges each year. Everyone else seemed to forget about the family living in the middle of the orange grove. The small two-room wooden house had no electricity and no running water. Kerosene lamps provided light for the rooms. Each week, the ice man delivered 75 pounds of ice blocks to put in the icebox to keep the meat from spoiling. The boys helped cut wood to use in the iron heater used for cooking and warming the house. Behind the house was an outhouse. Whenever there was a light breeze on a hot summer day, the odor gave away its location. At night, the preference was to hold it, rather than face the unknown. Elena kept the grassless front yard looking nice by sweeping the prettiest patterns in the dirt with a broom made of dog fennels.

When Inez returned, Belinda was standing in the bedroom looking around as if she was lost in time. "Have a seat," Inez said, pointing to the chair. She handed Belinda a glass of tea. It was the perfect blend and sweetened just right like it was sun brewed. Inez sat on the side of the bed and listened to Belinda talk about her grandparents.

"My Grandfather Bobby, Mama, and their remaining nine children moved from the little house in "the bottom" into this little three-room house by the railroad tracks in 1950. You always knew what time it was by the rumbling of the train passing by the house and the whistle blowing as it crossed the tracks by the highway. It was always on schedule. With five girls and four boys, the family survived off government handouts, the generosity of neighbors, and the vegetables Bobby grew in the garden. Bobby also fished – bringing home catfish and brim. Occasionally, an unlucky rabbit hopped in the wrong direction and became Sunday dinner. Elena made dresses for the girls out of empty flour sacks. Sometimes the boys wore those same flour-sack garments while their pants were drying on the clothesline.

In 1962, when I was born, John F. Kennedy was the 35th President of the United States. For as long as I can remember, Mama had a picture of President Kennedy and one of Dr. Martin

Luther King Jr. hanging on the living room wall. For Mama, they were the two people who had done their best to help Black people in this country."

"I agree with your grandmother on that. They were both taken from us too soon," Inez said. "So, how did you end up living with your grandmother?"

"I learned just recently that Mama wouldn't let Roberta take me with her when she left home," Belinda said. I always thought she just left me behind because she was too young to take care of a child. She was seventeen when I was born. My grandmother raised me in this house with my Aunts Maxine and Doris, and my Uncles Johnny and Chris. They all tell me I was more like their younger sister than their niece. Chris, who was the youngest and closest to my age was still ten years older than me. Since there was such a wide gap in our ages, I was essentially an only child as the only grandchild being raised by my grandmother. There were no other children my age around. All I remember is living in a house full of people and being alone most of the time. I knew they loved me because they took care of me, but nobody said it. Back then, children weren't given hugs and kisses, tucked in bed at night, or celebrated with birthday parties. If you ate and had a roof over your head that meant you were loved."

"Did you ever see your mother after she left?"

"I know Roberta must have come home for Christmas and other holidays, but those events are not etched in my memories. Mama would often say to me, 'Don't forget your Mama. She's the only Mama you got.' As much as I appreciated Mama's counsel, I couldn't forget Roberta because I hardly knew her. You can't forget someone you don't know.

Inez took a sip of her iced tea. "Your grandmother sounds like a beautiful, wise woman."

"Yes, she was," Belinda said as she continued to reminisce. "My Aunt Maxine told me that when I was a baby, Mama used to lay me in a big overstuffed recliner chair in the corner of her bedroom. She'd put a pillow in front of me to keep me from rolling out of the chair. That chair was my bed until I outgrew it. I can't remember sleeping in the chair, but I do remember the little roll-up cot I used to sleep on and later sleeping in the back bedroom with the others."

"This house has a lot of memories for you."

"Yes, I just wish I could remember more," Belinda said. "I guess that's also part of the reason why I needed to come here. One day Mama asked me, 'Have you ever heard God call your name?'

I told her, 'No Mama, I never heard God call my name.'

"Well one day you might," Mama said. "You might hear God calling out your name, and when He calls you, it won't be loud. It's just going to be a small whisper."

"Sitting here today, it's like I can still hear Mama's voice."

Turning the focus of the conversation back to Inez, Belinda asked, "What brought you to Cambleton?"

"My oldest sister Mercedes," Inez said. "She left Jamaica about ten years ago and moved to Florida. Other members of my family soon followed. They were seeking jobs and a better life. For me to be close to them, I made the only logical decision I could and moved here too."

"Yeah, it's important to have your family close by."

"I didn't realize how much until I came," Inez said.

"You've really taken care of this house."

"I do my best. I'm the only one who lives here, so that makes it easy-not having anyone else to clean after. How about you? Do you have any children?"

"Yes, my husband and I have four children. All of them are adults now, and the youngest is in college."

"What do you do for a living? May I ask?"

"Sure, I'm a police officer."

Inez laughed. "Wow! I'm glad I hadn't done anything wrong or else I guess I should be more careful about talking so much."

"No, it's not like that," Belinda said, laughing along with Inez. Besides, this is out of my jurisdiction. If anything happens here, all I can do is be a good witness. Plus, I didn't come here looking to find anything wrong. I came because I wanted to see the house."

"I think that's wonderful, you being a lady cop. Is your husband a policeman too?"

"No, he is self-employed."

"Well, your family must be proud of you. How does your husband feel about you being an officer of the law?"

"I think he's okay with it. We were both working as military police officers in the Army when we met. So, he's used to me carrying a gun. As for him being proud of me or even wanting to see me again, right now, I'm not so sure." Shifting the conversation again, Belinda said, "Inez, I want to thank you for allowing me to visit like this."

"Don't mention it. The truth is I was expecting you."

"What do you mean? I just met you, and I didn't know I was coming here today. I didn't tell anyone I was coming here either."

"Well, that may be true, but the Lord has a way of showing things to this old Jamaican woman. So, I'm not one bit surprised to see you. If it wasn't today, I knew you were gonna come here one day. Like I said, the Lord shows me things. Often, it's in my dreams at night."

"I don't know how you were expecting me, but my coming here has been a long time in the making." Belinda let out a deep sigh. "I knew I needed to come back here before I could do anything else."

"And now that you're here, what will you do?" Inez asked.

"Well, that's the question of the day. I'm not sure. I can go back to the physical place where I came from but going back to the person I was before is not an option." Then, whether she found Inez to be someone safe to talk to or if she simply needed to tell someone, Belinda shared with Inez how she arrived in

Cambleton, over 100 miles away from home. It all started with her living in that little three-room house back in 1962.

3

1969 | Cambleton, Florida

WHILE OTHER LITTLE GIRLS in Cambleton were playing
with dolls and learning how to do french braids, seven-year-old
Belinda was climbing trees and shooting marbles. The boy, who
lived with his uncle in the house next door, taught her how to use
a bb gun to shoot tin cans lined across the backyard. Sometimes,
she played kickball with the neighborhood children. If allowed,
Belinda would stay outside and play all day. The only street lights
that came on to warn her that it was time to go inside were the
natural lights illuminating from the lightning bugs at dusk.

Belinda came bursting through the front door and slammed
it shut behind her. Safe inside the house, she leaned her little 50-
pound body up against the back of the door and held it shut to
keep out whoever was chasing her. Only there was no one behind
her except the memory of Elena telling her to make sure she was
inside of the house before dark. Belinda stood there for a few
seconds to catch her breath. Then she plopped down on the
padded vinyl chair at the kitchen table.

Elena, wearing a green loose-fitting floral print duster, was standing at the stove stirring the gravy in the pan. The fried chicken and onion gravy reminded Belinda she hadn't eaten in several hours. Placing the pot top on the frying pan and wiping her hands on the flour-dusted apron, Elena spoke to Belinda. "Hello! And where have you been?"

Belinda looked down towards the floor. "Nowhere."

"What do you mean nowhere? And why are you running so fast like somebody after you?"

"I was trying to get home before dark."

"Look at your ashy legs and dirty feet. Why are you running around barefoot? Where your shoes at?"

"I forgot and left them on the porch."

"Where you say you been again?"

"I was right outside, playing kickball."

"And where else have you been, because I just looked outside and called you a little while ago and you were nowhere to be found?"

"I went down to the lake, but I didn't get into the water like you told me not to. I was just sitting on the side, watching everybody else."

The lake, which was only a pond, was a place for the children to cool off from the Florida heat. The teenagers liked to hang out there on the weekends. They huddled on the bank, listened to music, and drank beer that they stole from their father's stash or from one of the local winos too drunk to notice. The boys entertained themselves by tossing their friends who couldn't swim into the water. They watched them frantically flail their arms and kick their legs before they would jump in at the last minute to help them. All of Belinda's uncles learned to swim by being thrown into the water. Elena kept the girls away from the lake. She was even more protective of Belinda.

"Next time make sure you are inside this house before the sun goes down," Elena said.

"Yes, Ma'am."

"I know you don't want me to have to get my belt or a switch for you to know how to come home."

"No Ma'am."

"Good. Now go wash your hands so you can eat."

Belinda went outside to the faucet on the back porch and washed her hands using the small scale of soap on the wooden banister.

After dinner, she watched the Mob Squad on TV in Elena and Bobby's bedroom until her bath water was ready. When the picture on the TV became fuzzy, she scrunched the tin foil tighter around the antenna to get better reception. After pouring the hot water into the tin tub, Elena called Belinda into the kitchen for her bath. Then, dressed in a tee shirt that came to her knees, Belinda went into the back bedroom and hopped onto the bed. She dodged a spanking that day, but her luck would soon run out.

The Next Day | Cambleton

On Sundays, most of the neighborhood children went to church with their parents, so they didn't come outside to play until late in the afternoon. Elena rarely attended Sunday services apart from Easter Sunday or paying her respects at a funeral, but she read her Bible regularly. Without anyone else around to play with, Belinda played alone in the front yard. Fascinated by a beautiful monarch butterfly, she tried to catch it as it landed on a flower. The butterfly flew into the wooded field behind the house. It fluttered over the thick brush. Elena warned Belinda to stay away from the thick brush because it was full of scorpions and snakes. Belinda noticed a flock of mosquito hawks nearby. Heading Elena's warning she chose to chase them instead. Tired from running around, Belinda sat down to rest in a cleared area around the mouth of the trash pile. The County did not offer trash collecting services in Cambleton, so everyone dug a hole for burying their garbage.

While sitting on the ground, Belinda explored the little volcanic shaped pits in the sand looking for doodle bugs crawling beneath the surface. She took an empty vegetable can from the top of the trash pile to hold her bug collection. It wasn't long before she hit pay dirt. Placing several little roly-poly bugs in the can, Belinda proudly ran to the house to show off her collection to Elena, who was sitting at the kitchen table peeling potatoes.

"Isn't it hot out there in that sun? What are you doing out there?"

"I came inside the house to show you what I got. I found these little bugs in the sand. See!" Belinda lifted the can towards Elena's face.

"I see!" Elena said with a smile as she leaned back from the can held to her face. "What are you going to do with them?"

"I'm gonna get some grass to feed them and then let them go. I don't know," Belinda said ambivalently. "I might keep them for a little while though."

"Well, it's real hot out there. Don't you stay out there too long."

"Okay, Mama. Can I have some water?"

"Look over there on the counter by the stove. There's a cup you can use."

Belinda sat her bug collection on the countertop and took the cup. After quenching her thirst with water from the faucet, she sat the cup on the counter. Then, she saw a book of matches on the counter that Elena used to light the burner on the stove. Elena was paying more attention to peeling the potatoes than watching to see what Belinda was doing. Belinda took the book of matches and quickly dropped them in the can with the rolly pollies. As the screen door closed behind Belinda on her way out, Elena yelled, "Be careful out there."

Back at the trash pile, Belinda sat the can of rolly pollies on the ground. Taking another empty vegetable can from the trash pile, she peeled off the label. Then she lit one of the matches and set

23

the paper on fire. Feeling the heat from the fire as it neared her fingertips, Belinda dropped the paper, and it landed on top of the trash pile. The trash in the hole caught on fire, burning low for the first few seconds. She tried kicking dirt in the hole, but it was no use. The fire grew quickly, bursting into flames. Surprised by the fire, Belinda screamed and jumped back from the trash pile. The entire trash pile was ablaze with orange and blue flames, mixed with black smoke, reaching up to the sky. Sparks flew as popping sounds came from glass bottles, cans, and other debris on fire inside the hole.

Elena ran into the yard yelling for help. Johnny joined her, running from the back bedroom. Seeing Elena and Johnny, Belinda ran away from the fire towards the woods. For a few seconds, snakes and scorpions seemed like a small compromise to escape from the trouble she was in, but the thick grass was too tall.

Elena connected the water hose and stretched it across the yard to put out the fire. She yelled at Belinda to come back, but Belinda ran farther away. Once the fire was out Elena went after Belinda. Johnny advanced towards her from the opposite direction. Belinda was like a baseball player caught between first and second base with nowhere to escape. It didn't take long for Johnny to catch her. He picked her up and carried her back to the house with her little legs kicking wildly. Without saying a word, Elena walked over to the oak tree, tore off a small limb, and stripped it of its leaves. Pleading for Elena not to spank her, Belinda said, "I won't do it again. I promise."

"Belinda, I can't imagine what would have happened if I hadn't smelled the smoke and looked outside. You know how dangerous it is to play with fire like that. If that fire would have gotten away from us, I don't know what we would have done," Elena said.

Belinda danced around on the porch to try and keep the switch from contacting her bare legs, but there was no escape from the verbal chastisement. Most of the licks made contact and Elena's words were in unison with each one. From that day on, Belinda never played with matches again, but fire came in other forms.

4

MARY, ELENA'S SECOND oldest daughter, was always close to her mother. She lived in Dalton, which was only six miles away, so she came home often. One evening while Mary was visiting, Elena kept looking out the window, but there was no sign of Bobby. An hour earlier, Buster walked past the house with his orange sack slung over his shoulder, so Elena knew the work crew was back from the field.

"Mama, you keep looking out the window. You can't let yourself get all worked up worrying about Daddy. It's not unusual for him to get home late on Fridays."

"Mary, I know, but it's not like him to be this late. Besides, you know how your Daddy can get sometimes."

"Yeah, I know, that's why I like to be here on Fridays when he gets home," Mary said. "I wish Johnny was here more often. Chris and Doris are both out and gone this evening, but it don't matter. Neither one of them can do anything with Daddy when he's carrying on."

Chris, Doris, and Belinda were the children still living at home. Maxine finished school and joined the Job Corps, following in the footsteps of her older brother Calvin. At seventeen, Johnny hadn't officially left home, but he spent more time with his girlfriend than he spent at the house. Johnny and Bobby didn't always get along, especially on the weekends, when Bobby drank and argued with Elena. Fearing what might happen the next time he got into an argument with Bobby, Johnny tried to stay out of his way.

Every weekend men gathered at the picnic tables under the tree by Turner's Country Store to play checkers and dominoes, using empty barrels to hold the game boards. One of the rooms in the back of the store was reserved for a friendly game of cards, usually for a small wager. Sometimes Bobby earned a few extra dollars playing cards. Most of the time, he lost more money than he could afford. Those were the times when he came home and started an argument with Elena because he was angry with himself.

Gerald, one of Joe Turner's boys, knocked at the front door.

Elena answered the door.

"Ms. Elena, my Dad sent me here. He said to tell you someone needs to come and get Bobby before he gets himself in trouble with the law, or worse than that before he gets himself hurt. He's having a problem with one of the men down at the store."

"Okay, we'll get somebody down there and tell your Daddy I thank him for sending the message."

When Gerald left, Elena called Johnny from the back bedroom. Belinda came into the kitchen along with Johnny. After telling both Mary and Johnny what Gerald said, Elena sent Johnny to check on Bobby.

Joe Turner Store | Cambleton

When Johnny arrived, he found Bobby standing in the parking lot shaking his fists and yelling obscenities directed at someone inside the store. One of the men standing underneath the tree next to the store shouted, "Somebody needs to get that old drunken fool and take him home before he gets hurt."

Johnny walked over to Bobby and tapped him on the shoulder. "Come on Daddy, let's go home," Johnny said.

Bobby whirled around, surprised to see Johnny. "What are you doing here?"

"Mama sent me to ask if you could come home. Can we just go home now?"

"What are you talking about- 'just go home?' You think I'm gonna just leave here and let them cheat me out of my money?"

"Daddy, I don't know what's going on, but Mama's worried about you. That's why she sent me to come and get you."

"I don't need for you to come get me. All I need right now is the money Georgia Boy owes me." Bobby protested. Then, suddenly, as if he received a new revelation, Bobby said, "Alright, I will go home, but I'm also going to come back down here get my money. They gonna give me my money or I'm gonna blow they head off."

"Daddy, listen to what you're saying. What are you going to do?"

"I'm going to get my money back from them crooks, one way, or another. That's what I'm going to do. And you're going to help me."

"How am I going to do that? They ain't going to listen to me," Johnny said.

"Oh yeah, they will. Come on let's go."

It took ten minutes to walk back to the house. Johnny waited at the corner of the house while Bobby went to the tool shed. He dropped his orange sack on the ground and took a large hammer from the shed. Unzipping his jacket, he stuck the hammer down the front of his jacket and rezipped it. It was hard to identify the object underneath Bobby's jacket, but from the imprint, it was apparent there was something there. "Now, we gonna go get my money," Bobby told Johnny. "And you're going to go in there and get it for me."

"Daddy, I can't go in there."

"Yes, you can. You gonna go get my money, or you're gonna have to deal with me."

Bobby used a string of four-letter words that let Johnny know he didn't have a choice. Reluctantly, he walked back to the store with Bobby. The same men they passed by, who were standing under the tree earlier, were still there.

"Look who's back," yelled the man who called out to them before. Then, the man looked to his friend and said, "I don't know if I've ever seen him this mad. He looks like he's got steam coming out his ears."

Bobby staggered a little, but he walked like he was on a mission with Johnny following right behind him.

"He ain't playing this time," another man said. "It looks like he's holding something, but I can't tell what it is."

Once again, Bobby stood in the parking lot in front of the store.

"Georgia Boy!" Bobby yelled.

A tall brown skin man in his early forties, wearing a pair of maroon knit pants and a light tan jacket came and stood in the doorway. "Bobby, I thought you was done gone home. What are you doing back down here causing trouble again?" Georgia Boy said.

"There will not be any trouble if you do what's right. I brought my boy down here to get my money. If you all don't give it to him, I'm going to have to take it."

"Bobby, you're talking crazy. I came out here to talk with you man-to-man about this. It ain't got to come to all this. You say you were cheated, but we won that money fair and square."

"There ain't no way you could win fair and square with a marked deck of cards," Bobby said.

"The cards weren't marked and to satisfy you; we got rid of those cards. Remember? That's a fresh deck we were using, and you lost. That's all to it."

"Georgia Boy, I ain't gonna tell you no more," Bobby said while holding the front of his jacket, grasping the hammer. He pushed the end of the hammer up far enough so that the tip of the hammer was barely showing. Georgia Boy's eyes widened.

31

"Johnny, go on in there and get my money," Bobby said. "Georgia Boy, if you move or if anybody else tries to hurt my boy, you're a dead man." Another man who played cards with Bobby and Georgia Boy came to the doorway.

"Okay, Bobby, go on and take what you need?" Georgia Boy said, stuttering as he spoke. Then he muttered, "Bobby, you're crazy, ain't nobody got to get hurt over no fifty dollars."

"Johnny, go in there and get my money off that table," Bobby yelled.

Georgia Boy and the other man stepped to the side to make room for Johnny to pass. "Go ahead, son. Nobody's going to mess with you," Georgia Boy said.

Johnny was shaking so bad he could hardly walk, but he did as he was told. The table was just inside the room. After taking the money, Johnny walked briskly, almost running back to where Bobby was standing and handed him the money. Bobby shoved it into his front pants pocket. Then he stepped back a few steps, holding on to the front of his jacket while keeping an eye on Georgia Boy.

"Nobody wants to hurt you and your boy, Bobby. I can't believe you go do this," Georgia Boy said. "I thought you and me were alright."

"That was before you tried to cheat me out of my money," Bobby said.

He and Johnny turned around and walked swiftly; until the store was no longer in sight and they were almost home. Bobby didn't remove the hammer from his jacket until they were home.

"That's what you had all this time?" Johnny asked while standing on the front porch of the house, sweating underneath his jacket. "I thought you had a gun. I could have gotten killed back there" Johnny yelled. "What were you going to do if those men didn't do what you asked?"

"I was gonna to put something on 'em with this hammer. That's what I was gonna to do."

"I swear. I can't believe you," Johnny muttered under his breath.

Johnny stomped into the house. He moved so fast through the kitchen to the back bedroom that Elena didn't have time to ask him what happened. Bobby staggered in the house behind Johnny. The sour smelling mixture of sweat, oranges, and alcohol emanating from his body filled the room.

"What happened at the store?" Elena asked in a concerned voice. "Joe Turner sent his boy here to say there was trouble. Now, you and Johnny get here, and he runs into the bedroom without saying anything."

"Nothing to worry about," Bobby said. "Hey, Mary. How you? I didn't know you was here."

"I'm doing okay Daddy. We were worried about you," Mary said.

"I'm okay, and I'll be even better as soon as I get some supper."

Elena placed Bobby's plate on the table. "Bobby, I've been sitting here waiting for you to get here. You promised we would try to go grocery shopping this evening." She tried to speak as polite and as well-mannered as she could. "I saw Buster over two hours ago. You're just now getting here, and I have no idea of what went on down there underneath the tree." Elena said.

"Woman don't you start with me." Dropping his fork, Bobby slammed his fist on the table so hard that it shook the glass of water. "I was just having a drink and playing cards. Can't a man have one minute to himself after working hard all week?"

Mary leaned back to keep from herself getting wet from the water that flew from Bobby's glass. She stood to get a dish rag from the counter, but Elena motioned for her to sit back down. As if nothing had happened, Bobby took his fork and put another bite of food in his mouth. Elena got the dish rag and wiped the spilled water.

"That's fine Bobby, but you know we got bills to pay," Elena said. "I need to know how much we're going to have so I can figure how we are going to pay what we owe and buy-."

Before she could finish the sentence, Bobby stood and lunged angrily towards Elena, as if he was going to hit her. She jumped back, trying to get out of his way, screaming, "Bobby, No!"

He grabbed her by the throat and held her against the wall, while he braced himself by leaning his elbow on the wall and Elena. "Woman, don't you fuss at me, I'll cut your head off," he said, using several expletives.

Johnny ran from the bedroom and grabbed Bobby by the arm to pull him away from Elena, while Mary tried to reach for Bobby's other arm. Seeing that she was in Johnny's way, she moved back to give him more room.

"Daddy, don't you hurt Mama," Mary cried. "I'm not gonna stand by and let you hurt Mama."

Johnny firmly guided Bobby back down in his chair, but Bobby yanked his arm free from Johnny's grip as he sat down. "I'll cut your head off," he said. His thick and slurred verbal threats lingered in the air briefly and then drifted away like a deflated balloon. He was too tired and too drunk to be any match for Johnny, who stood beside him ready to act if needed.

While watching what was happening, Belinda cowered in the corner by the refrigerator. Elena noticed Belinda and told her to go back to the bedroom.

When Belinda didn't move, Mary grabbed Belinda's arm and pulled Belinda over beside her.

"Daddy, you're always talking about how you're going to cut somebody's head off," Mary said. "Ain't nobody done nothing to you and you ain't gonna hurt nobody. All Mama did was ask you about the grocery money."

"This ain't got nothing to do with you Mary, and I don't need for you to say nothing to me."

"Yes, it do have something to do with me. That's my Mama." Her voice cracked with emotion.

Bobby leaned back in the chair, reached into his pocket, and pulled out his money. "This is all I have. That's a hundred and fifty-seven dollars. Part of that is twenty dollars I got from Buster for what he owed me." Bobby slapped the money on the table. "Here you go, Elena. Take this. Take it and leave me alone," he yelled as he used several more four-letter words.

Elena looked nervously at the money on the table. She asked, "Bobby, why you got to act like this?"

"I'm tired and just want to go and lay down. Can I do that?" Bobby said, looking at Elena and Johnny. Then he stood from the kitchen table. "Woman, just take the money. Why don't you?" He said as he shuffled his way from the kitchen to the bedroom.

It wasn't long before they heard the rhythmic sound of snoring coming from the bedroom. Mary and Johnny, both satisfied things were calm for the evening, said their goodbyes. Mary needed to get back to Dalton before it got too late. Johnny went back to his girlfriend's house and stayed there for good this time.

Laying crossways on the bed is where Bobby stayed for the rest of the night. Elena sent Belinda to bed in the rear bedroom. Then, Elena took the money and put it away. She slept in the chair in the bedroom so she wouldn't risk waking Bobby. She knew he would start a fight with her and take back the money. During the night, Bobby woke up several times and punched the bedroom walls for no apparent reason. The next morning, he didn't remember half of what happened that evening. That's typical of the way things were most weekends.

5

Six Months Later | Cambleton

CHRIS RAN FROM THE HOUSE, kicking up dust as he went down the dirt road towards Joe Turner's house. "Where are you going?" Belinda yelled.

"Mama needs help with Daddy," he yelled back over his shoulder.

Belinda ran to the house.

"Hey, who's gonna cover third base?" Stephanie yelled, but Belinda didn't answer.

When Belinda came inside the house, Bobby was sitting in a chair in the kitchen leaning on Elena for support. Doris was standing on the other side of him. There was a strange look on his face that Belinda hadn't ever seen. Bobby reached out his arm as if he was looking for something to grab. Elena pressed her hand gently on his shoulder.

"Stay back over there out of the way Belinda," Elena said. "Bobby is not feeling well, and I need to try to keep him still."

"Okay Mama," Belinda said, as she stood by the door to watch without coming any closer.

Elena turned her attention back to Bobby. "You can't try to stand right this minute," Elena said. "Wait until Chris get back," she pleaded.

The more she tried to make him sit still the more he tried to get up. He stretched his leg out but couldn't bend his knee to get it in the right position to rise from the chair. He settled down a bit and stared at the wall.

Chris returned. Breathing hard from running, he said: "Mama, Mr. Joe Turner said he would be right here." He sent one of his boys to the house next door to get his wife to come and cover the store so he could leave.

A dark blue sedan appeared in the driveway. Joe Turner got out of the car and hurriedly approached the front door. He announced himself, knocked on the screen door, and pulled it open without waiting for anyone to answer.

"Come on in Joe, we're in here," Elena said.

"Elena, what's wrong?" Joe was wearing a pair of blue jeans and a long-sleeve denim button-down shirt.

"Thanks for coming, Joe. I'm sorry to ask you leave your store like this, but I didn't know who else to call. Bobby needs to go to the doctor. I think he's had a stroke."

As Joe Turner was talking, Bobby looked in his direction and tried to get up again.

"Whoa, easy now," Joe said. He helped Elena and Doris hold Bobby steady. Then he and Chris raised Bobby out of the chair to help him walk. Going down the step on the front porch when they got outside was the most challenging part. Bobby made slow and deliberate steps as if he was making sure the ground was still underneath him with each step. Watching Bobby was like watching an infant trying to negotiate his first steps. Once on the ground, they managed to get Bobby over to the car. Joe helped get Bobby turned around and seated in the car.

Turning to Elena Joe asked, "What happened?"

"Like I said earlier, I believe he had a stroke," Elena said. "I came out the bedroom and found him lying on the kitchen floor. Chris helped me get him off the floor and onto the chair. When I asked Bobby what happened, he tried to talk but was struggling to get the words to come out. Those that did come out, I couldn't understand. That's when I told Chris to go and ask if you could come over to help us. I thank you again for coming."

"Don't worry Elena. We're going to get him to the hospital. You can sit in the backseat behind Bobby. Chris, you sit on the other side, behind me."

"We'll be back as soon as we can," Elena said to Belinda and Doris. They were standing on the front porch watching.

"Ok Mama," Belinda said as the car pulled out of the driveway. The children who were playing kickball moved to the side of the road as the car drove past them.

When Elena and Chris returned home, Doris and Belinda met them at the door.

"What are you all doing still up?" Elena asked. Without waiting for them to answer, she said, "Well, I guess Y'all couldn't sleep."

"Is Daddy going to be alright?" Doris asked.

"Don't you worry; he is going to be okay. The doctor confirmed that it was a stroke. He has to stay in the hospital for a few days.

Bobby stayed in the hospital for a week before being transferred to a rehab center. His speech was slower than usual, and he had difficulty moving his right arm. After two months of therapy, Bobby regained his strength and recovered the use of his arm. His ability to walk and his speech also improved, but Bobby never went back to work again. Elena's friend, Lula Mae, helped her get a job working in the housekeeping department at the hospital. Lula Mae also drove them to and from work. Elena took a second job on the weekends pulling weeds at the Experimental Farm. She needed to make up for the loss of income until Bobby could start receiving a disability check.

From then on, Bobby spent most of his time outside tending to his garden behind the house. Some days he seemed to be alright. Other times he would forget what day it was. He talked to himself more than he used to and more than he spoke to anyone else. Mary, who Elena could always count on to help wasn't able to be there when Bobby got out of the Rehabilitation Center. It was apple picking season, and Mary was in Virginia. She was the cook for the hundred men, who lived in the camp. LeRoy and Johnny were also with Melvin and Mary.

Working two jobs, Elena relied more on Doris to help take care of Belinda and keep an eye on Bobby, but Bobby didn't always cooperate. One Saturday evening when Elena came home Bobby was not outside working in his garden as usual, nor was he inside the house. Elena went into the back room to ask Doris where Bobby was.

"I thought he was outside in the garden," Doris said. "I've been in here with Belinda. He must have walked away again."

"What do you mean again?" Elena asked.

Elena didn't know it, but Bobby walked away from the house undetected several times in the past. Doris always noticed when he was gone and found him before he got too far from the house. By the time Elena got home, Bobby would always be safe at home.

Elena yelled, "Doris May, I left you here to keep an eye on him," she said. Now I just got home from work, and you're telling me you don't know where he is. Plus, this ain't the first time he's been missing. We have got to find him. I pray to God nothing's happened to him. Can't you do anything I tell you to do?"

Doris fired back, "He's always walking off down the road. I can't stop him. He's always saying I wasn't going to tell him what he could and couldn't do." Doris stormed out of the room.

"I can't deal with you right now," Elena said. She left the house and walked down the road, checking with everyone she saw to see if anyone had seen Bobby. Elena learned many people saw Bobby walking around town at one point or another, but today, no one could positively say that they remembered seeing him. After exhausting all ideas of where to look for him, Elena had no choice but to go back home and wait for someone to find him or for him to come home on his own. She prayed he would be found safe, wherever he was. A few hours later, Joe Turner located Bobby about a mile outside of town, walking on the side of Highway 40. Elena was so relieved and thankful again for Joe Turner for finding Bobby.

It would take a few more frightening incidents of Bobby wandering off before Elena would admit she could no longer take care of Bobby at home. At his next doctor's visit, she agreed to allow the doctor to have Bobby placed in the Oakview Manor nursing home.

Oakview Manor Nursing Home

The Oakview Manor nursing home was in Dalton. Elena went to visit Bobby whenever she could get someone to take her. With each visit, she noticed that Bobby's health seemed to be deteriorating. He appeared disoriented and confused. The times when he didn't know who she was outnumbered the times he recognized her.

One Sunday while Elena was in the lobby signing the visitor's log the social worker met her at the front desk.

"Mrs. Stephens?"

"Yes, that's me," Elena said.

"Hi, my name is Tara Carmichael. I'm the social worker here at Oakview. Bobby's doctor, Dr. Samuels, asked if he could speak with you when you came to visit. He wants to meet with you in the conference room. If you would like to follow me, I can show you where it is."

Pointing to the conference table, she said, "You can have a seat in here and relax while I go and let Dr. Samuels know you're here."

"Is there something wrong with Bobby," Elena asked.

"No. Bobby's fine Mrs. Stephens. Dr. Samuels would just like to speak to you about his care."

Ms. Carmichael returned accompanied by Dr. Samuels and the charge nurse, Ms. Lemons, who was pushing Bobby in a wheelchair.

Dr. Samuels began the conversation. "Hello Mrs. Stephens, I believe you know everyone here."

"Hello, Dr. Samuels," Elena said. Then, she looked at Bobby. They spoke to each other with their eyes.

"We brought Bobby in so he could be a part of this meeting since it is about him," Dr. Samuels said. "We also didn't want to cause your visit to be cut short."

"Okay. Is everything alright?"

"Mrs. Stephens, as you know when Bobby first came here in addition to being treated for his stroke, he was having some minor problems with his orientation. Over the last few months, we have noticed some changes in his condition. He's now to the point where we're not sure he knows where he's at or what year it is. That problem is not uncommon. Our elderly patients that have dementia can experience this type of memory loss. The situation we have with Bobby is that he becomes very aggressive. The nurses report that Bobby is violent towards them. One of them quit her job last week and cited an incident that happened with Bobby as one of the contributing factors.

"What happened?" Elena asked.

"One day he hit her with his cane when she was trying to take his blood pressure. He was saying things to her that a gentleman doesn't say to a lady and calling her by a name she didn't recognize. So, she knew he didn't know who she was. She doesn't think he would have tried to hurt her if he was thinking clearly. She believes he may have felt threatened and was trying to defend himself. The problem is that we don't have the staff that's trained to handle an aggressive client like Bobby. We would have to put somebody with him one-on-one for twenty-four hours. Also, I know, or rather, I don't think you can afford to hire a person to come in to sit with him either."

"No, you're right. I can't." Elena said. "I don't know what to say. I mean, I don't want to see anyone hurt. I certainly don't want Bobby to get hurt, and I can't afford to stop working to take care of him at home. What are you suggesting?"

"Our psychiatrist did a mental status examination on Bobby. He has diagnosed Bobby with paranoid schizophrenia and recommended transferring him to the State Mental Hospital.

With the diagnosis Bobby's been given, I can no longer keep him here legally. Our facility does not have a license for patients diagnosed with a severe mental illness."

"What are you saying? You think he's crazy?"

"No ma'am, I'm not saying that. I'm saying Bobby is a very sick man and we don't have the resources to take care of him."

"How much is this going to cost? I don't have any money."

"There's no extra cost, Ms. Stephens. By law, it's our responsibility to find a place for patients like Bobby. Once a mental illness is recorded, we can only extend his stay here for a week at a time while we look for a place that will take him. Patients sometimes stay here for up to three months while waiting for a bed to become available at the State Hospital. But, we got lucky with Bobby. There is a bed available for him, and they accepted as a patient. We can schedule his transfer for the day after tomorrow. We just needed to speak with you first. I've explained to Bobby what's happening. Although, I'm not sure how much he understands."

"Where is this place again?" Elena asked.

"That's the bad news," Dr. Samuels said. "It's in Riverdale, 250 miles north of here."

"Doctor, I have trouble getting someone to bring me here to this nursing home, and it's only five miles away. I don't know how I'm going to get all the way to Riverdale."

"I understand Mrs. Stephens, and I'm sorry, but there is nothing we can do. I spoke with our social worker Ms.

Carmichael here. We have a couple of bus vouchers. That will give you one trip to Riverdale and one to cover the bus fare for the trip back. You are welcome to take them."

"Okay, well thank you. I guess that's better than nothing."

After leaving the conference room, Elena continued her visit with Bobby in his room. She had less than two days to visit with him and pack all his belongings. After her visit on the next day, Elena came home and told everyone what happened and about Bobby's transfer.

Riverdale State Hospital

Elena visited Bobby once using the bus tickets she was given. She had to wait three months until Mary returned from Virginia before she could visit again. When Mary returned, she brought with her a used Ford Galaxy 500 that she purchased on credit for Elena. With Mary's help, Elena practiced driving and studied for the drivers' test. Once she was confident of her ability to parallel park, she took the test and got her drivers' license.

Mary accompanied Elena on the next trip to Riverdale. The Riverdale State Hospital looked nothing like the brightly decorated nursing home in Dalton. Visitors weren't allowed to take their purses with them, and they had to be buzzed through a set of secured doors. As they walked down the hallways, they could smell the sickness. There were no tapestries or decorative artwork with the inspirational messages they saw at the nursing home in Dalton. Instead of sage green painted walls and matching floral print bedspreads, the walls were a dull tan with the same colored light wool blankets. Patients walked around in hospital gowns with untied straps and no robes.

When Elena and Mary saw Bobby, it was almost unbearable. He was in a room alone, sitting in a wheelchair, staring at the wall. His hair wasn't combed, and he was unshaven. For the first time, Elena saw him with his legs amputated below the knee. The doctor said it had to be done because of gangrene. Even though the doctor had called and gotten Elena's permission for the operation, it still was a shock for her to see him without his legs. When Elena called Bobby's name, his reaction was slow, but she was happy with what she got. Mary and Elena sat and talked with Bobby about what was happening at home, showing him as much love as they could. They didn't know how much he understood, but it didn't matter. They knew he felt their love. That was the last time they saw Bobby alive. Two months later, Elena received a phone call from the State Hospital notifying her of Bobby's death. The official cause of death was a heart attack. The family arranged for Bobby's body to be transported back to Cambleton where he was buried in the local cemetery.

6

ELENA SAT ON THE EDGE of her bed looking at a Polaroid photograph. It was one of only a few pictures she had that was in color. The heavyset bright skinned woman in the picture sat on a sofa along with a man holding a small child. Another child was seated beside him.

Belinda was sitting on the bed, looking at the other pictures in Elena's shoe box. "Who are these people?" Belinda asked.

"That's my oldest sister Cora, my brother Frank and his two children. They live in New Jersey. It had been almost fifteen years since I've had seen her. We talked after your grandpa Bobby died, but she couldn't come to the funeral because of finances. Cora called last night to say they were coming to visit. She's got two grandchildren about your age that she'll be bringing along with her."

"Are they in the fourth grade like me?"

"They should be, but I don't know how the school system works where they live. If they not in the same grade, it should only be about one grade off."

Anticipating their arrival, whenever Belinda heard a car coming down the road Belinda looked to see if it was them. There wasn't much unrecognizable vehicular traffic that traveled through town.

Finally, the day came when a four-door Lincoln Continental with a New Jersey license plate pulled into the yard and parked. Belinda was outside swinging on her swing set that she had gotten for Christmas that past year. Jumping off the swing, she ran inside the house to get Elena.

"Mama, they are here!" she shouted.

"Who's here? What are you talking about?"

"Your sister, she's here. Their car is outside."

Hurriedly, Elena brushed the flour off her hands. Laying her apron on the counter, she joined Belinda outside to greet her relatives. The car doors opened and Willie Mae, Elena's oldest daughter, emerged from the driver's seat.

"Hello, Mama. Surprise!"

"Yes, this is a surprise," said Elena, grinning from ear to ear. "Cora didn't tell me you were coming."

"Who did you think was going to bring them here?" Willie Mae asked as she hugged her mother.

Joyous tears moistened Elena's eyes as she hugged Willie Mae and her other relatives. "Cora, it's so good to see you."

"I'm glad to make it here finally, Elena," Cora said.

"And Frank, what a sight for sore eyes!" Elena hugged her brother tight.

"Now these two fine looking children must be your grandchildren."

"Yes, these are Dorothy's children, Arthur and Jessica," Cora said. "I've been taking care of them ever since they were babies."

"How is Dorothy?"

"That's a story in itself. We can talk about that later."

"This is my granddaughter Belinda," Elena said, placing her hand on Belinda's shoulder.

"Hello, Ms. Belinda. It's sure nice to meet you finally," Cora said.

Belinda returned the greeting. Then Elena invited everyone inside the house where the reunion celebration continued. After the adults settled, Elena suggested that Belinda take Arthur and Jessica outside to play on the swing set. They followed her out and ran over to the swing set. Belinda jumped on one of the single seats and started swinging. Arthur stopped suddenly and yelled at Jessica. "Wait. Jessie. Stop!" He stood beside the swing seat. Jessica stopped before getting on the swing and stood beside her brother. Arthur bent over to smell one of the seats.

"Oooh! This swing set stinks. Jessica, do you smell that? I don't want to play on no smelly swing, do you Jess?"

"No, I don't want to play on no smelly swing set either," Jessica said.

Then Arthur walked around the yard and found a large stick laying in the yard.

"Jess, I'd rather play with this stick." He took a rock from the dirt and threw it into the air, using the stick to hit it, as if he was swinging a baseball bat. Jessica sat down on one of the swing seats and let her toes drag in the sand.

Belinda stopped swinging when she heard Arthur's comments. "You can swing if you want to. Just because he don't want to swing don't mean you can't."

Jessica sat looking down at the ground while Arthur called Belinda names and made insulting comments about her swing.

Belinda started swinging again, this time, as high as she could. She was trying her best to ignore Arthur and the things he was saying. Belinda began to cry, wiping the tears from her face with her arm. Then she got off the swing and went and sat on the porch. Arthur went over to where she was sitting. "Look at the little cry-baby," he said. "I don't like your swing, and I don't like you." Belinda stood to move away from him. Then he shoved her so hard she fell in the dirt. The back of her head landed on a shovel that was sticking out from underneath the house. Fortunately, the shovel was turned over so that the sharp tip of the shovel was sticking down in the sand. Belinda ran inside the house crying. The adults were engrossed in their conversation and did not pay attention to her as she sat down on the floor beside Elena.

After a while, Elena noticed her. "Where's Arthur and Jessica, and why aren't you outside playing with them?"

While wiping tears from her eyes, Belinda said, "They don't like me and don't want to play with me. Arthur pushed me down, and I hit my head on the shovel."

"Come here. Let me see your head." After examining the back of her head, Elena said, "You're not bleeding anywhere. I don't see anything. Are you sure they pushed you down?" Elena asked.

"Yes, they pushed me down." Belinda couldn't understand why Elena didn't believe her.

"You just met them. Why would they want to push you down? It probably takes a little while for you to get to know them, that's all. Go back outside and try to get along with them. Those children are City children from up north. You just didn't understand them. They play different in the north. They are used to playing hard. You think they're fighting with you, but that's just the way they play. Go back outside."

Wiping the tears that she couldn't stifle; Belinda went back outside.

Arthur and Jessica were swinging on the swing set when Belinda returned. Belinda sat on the steps watching. Arthur snarled at her, "You're nothing but a cry-baby, and your swing still stinks."

Belinda stayed on the steps away from them until Aunt Cora, Willie Mae, and Uncle Frank came out onto the porch, and everyone said their goodbyes. Before getting in the car and at the prompting of Aunt Cora, Arthur and Jessica thanked Belinda for letting them swing on her swing set. Belinda was glad to know she had relatives who lived in the north. She was also as equally happy to see those relatives go back north.

7

MARY HELPED ELENA find a house to rent in Dalton. She was worried about them living alone in the country without a man in the house after Chris left home to go live with Maxine.

Doris didn't want to go to Dalton, so she moved in temporarily with another family in Cambleton. She was upset because she felt Elena treated her unfairly. Doris did her best to help look after Bobby, but she was only a young child and couldn't control Bobby. Plus, right before Bobby became sick, a talent scout from a modeling agency invited Doris to go to New York. Elena wouldn't grant her permission to go and made it clear that she didn't have to explain her decision. Once Elena needed Doris to help take care of Belinda and Bobby, Doris never got another opportunity to do something that she wanted to do. Now, Doris was six months pregnant. Therefore, she would have been moving out soon anyway. The County housing agency had already approved Doris for government-subsidized housing, but she couldn't move into a place until the baby was born.

Joe Turner hated to lose a tenant, but he agreed to help Elena move. He backed his 1968 Chevy Pick-up truck right next to the porch so they wouldn't have far to carry the furniture. The house was twice as large as the house they moved from. The screened-in porch alone was as big as the rear bedroom in the old house. The two bedrooms, living room, kitchen, and an indoor bathroom, made the house feel like a mansion. Although they didn't have a washing machine, the back porch was equipped for one. Belinda's bedroom was the second room on the right.

At ten years old, Belinda liked having her own bedroom and a closet to hang her clothes. The full-sized metal cast iron frame bed with springs that popped through the mattress and pinched her at night took up most of the space in the room. Sticks propped up the windows to allow a cool breeze to circulate through the house. The best part about the new house was the indoor bathroom, with a toilet, sink, and a bathtub. Eventually, they got a telephone with a party line.

Elena continued to work in the housekeeping department at the hospital during the week and the Experimental Farm on the weekends. Now that she had the Ford Galaxy 500 she got from Mary and Melvin, Elena was able to drive herself to work. Belinda enjoyed the muscadines and other fruit Elena brought home from work.

The school bus stop was across the road from the house. Belinda would wait at the bus with the other fifth graders who attended Dalton Elementary School. Because Elena had to work, most days Belinda was home alone after school and on the weekends. Sometimes Elena arranged for Belinda to stay at Miss Viola's house after school. Miss Viola had two grandchildren Belinda's age, Ashley and Vincent, who lived with her. Belinda liked visiting with Ashley, but every other weekend, Ashley and her brother went to stay with their father. During the week, Ashley was busy with Girl Scout meetings, piano lessons, and swimming lessons. Therefore, Belinda became discouraged and resolved to spend her afternoons alone. Most of the time, she just walked around the neighborhood, going no place specific.

Belinda wished she had a family like Ashley's. She saw how Ashley knelt at her Grandmother Viola's knee to say her prayers at night before going to bed. Ashley spent time with both her mother and father on the weekends. Belinda never considered the possibility of her having a loving family like Ashley's. Once, when her teacher asked if her father would be attending a school function, Belinda responded, "I live with my Grandmother, and I don't have a father."

One Saturday morning, while Elena was sitting on the front porch reading her Bible, the noise from a car door closing caused her to look up. "Well, look what the cat done drug in," Elena said as she got up to open the door for Roberta. "Oh, my goodness!" she continued with a huge grin on her face. "How you happen to show up? Whatever it is, I'm sure glad to see you. Come on in."

"Hey Mama, I just thought I'd come and see how you were doing. I heard you had moved." Roberta was carrying two black large heavy-duty garbage bags.

Elena turned and yelled for Belinda who was watching Bugs Bunny cartoons. "Belinda your Ma is here. Come on out to see her."

"Hey Belinda," Roberta said. "How are you doing?"

"Aren't you going to give your mother a hug?" Elena asked.

Belinda loosely hugged Roberta.

"Come here. Look at what I brought you." Roberta said as she pulled out some clothes and stuffed animals from one of the large plastic bags. She held a pair of pants against the front of Belinda's body. "Go try these on and see if they fit. In that other bag, you'll find some more clothes and some dress shoes."

Belinda took the pants and went inside the house to try them on.

Elena asked Roberta, "Where you get this stuff from?"

"The Waverlys sent these to Belinda. Most of this stuff has hardly been touched. If it was ever worn, it wasn't much. Those children-Christie and Jack's two kids got so much stuff they don't know what to do with it."

"You've been working for them for a long time now."

"Yeah, it's been over five years."

Belinda returned with the pants on and stood in front of Roberta and Elena. "Those fit nicely," Roberta said. "They are just a little bit too long and need to be hemmed. That's all."

Elena pulled Belinda towards her. "Come here Belinda, let me see," Elena said. "That little bit of length right there, you can hardly notice it. You can just roll them up, and nobody will ever know. Look like you got yourself a new wardrobe just in time for school. What a blessing! Now we don't have as much to buy when school starts. Take the rest of these clothes inside so you can try them on. Then, put them up in your closet."

Belinda never met the Waverlys. She only knew who they were because Elena told her they were the family that Roberta worked for cleaning their house. Belinda wanted some new clothes but was glad to get the clothes Roberta brought, even if they once belonged to someone else. They were still new to her. She took the clothes and went inside, while Elena and Roberta stayed outside on the porch to talk.

"How's my baby doing and, where is she?" Elena asked.

"She's doing fine. I left her with Ms. Martha, her other grandmother. They can do something for her sometime. Henry, he don't ever give her anything."

"When was the last time you seen him?"

"To tell the truth it's been so long I don't even know. The rumor is he's remarried, and his wife is pregnant. He's not going to take care of her either. He may be there now, but I'm gonna see what happens after that baby come."

"Long as my baby alright, that's all I care about. How old is she now, Roberta?"

"She's two and a half."

"Make sure you don't let anybody mistreat her. Next time, you bring her to see me so she can know who we are. Plus, she needs to get to know her big sister."

"Tonya knows who Belinda is. I show her Belinda's picture, and she points to it when she hears Belinda's name."

"Still, try and bring her with you next time. How long are you going to be in town?"

"I'll probably leave tomorrow or the next day. I just wanted to come and see you all and find out where you were living." Roberta looked inside the house. "This is nice Mama."

"Thank the Lord; it's a lot better than where we come from. Come on inside."

After spending the night, Roberta left the next morning to go back to Wakefield.

8

THE ONLY TIME Mary didn't visit with Elena were the months when she and Melvin were traveling north during the season to pick apples or some other part of the country to harvest whatever fruit or vegetable farm that needed a crew of men to pick the fields for them. Melvin, her common-law husband, was thirty years her senior and the contractor in charge of the fruit harvesting crew. If Mary didn't stop by the house to see Elena, she would call her on the phone. One day Mary was at the house when Belinda got out of school. When Mary took her keys from the table that was Belinda's cue to ask to go home with her.

"If it's okay with Mama, I don't care," Mary said.

Belinda looked at Elena hoping she would say that it was alright.

"It's okay, I reckon, if Mary don't mind putting up with you," Elena said.

"It's no bother. I'm not doing anything the rest of the day where she can't come over. Tomorrow is Saturday, so there's no school."

"Go and get some clothes to wear then," Elena said.

"Okay!" Belinda ran to put a change of clothes in a bag. Fifteen minutes later they were pulling into the driveway of Mary's house. She lived in a gray colored, two-bedroom, shotgun-style house, near Dalton Elementary School. Walking through the house was like walking through the boxcars of a train. Except for the bathroom, every room was in a straight row.

Mary didn't have any children. The ones Melvin had from his first wife were grown men and women, who were just as old as Mary. Melvin was a light-skinned, heavy set, biracial man. His birth mother was rumored to be a White woman whose birth of her son caused his father to be killed. An Aunt on his father's side of the family raised Melvin. None of his children, nor Mary, ever met anyone from the other side of the family.

Melvin's bedroom was the room between Mary's bedroom and the living room. He spent most of his time in bed watching cowboy and western shows, drinking sodas and eating candy. He had a serving tray that set next to the bed, so he didn't even have to leave his room when it was time to eat dinner.

When he wasn't at home, Melvin was out on the lake fishing or working in his garden. He wasn't much of a swimmer, but that didn't stop him from going on the lake to fish. He would put on his life vest and get into that small fishing boat and go right out in the middle of the lake. One day the boat turned over and some men, nearby fishing in a bigger boat, jumped in the water and pulled him out. That didn't stop him. The very next week, he was right back out on the lake. Mary cooked fish for dinner every Friday. If Melvin didn't catch any fish that week, he would buy some from the local market.

Belinda spent the day alternating between watching movies on cable TV and watching Mary cook in the kitchen. "Belinda, I have you with me so much that people sometimes think that you're my daughter. I have to remind them that Roberta is your mother," Mary said. "I know you call Mama – 'Mama,' but that's my Mama. That's not your Mama, Roberta is your Mama."

Even though Mary frequently reminded Belinda that she wasn't Belinda's mother, and neither was Elena, Belinda enjoyed the one-on-one attention she got when she visited Mary. No children lived on Mary's street, so Belinda didn't spend much time outside. The only time other children came around was when the lady who lived in the house next door had a supply of twenty-five cents frozen cups. The frozen cups were made of different flavored sugary drink mixes, and they sold fast. Mary saved the Michael Jackson records from the back of the cereal boxes for Belinda, and she would play them on Mary's stereo. To help combat the heat, Mary had a window air conditioner.

The last piece of fish was frying in the hot grease when Melvin called for Mary.

"Just a minute, Melvin, I'll be there in a minute," she yelled back. Once the fish in the pan was done, Mary moved the pan from the stove. She asked Belinda to watch the pot of rice and tell her if it started to boil over, while she went to see what Melvin wanted.

"Will you bring me a drink of water, please Ma'am. I'm so thirsty."

"Okay, wait a minute," Mary said. Back in the kitchen, Mary poured a tall glass of water filled with ice. She placed a napkin on the bottom of the glass and gave it to Belinda. "Would you take this glass of water to Melvin?"

Belinda took the glass of water to the bedroom.

"Here go your water," she said.

"Oh, thank you, Ma'am. Just set it right there on the table, and I can get it from there."

She put the glass of water down on the serving tray. "You like Hersey kisses?" Melvin asked.

"Uh huh," Belinda said, shaking her head up and down.

"Here, you can have these." Melvin handed her five pieces of candy. She thanked him and hurried back to the kitchen to show Mary what Melvin gave her.

Belinda sat at the table drawing cartoons on a tablet, while Mary finished cooking. Mary fixed Melvin's plate and took it to the bedroom. Then, she and Belinda sat down together at the kitchen table and ate their dinner. Afterwards, they tiptoed through the room past Melvin, back to the living room to watch television.

Melvin was always nice to Belinda, giving her sodas and candy. If there was no candy on his serving cart, there were bags of candy stored in the refrigerator. He kept at least two cases of sodas in the bottom of the refrigerator. Even though Melvin gave them to her, Mary admonished Belinda not to drink all of

Melvin's sodas that were in the refrigerator and not to mess with his candy.

The next morning, Mary prepared a grocery list of items she needed for dinner. "Belinda, do you want to go with me to the store or stay here?" she asked.

"Are you going anywhere else?"

"No, I'm just going to run to the store, and I'll be right back."

"I want to stay here and watch cartoons."

"Melvin's back in the room there. Don't mess with none of his stuff in the refrigerator."

"Okay," Belinda said. She stayed on the sofa in the living room, watching TV after Mary left.

Mary was gone for about fifteen minutes when Melvin called for her. When she didn't answer, Melvin called her name out again.

"Mary is not here," Belinda said. "She went to the store."

"Who that? Is that you Belinda?"

"Yeah!"

"Could you come here please?"

She went into the room to see what he wanted.

"How about bringing me a tall cold glass of ice water, please Ma'am?"

"Okay," Belinda said.

When she brought the glass of water back to Melvin, she asked, "Do you want me to put it on the tray?"

"Yes, please Ma'am and I'll get it from there."

Belinda sat the water on the tray. Before she could step back, Melvin reached out his hand as if he was reaching for the glass of water but took Belinda's hand instead. With his other hand, he took the drink from her and sat it on the tray. "Come here, let me feel you," he said while pulling her towards him. She tensed up very stiff and took a short half step to maintain her balance. Melvin gently, inappropriately touched her developing body. With his eyes fixed on her chest area, Belinda stood frozen. She took another step backward as if she was about to run. He quickly grabbed her by the wrist to stop her. Touching her bare skin, she flinched. "It's alright," he whispered. Then he stopped abruptly, let go of her hand. "You can go now," he said.

Belinda hurried back into the living room. She sat on the sofa, staring at the TV until Mary returned. She knew she had done something wrong by letting Melvin touch her, but she couldn't tell Mary what happened.

"Belinda, I'm back," Mary said as she unlocked the front door. "Come and help me take the groceries out of the car."

Belinda went outside and grabbed two of the grocery bags and carried them inside the house. She walked behind Mary through the long narrow house, past Melvin still lying in bed. Mary talked about how busy the store was and how much money she spent when her intentions were only to purchase a few items. Belinda helped her put away the groceries in silence.

Another incident with Melvin happened a weeks later. That time Mary was in the kitchen at the opposite end of the house while Belinda was in the living room. It only took a few moments for Melvin to commit the act and go back into the bedroom. Melvin looked for opportunities to catch Belinda alone, telling her it was their little secret. He barely spoke to her when other people were around.

9

BELINDA PLACED HER completed assignment on Mrs. Whitfield's desk just as the bell to change classes rang. By the time she got back to her desk to grab her books, all the other students were gone.

"Belinda, wait a minute, please," Mrs. Whitfield said. "I want to give you something." She handed Belinda a piece of paper with her name, phone number, and address on it. "My husband Donald and I are planning to have a picnic this weekend. We will be taking the boat out for a ride. I was wondering if you would like to come."

Denise Whitfield was Belinda's sixth-grade home-room teacher.

"If you're interested, take this paper with my address and phone number and give it to your grandmother. Ask her to call me to let me know if you have her permission to come. I will also answer any questions she might have."

"Yes, ma'am, I'd like to come," Belinda said, beaming with excitement, "but I've never been on a boat before, and I can't swim."

"That's alright. The boat is a pretty good size, and we all wear life jackets, whether we can swim or not. I think you will feel safe."

The idea of going on a boat ride was exciting to Belinda. With Elena working almost every day, she still spent most days alone, to include the weekends. Sometimes, she went to Mary's house to visit, but the idea of watching cartoons and cable TV was not as appealing to her as much as it was before. Belinda stayed away from Melvin as much as she could. He hadn't tried to touch her anymore, but she also hadn't told anyone about the incidents that had already taken place.

As her twelve-year-old body continued to develop Belinda received her first training bra as well as attention from the neighborhood boys. Elena left strict instructions that no one was to be at the house when she wasn't at home, especially young boys. Belinda found it hard to resist their attention. Being somewhat of a tomboy, she enjoyed hanging out with the boys, even if the motive of their invitation for her to join them wasn't always pure motives. Unlike with Melvin, the contact she had with the boys around her age did not go beneath the clothing.

When Belinda got home, she handed the note to Elena and asked if she could spend the weekend with Mrs. Whitfield.

"Why does your teacher want to take you home? Does she have any children of her own?" Elena asked.

"No, she doesn't have any children. She said we would go on a picnic and I would be able to go out on the boat ride. Can I go?"

"I don't know, Belinda. I want to see what your Ma think."

Elena called Mary on the phone. "Mary, Belinda came home from school today and said her teacher asked her if she could go home with her this weekend. What do you think about letting her go and spend the weekend with this woman?"

Belinda stood by while Elena talked with Mary on the phone. Elena told Mary that Mrs. Whitfield's note mentioned how much she admired Belinda. It said Belinda was a smart student and had a lot of potential, so she wanted to invite her over for a weekend picnic and boat ride. "According to this note, Mrs. Whitfield lives in Lake View. Elena told Mary she was going to call Roberta, but also wanted to know her opinion."

When Elena finished talking to Mary, she called Roberta. Belinda waited anxiously while Elena spoke with Roberta. Whenever Belinda asked to do something, Elena called Mary, Roberta, or Maxine, and sometimes one of Belinda's Uncles before she would give her an answer. Belinda wanted Elena to decide without consulting everyone else. She felt like the family conference phone calls seldom turned out in her favor. That was the case with Ms. Newsome, Ashley's Girl Scout troop leader.

Ms. Newsome approached Belinda about becoming a member of the Brownies. She told Elena she would be willing to take Belinda to the meetings if transportation was a problem. Ms. Newsome also offered to help Elena apply for a scholarship from a donor if the dues and uniforms were a problem. For Elena's part, she wouldn't have to host no more than one meeting. When

Elena talked to Roberta, Roberta told Elena that she shouldn't allow Belinda to join, because they didn't have enough money to buy the uniforms. Plus, organizations like the Girl Scouts and Brownies were always having meetings, doing fundraisers, and going places. Roberta told Elena she would have to host meetings at the house and participate in the activities. Belinda was heartbroken because Ms. Newsome was willing to help with the things Roberta objected to. Roberta never spoke with Ms. Newsome to find out about the help she promised. Belinda never asked to join any other organization.

After speaking with Mary and the phone conference with Roberta, Belinda was surprised when Elena said, "Your Ma said I should let you go. Just make sure you keep mine and Mary's phone number with you in case you need to call for somebody to come and pick you up."

Then, Elena phoned Mrs. Whitfield to give her permission to come and get Belinda that weekend. Elena gave her address and phone number to Mrs. Whitefield and thanked her for taking a personal interest in Belinda.

As Mrs. Whitfield had stated, everyone on the boat wore a life jacket. So, Belinda was able to relax and enjoy the ride. That weekend, Belinda stayed in the guest room. She was free to watch movies, eat hamburgers for dinner and whatever she wanted to do. Donald and Denise Whitfield did what they could to help Belinda enjoy the weekend. They encouraged her to continue to do well in school. Belinda visited a couple of more weekends before being promoted to the next grade and a new teacher. The memories of Mrs. Whitefield stayed with her.

10

IT WAS THE BEGINNING of May and summer vacation was fast approaching. Belinda was sitting on the sofa studying for final exams.

"Belinda, school will be out soon, what you want to do this summer?" Elena asked.

"Can I go to Wakefield and stay with Maxine?"

"You can go to Wakefield, but don't you want to spend some time with your Ma? I bet she would like for you to come stay with her some," Elena said.

"I guess so, but there is nothing to do there. Roberta just works all the time."

"She works because she has to. You can go down and help by staying home with Tonya while she's at work. That way, she won't have to pay a babysitter. Maybe she can use some of the money she saves to help buy you some new school clothes. You can also get to know Clyde. They've been married for a year now, and she wants him to get to know you too.

Two weeks later Belinda packed enough clothes to spend the summer in Wakefield. With Mary driving, two and a half hours later they arrived at Roberta's house.

Summer 1974 | Wakefield

"Hello, we're here," Mary said as they approached the front door. The screen door was closed, but not locked.

"Y'all come on in. I figured you must be hungry," Roberta said, yelling from the kitchen.

"Yeah child. It sure smells good in here. What you cooking?"

"Some collard greens, cornbread, stew beef, rice, and gravy. I ain't got no macaroni and cheese this time though."

"That's alright. Everything you mentioned sounds good to me," Mary said.

Belinda entered the house carrying a small suitcase and laundry bags.

"Hi Belinda, you can put your clothes in that first room right there. Tonya's room is the one in the back," Roberta said.

"Okay."

Upon hearing her name, Tonya came from the bedroom. Her face lit up when she saw Belinda. She ran and wrapped her arms around Belinda. "Belinda! You finally made it. I'm so glad to see you."

"I'm glad to see you too," Belinda said.

"Come on let me show you where your room is," taking Belinda by the hand.

She went with Tonya to the bedroom, while the women visited with each other in the kitchen. Belinda put away her clothes in the dresser and sat on the bed to test the softness. Then she admonished her little sister, who was already exploring what was on top of Belinda's dresser, not to mess with her things.

It was getting close to six o'clock in the evening. Mary thanked Roberta for a wonderful meal and announced it was time to leave. Because she was no longer comfortable driving long distances at night, she wanted to make it back to Dalton before nightfall.

The first few weeks at Roberta's were noneventful. Belinda enjoyed being a big sister and having someone else around to talk to. However, she didn't like how Tonya would come into her room while she was gone and mess with the things on her dresser. Tonya would deny the accusations, but the smell of perfume and the spilled fingernail polish on the dresser was a dead give-a-way.

Clyde worked for the City's Sanitation Department, so he always got home before Roberta, even when Roberta didn't have to work late. Clyde made inappropriate comments to Belinda while Roberta was away. One day while Roberta was at work Clyde took Belinda into their bedroom and sexually assaulted her. He made her promise not to say anything, or he would tell Roberta it was her idea, and that she came into their bedroom flirting with him.

Roberta came into the house as Belinda was coming out of the bedroom. Belinda left the house and stayed the night at Maxine's apartment. Each time Belinda spent the night at Maxine's she took enough of her clothes with her until eventually, she didn't have to go back to Roberta's. Roberta accused Belinda of thinking only of herself and not wanting to stay at the house to help with the house chores or look after Tonya. An argument between the two of them ended with Belinda slamming the door and telling Roberta that she never wanted to stay with her in the first place.

Belinda was happier at Maxine's. There was no one there to pressure her or try and take advantage of her. When Maxine was at home, she spent time talking with Belinda about different things, unlike Roberta who spent all her free time with Clyde. When summer ended, Belinda returned to Dalton.

Back home, Belinda began having excruciating tension headaches and nightmares. Elena took Belinda to the doctor, but he was unable to determine a cause for the headaches. The doctor suggested sending Belinda to counseling and prescribed Fiorinal for her headaches. Elena took Belinda to an appointment with the case manager that was provided through the County Health Department. The counselor could not identify any problems Belinda was having that would cause the headaches.

11

1975 | Dalton

THE PINCH-A-PENNEY grocery store in Dalton was busy on Friday afternoons with its regular weekly shoppers. This Friday the store seemed even busier. Many of the shoppers had just gotten off work and were cashing their checks in addition to grocery shopping. It was the first weekend of the month, which meant a lot of them were cashing their social security checks, welfare checks, and retirement checks. By the size of the crowd, it appeared everyone had the same idea. The cashier at the service counter checked out customers to help shorten the express lines. Other customers lined up at the counter to purchase cigarettes.

"Belinda, I'm not ready to buy grocery yet," Mary said. "I just need to pick up a few things we need so I can cook this evening. I don't feel like standing in no long lines, so I'm gonna make sure I don't get over ten items."

Mary and Belinda walked down the grocery aisles beginning with the canned vegetables, picking up the items on Mary's list. A light-skinned black male, in his mid-thirties, with dark curly hair, walked past the aisle. He was looking in the opposite direction, so he did not see them. When Mary finished selecting the items she needed they went to the check-out line.

While they were standing in the check-out line, they saw the same man from earlier waiting in the check-out line on the next aisle. Mary said, "See that man over there with the blue shirt on?"

"Where?" Belinda asked.

"He's in the line over there, standing behind the White man with the black shirt on." The man was bending over looking at some of the items in his cart.

"Yeah, I see him."

"His name is Michael. That's who they say your Daddy is."

As she spoke, the man looked towards them. Noticing Mary, he called her name. "Is that you Mary?"

"Hey Michael, I knew that looked like you."

"Yeah, it's me."

"How long you been in town? Child, I haven't seen you in ages."

"I know. It's been a while. I ain't been back too long. I just got in town last week. I came down to help Daddy. He's getting up there in age."

"How is your Daddy?"

"Oh, he's doing alright. He just needs someone to help him out around the first of the month to buy grocery, take him to the doctor and what not. But, health-wise, he's doing well."

"Well Michael, you must be taking good care of yourself. You still look good."

Laughingly, he said, "I try. It gets hard sometimes though." He looked at Belinda. "Well, who is this you got with you?"

"That's Belinda!" His mouth fell open. "No, no way," he exclaimed! "Look how big you've gotten," he said to her. "You were a little bitty toddler running around the last time I saw you. Now, look at you. How old are you now?"

"She's thirteen," Mary said.

"You don't know who I am, do you?"

"No," Belinda said, shaking her head from side to side.

"Let me introduce myself to you. I'm Michael Dawson. I'm your father."

Belinda did not know how to respond. She tried not to display any feelings at all, but she couldn't keep from being nervous. Michael and Mary talked a few more minutes. When he got ready to leave, Michael asked, "Can I come by to visit with you later, so we can get to know each other?"

Not knowing how to answer, Belinda looked at Mary.

"Yeah, you can come by," she said. "I still stay in the same place. Belinda, she stays with Mama over on Tally Street."

"How is Mrs. Elena?"

"She's doing well."

"Here, let me give you my phone number." Michael wrote his phone number on the back of an old business card and handed the card to Belinda.

"What's your number so I can call before I come?"

Belinda told him their phone number.

"That's Mama's number," Mary said.

"I look forward to seeing you," Michael said. "Tell your mother I asked about her."

"Okay, we'll let her know," Mary said.

After Michael finished paying for his groceries, he left the store. Mary and Belinda were not too far behind him, as they walked to their car parked on the side of the building. Then Belinda watched as Michael turned to go to his car on the other side of the parking lot. She wondered about this stranger she had never met before. Would she ever see him again?

Later that evening, while back at home with Elena, Belinda told her, "I met my dad today."

"Yeah, Mary told me. What do you think of him?"

"I think he was nice."

Elena only grunted at her response.

12

MICHAEL PARKED HIS 1975 white Pontiac Grand Prix in front of the house. He knocked on the front door. "Good afternoon Mrs. Stephens, remember me?"

"Hello, Michael. Belinda told me they ran into you yesterday. Come on in."

"Yeah, I met Belinda and Mary at the store. She's gotten so big. I almost didn't know who she was."

"Time don't stand still. They grow up."

"Yes. They do."

"Where you stay at now? Have you moved back in town?"

"No, I live over in Hampton with my wife and daughter. I come over here at least once or twice a month to check on Daddy to make sure he's alright. I take him to buy his grocery and make sure he gets to the doctor. Otherwise, he wouldn't go. He's stubborn and don't like doctors."

Belinda joined Elena and Michael outside on the porch.

Michael smiled. "Well hello again."

Belinda shyly smiled back and returned the greeting.

"I promised you I would come to see you before I left. Here I am. Unfortunately, I'm not going to be able to stay as long as I like, because I have to get back to Hampton. But, I wanted to keep my promise. The next time I come to town, if it's alright with your grandmother, I want you to go with me so you can meet Daddy. You have a grandfather, Michael Dawson Sr., who lives not too far from here and wants to meet you."

Belinda said okay, learning she had a grandfather she'd never met, who's lived less than five miles away from her all her life.

"Does your daddy still live down on Wood Street?" Elena asked.

"Yes, he still lives in that same little house. It's been over forty years now."

"Then, I guess it's okay," Elena said.

After visiting with Belinda for about an hour, Michael left to return to Hampton. The joy of knowing she had a father and grandfather overpowered any feelings of confusion Belinda had about the whole situation. She was happy to have someone who would be there for her finally. She wished she had a father like Ashley and Vincent. Now, her wish had come true.

Michael returned the following weekend. As promised he took Belinda to meet her grandfather. While on their way to Dawson Senior's house Belinda asked Michael, "If you lived in Florida all this time, how come you never came to see me?"

"I didn't know where you were, or I would have. When you were small, I tried to see you, but your mother wouldn't let me."

Not having any information to counter the claim, Belinda accepted his explanation. Before now, Roberta never spoke about Michael to Belinda, nor did anyone else. It was as if Michael didn't exist. When anyone asked Belinda about her father, she told them she didn't have one. The sad truth is that she meant it. Even after she met Michael, she knew Elena kept Roberta informed of their activities, but Roberta still never talked about him with Belinda.

Michael alternated between regular visits with Belinda and extended periods of absence in between. It didn't matter how much he was gone, Belinda looked forward to spending time with him. Michael treated her like his princess, filling an emotional void in her life. Whatever she wanted to do, he would make it happen for her, whether it was going to the movies, high school football games, or taking walks in the park. It didn't matter.

Belinda's favorite place was Violet Rose Park. Michael took her there often. They walked among majestic oak trees, whose branches spread out like umbrellas inviting rest in their shade or shelter during a light rain shower. The trees' reflections in the water were a picture of calmness and stability. When the wind blew, the flowing beauty of moss swayed from the branches, showing the wisdom of the trees and the history of their roots. People jogged along the trails. Some stopped to exercise at the various stations. Others fished. Warning signs prohibited alcoholic beverages, feeding of the alligators and other wildlife. Several gazeboes were scattered throughout the park for families to enjoy an afternoon picnic, barbeque, or birthday party.

One Saturday, while she was waiting for Michael to arrive, Elena came out on the porch to talk to her.

"How can you love someone who has not been around at all and all of a sudden one day just show up?" Elena asked. "He has never done anything for you."

Belinda starred emotionless towards Elena as she spoke.

"I see you sitting awfully close to Michael when the two of you are in the car together. There is no father and daughter that should be that close. If you ask me, you must be going together."

Belinda was surprised to hear Elena saying those things. She knew she was guilty of receiving Michael's affection. There was no defense. She also knew she couldn't make Elena understand how lonely she was before Michael came and how much he meant to her. Having a father made her feel almost normal, like other kids, and like there wasn't something wrong with her. Michael always put his arm around her and held her hand as they walked together. To Belinda, that was just his way of letting her know how much he cared for her. Meeting Michael filled a void for Belinda of having someone who was there on her side. She was secretly and silently hurt and couldn't understand why Elena was trying to turn his love for her into something ugly.

Belinda didn't expect Michael to pay child support or give her Grandmother any money. He told her he was temporarily unemployed and looking for work. Unlike the rest of her family, Michael talked with Belinda and explained things to her. Consequently, she believed everything he said.

During the times when Michael was not around, Belinda went to the park or found other places to sit and meditate. Sometimes she would walk to Dawson Sr.'s house. It was only a few blocks from Violet Rose Park on Wood Street. The area was famous for the town's bars and juke joints. Anytime, day or night, winos staggered out of one of the buildings close to Dawson Sr.'s house. Some wino with disheveled clothes, unkempt hair, and a glazed look on their face, and in some permanent state of intoxication was always standing on the nearby corner.

Dawson Sr. was always happy to see Belinda. They watched television, and she listened to him talk about things that interested him. However, he never talked about his wife, Michael's mother, except she died when Michael was young. Dawson never remarried. A rumor around town was that Dawson shot and killed his wife during a heated argument and that then nine-year-old Michael witnessed the incident.

Belinda visited Dawson regularly over the next two years. One spring day in March, Dawson died quietly in his sleep. For the funeral, Michael dressed Belinda and his other three daughters, whom Belinda met for the first time at the funeral, in identical yellow dresses like they were flower maids in a wedding. Yellow was Dawson Sr.'s favorite color, and it was almost Easter. Michael thought it was the fitting thing to do.

13

THE NEXT SUMMER when school was out, Belinda went back to Wakefield to spend the summer with Maxine. Even though Roberta was no longer living with Clyde, Belinda had no interest in staying with her.

Raymond Jones, a sixteen-year-old high school junior, lived in one of the upstairs apartments behind Maxine. Raymond was tall, good-looking, and quiet. She admired his neatly trimmed afro and mustache, but it was his brown eyes that held her captive. One day he and a group of boys walked past the steps where she was sitting. She noticed him looking at her. When their eyes met, he winked. Belinda couldn't help but blush. She couldn't believe someone as nice looking as Raymond was interested in her. A few days later he asked her to go with him to the dance at the Rec Center. They danced throughout the night to the soulful sounds and during the slow dance, he held her close. From that day on they were inseparable.

One afternoon while walking through the mangos groves Raymond convinced Belinda if she loved him as much as she said, and as much as he loved her, she would show it by her actions.

Raymond was the first person she had feelings for that matched the physical attraction. He assured her the feelings were mutual. She was in love as much as a thirteen-year-old could be.

At the end of summer vacation, Belinda went back to Dalton for the start of the ninth grade. Two months into the school year she wasn't feeling well. A trip to the neighborhood clinic confirmed she was pregnant. Three months passed before Belinda said anything to Elena.

Elena took Belinda back to Wakefield to talk with Raymond and his parents. Raymond denied it was his child. Feeling the pain of rejection, Belinda gave him the excuse of being too immature for fatherhood. Someone once told her that girls mature faster than boys. Despite Raymond's reaction, his mother, sisters, and brothers embraced Belinda and rejoiced over the new addition to their family. After all, they had seen them together all summer.

Belinda was given the option of going to the adult alternative school to keep up with her school work. Because there was no school bus to the adult school, she had to walk or take a taxi. Sometimes Elena was able to drive her.

The next time Michael visited Belinda, she was six months pregnant. As usual, he took her out to dinner and then to see a movie. The ride to the restaurant was quiet until Michael broke the silence. "I see you already know about boys," he said. Then he asked her when the baby was due and offered her his support.

March 1977 | Dalton

ON THURSDAY at school, Belinda was feeling discomfort from light pains in her stomach all day. Since it was only embarrassing gas pains, she didn't mention it to anyone. Elena picked her up from school. She was well into her ninth month of pregnancy and Elena didn't want her to have to walk in that condition. When she got home, she went into the bathroom.

"You stayed in the bathroom quite a while. Is everything alright?" Elena asked.

"Yeah, I'm okay. My stomach's been hurting a little, that's all."

"What does it feel like?"

"It feels like gas pains, but it's getting worse."

"How long you been having pains in your stomach?"

"It started this morning, but it wasn't that bad. It just got worse after I got home."

From the look on Elena's face and the choreographed sharp pain that simultaneously hit her stomach, Belinda knew what she was experiencing was much more than gas or indigestion. She was having labor pains.

Elena grabbed the phone and called Mary.

"Mary, I think this child done gone into labor. Can you come over here and drive us to the hospital?" There was a pause as Elena paused to listen to Mary's response. She continued, "I just put a pot of greens on the stove. I'll cut everything off and get ready." Elena hung up the phone and told Belinda that Mary was on the way.

"Have you had another pain?" Elena asked. "You should start timing them to see how far apart they are. Go get your things together so we can be ready to go when Mary get here."

Belinda determined that the pains were about 15 minutes apart. She felt an urge to use the bathroom, but Elena had told her to try not to; but if she did, not to lock the door.

"I don't want to have to break the door down to go in there and get you," Elena said.

The next time Belinda went into the bathroom; her water broke. There was no mistake about her being in labor. She cleaned herself as best as she could and waited in her bedroom until Mary arrived.

"Mama, I got here as fast as I could," Mary said. "Where's Belinda?"

"She's back in the room, putting some things in her bag."

Mary's car was newer than Elena's, but they took Elena's car because it had almost a full tank of gas. Carrying her overnight bag, Belinda got into the back seat.

"My palms feel a little sweaty, and I'm starting to shake. Mary, will you drive, if you don't mind?"

"Yeah Mama, I'll drive."

Elena handed Mary the car keys and got in the front passenger seat. Mary drove about a quarter of a mile to the end of the street. While stopped at the red light, at the intersection of their street and the main highway, Elena asked her to turn around.

"I don't know if I cut the fire out from under them greens," Elena said.

"We'd better go back now and go check. If we don't, and the fire is still on, by the time we get all the way to Dalton hospital, a fire would have started for sure," Mary said.

When they got back to the house, Elena handed Mary the house key. Mary got out of the car, unlocked the front door, and went into the house. A few minutes later she came back to the car.

"It's a good thing we came back. The fire was still burning, and all the water was near 'bout cooked out of them," Mary said.

"Thank God, I thought about it before it was too late. The good Lord was watching over us that time."

"Mmm hmm," said Mary in agreement.

Belinda was still sitting in the back seat. The contractions were coming more frequent. The hospital was about 25 miles away on roads designated for business traffic. In the best traffic conditions, with all the red lights, it took a good forty-five minutes to get to the hospital. She was determined to stay calm when she saw how nervous her grandmother and aunt were. She never grunted, yelled, screamed, or cried. She simply bore the pain that she had brought upon herself.

A circular driveway at the emergency entrance of the hospital welcomed them. No one outside to show them where to go and they hadn't been there before. All of Belinda's doctor check-ups were at the health clinic in Dalton. Mary pulled the car over to the side of the driveway and parked. She tried to leave enough room for another vehicle to get by if necessary. She saw the no-parking sign, but under the circumstances, she didn't know what else to do. Belinda couldn't walk very far, and Elena needed Mary's help to figure out where they needed to go.

Belinda got out of the car holding the bottom of her stomach. Mary grabbed her overnight bag and carried it inside. Elena followed behind them.

"You all go on. I'm coming. Don't let me hold you up," Elena said.

Inside the building, a nurse noticed them coming down the hallway. She got up and grabbed a wheelchair. Pushing the wheelchair towards them, she said, "Let me guess, Labor and Delivery?" Mary answered. Her voice was loud and trembled with excitement. "Yes, this here is my niece and she's about to have a baby. Which way do we go?"

"Grab a seat young lady," the nurse told Belinda. Looking back at Elena and Mary, she said, "Y'all just follow me." She pushed Belinda midway down the hall, onto the elevator and up to the fifth floor, then through the gray double doors marked, "Labor and Delivery." She stopped in front of the nurses' station. "Here is where I depart. These ladies are going to take good care of you" she said while gesturing towards the nurses seated at the nurses' station. "Good luck to you," she said, as she turned to leave. Both Mary and Elena thanked her for the assistance.

One of the nurses came from behind the nurse's desk to meet Belinda. "Hi, my name is Jennifer," she said. "What's your name and can you tell me how far apart your contractions are?" Belinda couldn't answer her because she was in the middle of a contraction that very minute. "Take your time. It's all right. Breathe in-deep, breathe-then let it go." Belinda followed Nurse Jennifer's example. She answered when the pain from the contraction subsided.

"My name is Belinda Stephens. I'm not sure how far apart they are, but they feel closer now than when we left home."

Jennifer took her blood pressure, temperature, and checked her pulse. She wrote the vital signs down on her clipboard and checked the whiteboard to see which room was available. A security guard approached Elena and Mary. Looking at Mary, he asked, "Are you Mrs. Stephens?"

Elena answered, "I'm Mrs. Stephens. My granddaughter is having a baby."

"Ma'am your car is parked in a no parking zone. You have to go and move it if you don't want it to be towed away."

"Mama, you stay here. I'll go and move the car," Mary said. "Belinda, you're going to be alright. You're here in the hospital now. I'm going to go and park the car, and I'll be right back."

Belinda nodded her head, and then said "okay." She spoke in a tone so low that it looked like she was only mouthing the words. She had another contraction, just as strong as the ones a few minutes prior. Nurse Jennifer hurriedly wrote her name and information on the admission form. She filled in the time of arrival-seven o'clock pm.

"There is a waiting room right around the corner," Nurse Jennifer told Elena. "You can go and sit in there. We'll come and get you when this little angel gets here." Then she made sure Belinda's feet were up on the pedals of the wheelchair, unlocked the chair, and pushed her into examining room number three. "Go call Doctor Neumann," she yelled to one of the other nurses. "She's about to deliver."

One of the other nurses came into the exam room and helped Nurse Jennifer get Belinda undressed and up on the bed. They put in an IV and hooked her up to blood pressure and heart monitors. Dr. Neumann walked in while the nurses were prepping her for delivery. They had already transferred her over to the delivery table. He washed his hands at the sink and put on a pair of gloves.

"Hi Belinda, my name is Dr. Neumann. We're going to deliver your baby. Let's have a look." said Dr. Neumann; as he sat down to examine her. "The head is crowning. You are ready to deliver. You're going to push, but I don't want you to do it until I say so." he said.

Nurse Jennifer handed Dr. Neumann the tools he needed. There were two other nurses in the room to assist. Belinda was in so much pain that she forgot their names just as soon as they had introduced themselves to her. "I'm going to make a small incision to help the baby," Dr. Neumann said. Belinda nodded her head okay. Nurse Jennifer stood by her side and held her hand. Still, she never said a word. Lying on the table, surrounded by people she had just met only minutes ago, and in pain like she never imagined she pushed with the contractions. She let her body relax. Then she squeezed Nurse Jennifer's hand when the next contraction came. On the doctor's command, she pushed one more time. At 7:19 p.m. LeMarkus Stephens was born, a beautiful, healthy baby boy, 5 pounds, and 15 ounces, with all ten fingers and all ten toes. While lying on the bed, with the doctor stitching her, Belinda heard him cry for the first time. She felt an enormous surge of emotions come to the surface. Her eyes filled with tears and she wanted to cry also. Too heavy for her eyelids a single tear escaped and fell on her cheek. Nurse Jennifer was still holding her hand. In an effort to comfort her, she looked into Belinda's face and said, "The hard part is over Sweetheart, there's no need to cry now." And just like that, the tears were gone. Belinda began to smile.

Mary came back upstairs from parking the car. When she stepped off the elevator, she heard a baby crying. Joining Elena in the waiting room, she said to her, "I think I just heard the baby crying. Thank God, we made it in time."

After spending two days in the hospital, Belinda and her newborn baby were ready to come home. She was no longer alone in the world. She had a little person whom she would love and take care of.

14

September 1977

BELINDA DID ALL she could to take care of LeMarkus by herself. Elena guided Belinda but allowed Belinda to do things on her own. It was only late at night when Belinda grew too tired and sleepy that Elena took LeMarkus out of Belinda's arms so that she could get some rest.

The Aid to Families with Dependent Children (AFDC) check that Elena was receiving now came to Belinda with added funds included for LeMarkus. According to the government, at fourteen years old, Belinda was the head of the household for her and LeMarkus, although she was still a dependent herself.

She went with Elena to several recertification appointments where Elena had to report all her expenses and income to determine if she still qualified for support. Belinda did not want to live her life depending on a government welfare check and go through that kind of humiliation. The process of qualifying for government welfare made Belinda feel like she wasn't her own person. It felt like she belonged to the government.

Elena helped purchase whatever items for the baby that Belinda couldn't afford. Belinda received food stamps to help with the groceries. She managed her own budget, which included giving Elena money for rent. Belinda purchased clothes and food for LeMarkus and herself, plus whatever else she needed out of her check.

Raymond continued to deny that he was the father and refused to pay child support. In family court, the judge ordered Raymond to pay ten dollars a month for child support. He paid it one time. Whenever Belinda went to Wakefield, she took LeMarkus to see Raymond's mother. Raymond's sisters were always happy to see LeMarkus. They bragged about their beautiful nephew, played with him, and took pictures for their family album. As LeMarkus grew, looking at LeMarkus was like looking at a photograph of Raymond when he was LeMarkus' age.

Belinda had the option of staying in the adult school to get a GED, but as soon as the doctor cleared her, she went back to regular high school. She promised herself she would graduate with her senior class. One of the women from a church in the neighborhood ran a daycare center agreed to take care of LeMarkus while Belinda was in school.

Elena encouraged Belinda to go out with some of her friends. "You can't stay hidden in the house forever. I can keep LeMarkus while you go out some to be with your friends. Just don't stay out all night," Elena said. "I'll tell you like the old folks used to say, the first one is a mistake, but next one is on you. By then, you ought to know better."

Belinda went to the high school dance and the football games a few times but felt she didn't have much in common with the other students. The boys were only interested in something other than friendship. She didn't blame the girls at school for not wanting to be with her. Now that she was a teenage mother she was exactly the kind of girl good girls weren't supposed to hang around. Although Ashley continued to be her friend, she was busy with cheerleader practice, club meetings, or some function at their church.

When Michael returned to Dalton, LeMarkus was six months old. He visited Belinda and his new grandson regularly.

"Don't keep her out too late," Elena said one night as Michael and Belinda were leaving.

"I promise to have her back before midnight," Michael said.

After they were down the road a little way, Michael said, "What are you doing way over there? You know I missed seeing your beautiful face?"

Belinda scooted over closer to him. When he put his arm around her shoulder, Belinda felt safe, like all things were right with the world.

At the movie theater, Michael bought a large box of popcorn and two drinks. She wasn't hungry, but the movies didn't feel like the movies without popcorn. She laid her head on his shoulder as they watched the movie.

Afterwards, they walked around downtown, window shopping.

"I wish I could buy you everything you see that you like," Michael said. "You deserve every bit of it."

"I'm just glad you're here with me," Belinda said.

As promised at 11:30 p.m., way before midnight, Michael had her back home. He kissed her on the cheek. She unlocked the door and went inside the house. Her grandmother was sitting in the chair asleep. LeMarkus was asleep also, lying on top of Elena's chest. The television was playing the evening news. She picked up LeMarkus, Elena's eyes opened. Instinctively she grabbed LeMarkus as if she was trying to keep him from falling. With her eyes now open Elena said, "Oh, that you Belinda? Go on take him with you." She took LeMarkus and went into the bedroom and laid him down on the bed. Then she got ready for bed herself. Despite all the movement, LeMarkus never woke up.

During Spring break, Belinda got an opportunity to participate in a school work program as a cashier in one of the gift shops at Walt Disney World. The ride to Walt Disney World was an hour drive by charter bus. For the first time, she had a real job. Although the job was only temporary, it renewed her hope of doing something with her life other than collecting a government check.

15

WITHOUT A CAR, Belinda walked most places that she went. One day while walking from the store she caught the attention of Anthony Carmella, who recently moved into the area. Anthony was a 29-year-old divorced father with a seven-year-old son, Anthony Jr. They lived in his 1975 brown motorhome. Anthony offered Belinda a ride home. She agreed to meet him the next day, and they went out to dinner.

A month after Belinda began dating Anthony, Johnny stopped by the house. From her bedroom, Belinda heard Johnny yelling about some incident that happened earlier that day.

When she walked into the living room, Johnny said, "Belinda, I almost went to jail over you today girl. Everybody around town is talking about you running around town with some White guy name Anthony. I was down at the corner store when I heard these two men talking. I wasn't going to just stand by and let that White man talk about you, saying the things he was saying."

Johnny looked back at Elena. "Mama, I ended up getting into a fight. If my friend David hadn't pulled me out of there before the cops came, I'd be in jail right now."

Johnny continued, "Belinda, I don't know who this Anthony guy is, but I wish you would stop hanging around with him." Afterwards, he calmed down a little. Then he spent a few more minutes visiting with Elena before leaving.

The next day Mary stopped by the house. She heard about Johnny's fight with the man at the store. "Belinda, I'm very disappointed in you right now," Mary said. "I thought you were going to be the one to make something out of your life. You're smart and get good grades in school. None of us ever had the opportunities you've had and been able to do the things you've been able to do. But, it's just been one thing after another, and now you're running around town with some man and got people talking bad about you. I don't know what to say."

When Mary finished talking, Belinda asked Elena if she could watch LeMarkus for a few minutes. It was past midnight when Belinda returned. Elena was sitting in the living room when Belinda walked into the house.

"I'm glad you made it home. Just a few more minutes and you were gonna have to go back to where you came from," Elena said. "Here, come take your baby."

Belinda took LeMarkus, who was sound asleep and went straight to her bedroom without responding. When she changed into her night clothes, she noticed that her blouse was on inside out. "Did Elena notice her blouse? she wondered." If she had, she didn't say anything, but Belinda knew she would hear her talking about it with Mary later. They normally talked to each other about the things that were happening how disappointed they were in her.

Belinda continued to date Anthony until the day he told her he couldn't see her anymore. He said he didn't want to ruin her life any more than he had already. He left town the next day. Once again, Belinda spent most of her time in her bedroom. She didn't eat much and experienced chronic headaches. Nightmares kept her awake at night. She denied to everyone that there was anything wrong. The next month her period was late.

While she was lying on the sofa, Belinda overheard Elena talking with Roberta on the phone about a trip they were planning.

"I can't go all the way to Georgia and leave Belinda and the baby alone here in this house," Elena said. When Elena ended her conversation, she called Belinda into the room.

"Belinda, we're going with Roberta and Mary on a trip tomorrow. We're leaving real early in the morning, so the things you need to take for you and LeMarkus need to be ready tonight. You need to pack enough for at least two days."

"Where are we going?"

"We're going to Georgia. Roberta is going to come pick us up."

The next morning, they left before daybreak. Elena packed sandwiches and drinks in a cooler.

On the way to Georgia, the women talked about what they were going to discuss with the root-doctor once they got there.

"What are we going to do with Belinda while we go inside?" Elena asked.

"She might want to go in too. Young people have problems also," Roberta said.

Macon Georgia

When they reached Macon Georgia, they drove down a winding dirt road in the country to a secluded wooden house. Other cars with out-of-state tags were parked in the yard. Once inside, a middle-aged woman took their names and gave them a number. They waited in a small waiting room with other customers. One by one, they went in to talk to Dr. Nigel.

"What about her?" The lady asked, referring to Belinda. "Are you going to see the doctor too?"

"I'll pay for her if she wants to go in," Roberta said and gave the lady another twenty dollars.

The woman led Belinda into a room where an elderly man dressed in all black was waiting. He offered Belinda a seat on the sofa and introduced himself as a spiritual doctor. He explained he could help her with whatever might be troubling her. After answering some basic questions, Belinda talked about the headaches and nightmares she was having. She also told him she suspected she was pregnant again but hadn't taken a test yet.

"I can help you with your headaches and let you know whether or not you're pregnant if you want to know. I'm going to have to examine you, but my assistant will be standing by," Dr. Nigel said, referring to the woman who escorted Belinda to the room.

They took Belinda to a room with a twin bed, handed her a gown and instructed her to undress. Belinda did as she was told.

Dr. Nigel told Belinda someone placed a spell on her, but not to worry because he removed what they put inside her and reversed the spell. He also told her she was pregnant. He said her headaches and nightmares would stop. The words of her grandmother Elena echoed in Belinda's ears, "The first one is a mistake. The second one ain't a mistake." Belinda tried to be careful but was frequently away from home without her birth control pills, or she would forget to take them altogether. On the drive back to Florida, they talked about everything except Dr. Nigel.

The Next Day | Dalton

When they returned to Dalton, Belinda went to see Michael. He had been staying in the house that belonged to Dawson Sr. She knew she could count on him. It was past 10:00 p.m. when she arrived at the house. Regina, Michael's other sixteen-year-old daughter from one of his ex-wives, answered the door. "Who is it?" she asked.

"It's me, Belinda. I'm looking for my dad."

"He ain't here, said Regina. What you need him for anyway?"

"I just need to talk with him."

Two other girls joined Regina at the door. "Do you know where he is?" She asked.

"Yeah, he's over at the Club. He said he would be back in thirty minutes." The club was a few blocks away from the house.

"I think I'll wait for him here."

"Suit yourself," Regina said. When Belinda came inside the girls went back into the back room.

She heard the girls laughing over the music coming from the room. When the music stopped, Regina opened the door, and a cloud of marijuana smoke came out along with them. "Come on Y'all, let's get out of here, and go have some fun," Regina said. The giggling girls followed her, walking past Belinda towards the front door.

"Hey Regina, when did you say he was coming back? Shouldn't he be here by now?"

"He was supposed to be. I don't know what's taking so long," Regina said.

One of Regina's friends asked her, "You think he's gonna like me?"

"I know he will. You saw how he was looking at you earlier," Regina said.

"Yeah but, what if he don't like me and say I can't stay here anymore?"

"Look, girl, I already done told you, he like you," Regina said, as the front door slammed behind them.

Only one of the girls was with Regina when she returned about a half hour later. Michael finally came home. It was almost midnight. This time the peppermints were not enough to mask the odor of alcohol. Hearing Michael, Regina, and her friend came out of the room to meet him. "Hey, Daddy, I got a surprise for you," Regina said.

"Hello handsome," said Cathy. She walked over and stood beside him. Then she rubbed the back of his neck. "You look tired. You gonna let me give you a back massage?"

Michael took her hand and removed them from his neck.

"Hold on a minute, young lady. I don't even know who you are."

"That's my surprise for you, Daddy," Regina said. "This is my friend Cathy that I was telling you about."

"My surprise?"

"Yeah, Daddy."

"Okay, both of you young ladies need to go into the back bedroom there so that you can cool off."

Michael turned and saw Belinda sitting on the sofa. "Hello sweetheart," he said.

"Hi!"

"What brings you out so late?"

"I needed to talk to you."

"Okay, then, give me a minute while I go back here to see what's going on with your sister and her little friend."

Belinda went and sat down on the sofa out on the porch. The porch was screened-in and had curtains hung for privacy. About twenty minutes later, the two girls walked out of the house, cursing as they walked past her. Michael came out and joined her on the porch.

"I told them they were going to have to go somewhere else. That one, your sister Regina, is something else. The other one is her little friend, who's been trying to hook up with me."

"Her?" Belinda asked.

"Yeah, that's what I said. She's not my type anyway. They got no place to live, so they talked Regina into bringing them here. I ain't having any part of it. So, now my dear, what is so important that you come out here this time of night to see me?"

"I don't know how to tell you."

"Well, you just say what's on your mind," Michael said. "That's all. I can see it looks like you need a few minutes to gather your thoughts. I'm gonna go inside and get me a drink. Maybe you'll be ready to talk when I come back."

Michael stayed inside the house longer than Belinda expected. She called out to him. "Dad?"

"Yes dear, I'm right here. What's wrong?" He came out and sat beside her.

"Dad, I'm pregnant," she said. Tears were streaming down her cheeks.

Michael tried to comfort her by holding her close. He took his finger and wiped the tears from her face. "It's gonna be okay." He said. "Everything is going to be alright." She was sobbing with her face buried in his chest.

"As long as I'm here, I'm not going to let anything happen to you," Michael said. He held her tighter and then pushed back so he could see her face.

"Listen, you heard what your grandmother told me, "Don't bring her back here pregnant." They are going to blame me for this. They have already accused me of doing something that I have not done. I'm on parole for robbery. If they charge me with another crime, I'll go back to jail. If I have to go to prison, I want it to be for something that I have done. Plus, you're sixteen now. I love you more than anything in this whole world. He kissed her on the forehead and pulled her close to him again. Then he guided her down onto the sofa. Numb without emotions, without the presence of thought, motionless, and defenseless, she simply laid there as he undressed her and had his way with her.

This was not happening. This was her father. She thought, of all people, he would never hurt her like the others. He was the only person she knew she could count on; the only one she thought loved her unconditionally. Paralyzed and emotionless, she had no will to resist. She had no thoughts of being hurt physically because she had no thoughts at all. She was simply dead inside. Afterwards, he kissed her on the lips "I've always wanted to do that," he said. Then he left her to get dressed. From that point, all of life was even more of a nightmare.

Belinda stayed at the house with Michael the rest of the night. The next day, he told her that she needed to go home so that her grandmother would not have to come looking for her. She did not want to leave, but he insisted that it was the best thing for both of them. Belinda knew she couldn't say anything to anyone about what had happened. They would say that she wanted it to happen and that this wasn't the first time. Like Michael said, Elena and Mary had already accused her of sleeping with him. This time she was really alone, and it didn't matter what happened to her.

Her relationship with Michael was different now. She conceded to living life in the role of a daughter, who was in love with her father. She had seen stories on TV about a girl being in love with her father, but she never imagined that would be her. Michael assured her that their love was natural, and he would be willing to go through with any punishment as long as he could be with her. He promised to never leave her. Belinda didn't know what to think or feel, except she believed Michael would protect her. Besides, she had no place else to go. No one would understand. She didn't understand, so how could she make anyone else. Having Michael for a father was like a young person becoming part of a street gang that made them feel wanted when no one else did, only it was worse than that. Michael wasn't a substitute family; he was family. Her initiation was his love and affection. The next time Michael abused her and every time afterward, she did not resist, which made her a willing participant

16

BELINDA WENT BACK home the next day. A few days later she confessed to Elena that she was pregnant. Elena never asked who the father was, and Belinda never volunteered the information. She went to the county clinic for check-ups and prenatal care. At first, she went to school a couple of days a week to try to keep up. Eventually, she stopped going altogether. She spent her time sleeping, walking around town, or at the park sitting by the water. The more she stayed away from home, the more Elena took on the role of taking care of LeMarkus.

Michael promised her again that he would take care of her. He told her he would divorce his wife and move back to Dalton permanently to be with her. The next time he came to visit he brought a copy of a divorce petition. As the months passed, Belinda felt as if everyone in her neighborhood knew what was happening between her and Michael, but just wasn't saying anything. So, she spent as much time as she could in the predominantly White neighborhoods. There, nobody noticed her, cared who she was, or what she was doing. At least, that's what she thought. The chronic headaches and nightmares continued, which made it difficult to sleep at night. She stayed awake at night and slept during the daytime. She watched the TV evangelist and read the Bible looking for answers to her situation. She read where anyone who lay with their parents should be put to death. Right then, she knew there was no hope for her, and she deserved to die.

That Sunday morning Belinda got up and put on her blue dress, stockings, and black sandals. She didn't know what was propelling her, but she knew that she wanted to go to church and she knew that she wanted to be saved. She left the house and walked two miles downtown to the Freedom Baptist Church of Dalton. Belinda went inside the church and sat down. There must have been a thousand people present that Sunday morning. She did not know anyone there, but she knew they were supposed to be people who loved God. Since they loved God, they would be able to love her also. She took her seat as the usher directed her. She was uncomfortable because she didn't know anyone there, but she was not afraid. She looked around. A male seated on the third row may have been African American, but she wasn't sure. There was an African American couple in the mid-section to her right. The choir sang two selections that were peaceful to her soul. When the choir finished singing, Pastor Rosen delivered his message. At the end of the sermon, he extended the invitation to accept Jesus Christ as Lord and Savior. Belinda knew that was what she needed. She excused herself from stepping past the two people seated next to her and made her way to the aisle. She walked to the front of the church and stood in front of the preacher. He hugged her and congratulated her on her decision.

Pastor Rosen asked for her name and if she wanted to say anything. She did not address the congregation but spoke to Pastor Rosen. She said, "I have a little boy who was two years old. I have also been having a relationship with my father. I know that it is wrong, but I don't know what else to do. I have no one else who I can go to."

After she finished speaking, Pastor Rosen responded. "You don't have to worry about anything that happened in your past." Then he read from 2 Corinthians 5:17. "Therefore, if anyone is in Christ, the new creation has come: The old has gone, the new is here!"

"Belinda, I want you to know that God loves you and he forgives you of all of your sins. Today, you are a new creature in Christ. From this point on, your life has been made new."

Pastor Rosen hugged Belinda and held her hand. He asked her to turn and face the congregation. All the people clapped giving verbal praises to God. Some were wiping away tears. She felt as if a huge weight had lifted. It was something she had not felt before.

Belinda walked home after the service. Elena was outside pulling weeds out of the flower bed around the mailbox. LeMarkus came running to her. She picked him up, squeezed him tight, and gave him a big kiss on the cheeks. Then she put him down and walked over to where Elena was working.

"How was church?" Elena asked.

"It was good. I got saved today and joined the church."

"You did? That's wonderful news."

"Yeah, I did."

"What church is it?"

"It's the Freedom Baptist Church downtown."

"Ain't that, that big White church downtown? How happen you join that church?"

"I don't know. I just like it."

"Well, I'm happy for you."

Later that evening, Mary stopped by to visit. Belinda excitedly shared her good news about being saved with Mary.

"Belinda, I tell you that show is good news. I'm so happy for you. You'll see how the Lord will bless you when you do right and serve him." Mary said. Then she continued, as if she was embarrassed, "I know I should go to church more often. Ain't no excuse though, I know who He is, and I know that I can't make it to heaven without Him."

The next few days Belinda couldn't stop talking about surrendering her life to Christ. She told almost everyone she encountered about her good news. The following Sunday, Belinda took LeMarkus to church with her. They rode to church in a taxi. After church, Roger, one of the members who taught one of the midweek Bible study classes, gave them a ride home. He invited Belinda to come back to church on Wednesday evenings for Bible study.

Belinda attended church for a while, but it wasn't long before she stopped going. Transportation was one problem. The other problem was finding a group where she felt she belonged. She was a child living a grown-up life. She still had to deal with having a child, being pregnant again, and her father. No one ever asked her about the relationship she was involved in with her father, and she never mentioned it again. The good news was that Jesus now lived in her heart. That, she believed. And although things were not much different on the outside; Belinda knew she changed on the inside.

17

Dalton High School

IT WAS THE LAST week of final exams when Belinda went back to school. Mrs. Crosby, her 11th-grade guidance counselor, called her into the office.

"Belinda, I was hoping I would see you. So, I'm very glad you came today. I want to talk with you about your being able to pass this grade and being able to graduate. Our records show that you have not been in school for eight days. Altogether, you've missed 19 days out of this semester. If this continues, you will not be able to graduate. Is there something going on that we can help you with?"

"No Ma'am, there is nothing you can help me with. I just haven't been able to get here."

"Well, you are smart and a good student when you are here. As you know, this is the week of finals. You must pass the finals to pass to the next grade. Under the circumstances, I can give you a week extension, but no more than that. If you come back here and take your tests and pass them, you will go to the twelfth grade. Do you think you can do that?"

"Yeah, I can do that."

"I was also wondering if you have ever considered transferring to a new school. Maybe a new environment will help. Do you have some relatives somewhere else you might be able to go stay with for a while?"

"I don't know. I might be able to go and stay with my Aunt."

"I think it's something you should consider," Mrs. Crosby said.

Dalton

Belinda called Maxine that evening. She told Maxine what Mrs. Crosby said. Maxine let Belinda know that she wanted to help her, but she didn't want to cause any confusion with Roberta. So, Maxine suggested that Belinda ask Roberta if she could stay with her instead. Belinda took her advice. She contacted Roberta and Roberta agreed. As scheduled, the next week, Belinda met with Mrs. Crosby in her office and took the final exams. Belinda passed all her final exams. A week later she received a transfer letter to Wakefield High School. Elena agreed to take care of LeMarkus until Belinda could settle into her new environment.

1979 | Wakefield High School

At Wakefield High School, Belinda walked into the classroom and took the empty seat in the second row. She took out her English book, notepad, and pencil. She placed the rest of the books in the storage compartment underneath her desk. Mrs. Ramos, a Hispanic female in her mid-forties was at the podium trying to make sure the projector was working correctly. Belinda listened as the students engaged in conversations about how great their weekend was or how much it sucked because things didn't go their way.

The bell rang signaling it was time to start class and everyone not already present was late. Mrs. Ramos began calling the names on the roster.

"Jackie"

"Here"

"Marian"

"Here"

She continued until she called everyone's name on the roster. When she got to Belinda's name, Mrs. Ramos paused to introduce her and welcome her to the class as a new transfer student. Everyone smiled politely. The girl behind her leaned forward and tapped her on the shoulder.

"Hi, my name is Barbara. If you need anything or have any questions, let me know. I'll be happy to help you."

Belinda thanked her for the gesture. The rest of the day went well considering she was a senior in a new school taking a full load of classes needed to graduate. Most of the students in her classes were juniors. The seniors were on half-day schedules, taking only what classes they needed to graduate. No one said anything about her being pregnant. Most of her classmates just asked if she needed any help. Belinda was quiet and kept mostly to herself.

She had been attending Wakefield for about two months when she received a note one day to go to the office to speak with someone. When she arrived, a police officer was waiting to talk to her. He was in the office of one of the guidance counselors that was off work that day.

"Hi Belinda, my name is Officer Carson. Have a seat."

She returned the greeting as she sat down.

"Belinda, I'm sorry to have to pull you out of class like this."

"That's okay."

"Good, Belinda I'm here because we received a complaint that said someone was possibly abusing you. Is there something going on that you'd like to talk about?"

"No, nothing is going on."

"I know this may be a difficult subject, but are you sure nothing is going on with your father that you'd like to talk about?"

"No, there isn't."

"Okay then, here is my business card. If you ever want to talk, give me a call."

"Okay, I will."

When the officer left, Belinda went back to class. She was upset and embarrassed that the police showed up at her school to speak with her. So, she didn't say anything to anyone about the visit.

With everything going on, school was a safe haven for her. Belinda participated in everything the other students participated in. She had friends who talked to her about homework and school projects. She got to know a couple of the girls and visited with them at their home after school. For the most part, life was as normal as it could be while she was at school.

Wakefield

Life at home with Roberta was a different story. Roberta and Clyde remained separated, and Roberta was living in an apartment. Belinda felt as if Roberta didn't want her there and that Roberta only took her in because of Elena. Roberta and Belinda constantly argued although Roberta did most of the talking. Out of frustration, Roberta yelled and cursed at Belinda when Belinda didn't answer her questions. Belinda spent most of her time in her bedroom asleep when she wasn't in school. When Roberta came home from work, Belinda had not washed the dishes nor swept the floor. With a few exceptions, none of the chores Roberta left for Belinda were completed. Roberta constantly yelled and cursed while reminding Belinda of how grateful she should be to have a place to live.

When someone came to visit, Roberta's voice tone immediately changed. "I don't know what's wrong with her," she said in the nicest voice possible. "She won't do anything around here to help no matter what I do for her," Roberta would say to people about Belinda. That infuriated Belinda because, less than five minutes before the guest arrived, Roberta was cursing her in the most vulgar language possible. She was depressed and knew that was nothing she could do to make Roberta love her or feel any different about her.

A few weeks later, a police officer visited with Belinda at the house. He asked Roberta if he could speak with Belinda alone. He asked the same questions the first police officer asked. Belinda gave him the same response. Except when he got ready to leave, she asked him if he ever knew of any incidents where a girl and her father were married. Belinda had seen a recent news report on television about a girl marrying her father. Michael had convinced her that they were meant to be together and that their love for each other was natural. The officer told Belinda that he had not heard such a story and that it would be illegal. Later, Belinda overheard a phone conversation where Roberta was speaking with Mary. Roberta repeated the question Belinda had asked and the officer's response. Already, Belinda did not trust Roberta. She trusted Roberta even less after that.

18

IT WAS MID-MORNING when Belinda went to the Waterfront Park to meet Michael. The sky was a chamber of commerce blue with a few cumulus clouds dispersed throughout. The smell of fish in the air explained the activity of the seagulls flying overhead, diving in and out of the water. Belinda sat down on one of the park benches between two twenty-foot-tall skinny palm trees. The branches of the trees swayed back and forth in the wind. Belinda watched the boats and listened to the waves. She dreamed of being in faraway places, if only for a moment. Belinda wondered what type of people lived in the big mansions that lined the street opposite the bay and whether any of them were truly happy.

"Hello, Sweetheart. I got here as fast as I could. You said it was urgent and I could hear it in your voice. Plus, I couldn't go anywhere without somebody telling me you called. So, I pretty much got here. You said you needed to talk?" Michael put his arm around Belinda and kissed her. "I can't tell you how much I missed you. Tell me what's going on that has you so upset."

Belinda leaned back, breaking the grip of his embrace.

"Roberta came home yesterday and played the tape of you and her together."

"What tape?"

"I don't know if you knew you were being recorded. It sounded like you had been drinking. It was the tape of you and her having sex together. You lied to me. You told me you couldn't come here for another two weeks, but you were here already. You were with her. How could you lie to me?"

"Hey, wait, hold on. I didn't lie to you. I have not been with Roberta."

"Then, how did she make the tape?"

"I don't know what you are talking about," Michael insisted. "I have not seen your mother, and I certainly have not done what you're talking about."

"Dad, I know what I heard, and it was you. You sounded like you were drunk, but it was you."

"If you heard me on a tape with your mother, I must have been drunk. But, I assure you dear, I have not been with Roberta."

"It's okay Dad. I don't care. Just get me out of here."

"What do you mean?"

"I can't stay there anymore. She hates me. You should see how she treats me when no one else is around."

"Okay, Okay, Shhh. Listen. I'll stay, but it is gonna take me some time to find a job and a place to live. But, I'll stay. I love you, and I promised to take care of you. If you need me, I'm here."

"I don't want to go back tonight."

"You got to go back. You have to get your clothes and your school books. You're gonna need them to go to school. Why don't you go back and take care of what you need to and meet me back here at six o 'clock."

"Okay. I love you. I'll see you back here this evening."

That evening Belinda was sitting on the retention wall with her gym bag on the ground in front of her. A 1978 four-door Buick Regal with dark tinted windows pulled up on the street in front of the bench where she was sitting. Michael rolled down the rear window so that Belinda could see him.

"Belinda, it's me. Come on and get in."

Belinda jumped got down off the retention wall. Michael got out and helped Belinda with her bag, while she got into the car.

"I want you to meet some friends of mine; this here is Larry and Loretta."

Loretta looked over her shoulder to the back seat and spoke to Belinda. "Hi, I'm pleased to meet you. I've heard so much about you," Larry spoke also.

"Good things, I hope," Belinda said.

"Oh, nothing but good, your father adores you, and he is so proud of you. He tells us all about how well you are doing in school. You keep at it, and you're going to be very successful one day."

They drove to a condominium on Finlay Beach. Michael showed Belinda to a bedroom where she could put her things.

"We're gonna stay here a few days till I can get things straightened out."

"Wow! This place is nice. I wish we could stay here forever."

"Me too, but we both know that ain't gonna happen. So, enjoy it while you can."

Michael and Belinda stayed with Larry and Loretta for two weeks. At the end of the second week, Belinda overheard Larry telling Michael he was going to have to find another place to live. He said he wasn't supposed to have any visitors in the condo, as part of his lease. He didn't want his landlord to find out they were staying there. He explained that people had been asking questions.

"It's okay man, I understand," Michael said. "Friday, I should get paid, and I can get a place. I appreciate what you guys have done for us."

"Michael, man I hate to do it, but I- If there were anything else I could do to help you and your daughter, you know I would."

"Hey man, we cool. You did a lot."

That Friday evening, when Michael got off work, Larry gave Belinda and Michael a ride to a motel on 9th Avenue. They had packed up their things the night before. Michael registered at the front desk and received the key to room #15. They stayed at the motel for almost a month. Michael was still working day labor construction jobs so that he could afford the motel, but he still had to save enough for an apartment. From the motel, Belinda was able to walk to school. She'd only missed a couple of days from school while staying at the condo. During the afternoons she went to the library to work on her homework until it was almost time for Michael to get home.

Belinda called and spoke with Elena from the phone in the motel room.

"How are you getting along, Belinda?"

"I'm okay."

"Where are you?"

"I'm staying with Michael. He's working. We're staying in a motel room, but he's saving up enough money to get an apartment closer to the school. How's is LeMarkus?"

"He's doing fine. He's been asking about you. You want to talk to him?"

"Yeah"

"Hello, who is this?" asked LeMarkus.

"Hello, LeMarkus. How are you doing?"

"Okay. Mama! He said, excitedly. I got a new toy truck."

"You got a new truck? What kind of truck is it?"

"It's a dump truck. I can haul lots of stuff, then dump it all out and watch it fall."

"Wow, that sounds like fun. I wish I could play with it."

"I can let you play with it when you get home."

"You will?"

"Yeah, Grandma said you have to go away to study for school. When you coming home?"

"I hope to be home soon."

"You want to talk to Grandma again?"

"Yeah, let me talk to her again. I miss you. I love you."

"Grandma... she wants to talk to you."

Elena came back on the phone. "He asks about you all the time. I hope everything works out okay."

"It will. I just wanted to say hello and talk to LeMarkus. I'll talk to you later."

"Okay, you take care of yourself."

"I will. Bye Mama."

Michael came home covered in concrete dust. He arrived later than usual because he had to wait for his paycheck. After eating burgers and fries that Michael brought home, they went out to the movies.

Belinda didn't have to go to school the next day, so she went to visit Maxine.

"Well, well...Hello Ms. Belinda. I was wondering when I was going to see you."

"Hi"

"What you been up to?"

"Nothing, just going to school."

"How's Michael?"

"He's doing alright. He's working right now."

"They work on Saturdays, huh?"

"Yeah, he works every day except Sunday."

"I'm glad you came by. I wanted to let you know that one of those apartments behind me just became empty. It's the one on the corner. The landlord said he would let someone have it without paying the full deposit if they needed somewhere to stay.

Course now, I'm not trying to get in your business. If y'all already found a place, I'll tell him never mind."

"No, we haven't found anywhere yet. I can tell Michael."

Belinda stayed and visited for a while with Maxine. Belinda knew that although Maxine didn't have any problems voicing her opinions, she would allow Belinda to express her feelings without passing judgment.

19

MICHAEL PAID THE first month's rent for the two-bedroom apartment behind Maxine's apartment. The apartment was close to Belinda's school and the health clinic where she went for prenatal care. It was comforting knowing that Maxine was close by in case something happened where she needed help. That next weekend, Michael and Belinda moved into the apartment. A young couple moving out of one of the upstairs apartments that same weekend, gave Michael a sofa, lounge chair and a coffee table for the living room. Michael purchased a mattress and two lamps. That was the extent of their furniture. Using sheets and a blanket that Maxine gave them, they slept on the mattress on the floor in the living room.

Monday afternoon, when Belinda returned home from school, the aroma of pinto beans seasoned with ham hocks filled the house. Michael left them cooking in a crock pot before he left for work. He cooked a pot of rice when he got home. The beans and rice were their first meal together in their new apartment.

A month later, Belinda went into labor four weeks before her due date. Michael called Larry, who drove them to Wakefield Memorial Hospital where Belinda gave birth to a baby girl. Although there were no signs of anything being wrong, the baby only weighed one pound and thirteen-ounces. Belinda named her Maxine Rosalina Stephens, after her aunt Maxine and Michael's mother, Rosalina.

Wakefield Memorial Hospital

"Congratulations! You have a beautiful baby girl," the doctor said. "You will be able to see her in just a little bit. You've had quite a day, but you handled it beautifully. You can be proud." In a more serious tone, the doctor said, "She does have some complications though. That's what I want to talk with you about. She is doing so much better right now, but already we have had to give her a blood transfusion. We will continue to monitor her throughout the night to see how she's doing. I've instructed the nurses to call me personally if anything changes in her condition. I have arranged for her to be transferred to Wakefield's Neonatal Care Unit, located on the other side of town. I just need a signature from you to make that possible. We don't have the equipment here to give her the type of special care she needs for a baby her size. She will get that from the specialists at the Neonatal Unit. I know I've given you a lot of information. Do you have any questions?"

Belinda nodded her head from side to side, indicating she did not have any questions. "Well, if you think of any after you have had a chance to take all of this in, don't hesitate to ask. Now, let's let you visit with this little angel of yours."

The nurse pushed baby Rosie in the room in a baby incubator. There were two little round holes in the bottom so Belinda could stick her hand inside to touch her baby. Rosie had wires and tubing sticking from everywhere imaginable. The wires were taped around her nose and mouth, holding down the breathing tube stuck inside of her. Belinda reached inside the stroller and touched her tiny fingers. She held on to the index finger on her right hand, which gripped Belinda's hand with the tightest grip little Rosie could make. It was frightening to see her with all the tubes sticking out of her mouth and nose. The heart monitor and blood pressure machine were beeping with every heartbeat. Belinda stared at her baby. She would love and care for her the rest of her life.

20

Wakefield

MICHAEL BORROWED Larry's car to take Belinda to the hospital to see Rosie. This time she was able to hold Rosie for a few minutes before she had to put her back in the incubator.

"She's doing a lot better," the nurse said. "The first night started out a little rough, but she's a fighter. She's got a strong will."

For the next three weeks, Belinda took a taxi to go and visit with Rosie. Since she was born a few weeks early, Belinda did not have a crib, baby clothes, diapers, or anything.

"We can fix the extra bedroom for Rosie when we know for sure when she's coming home," Michael said. "Then we'll go shopping." He bought her a little dress for her to wear home. Maxine and others gave Belinda some diapers and little onesies outfits.

On Valentine's Day, the nurses dressed Rosie in a little red and white dress. They took a picture of her and gave it to Belinda inside of a large Valentine's Day card. The card said, "I love you Mommy, Rosie." Belinda thanked the nurse for the card and the picture. She treasured the card and couldn't thank the nurses enough for the love and care they provided.

Two months later, Rosie was still in the hospital. The phone rang, and it was Dr. Bowman.

"Belinda, I'm afraid I have some bad news. Rosie had a rough night, and she needs another blood transfusion. We need your permission to treat her. Do we have that?"

"Yes. Do I have to sign the paperwork?" This wasn't the first time, so Belinda knew the drill by now.

"Your verbal permission is okay right now because it is an emergency. We'll keep you posted on your daughter's progress. I know it's difficult for you to get here. You come over when you can."

It was two days later before Maxine was able to give Belinda a ride to the hospital. The nurse greeted Belinda when she arrived.

"Hi Belinda, come on in. You can take a seat in the lounge. Is this your mother?"

"No, this is my Aunt Maxine."

"So, Rosie is named after you."

"Maxine smiled, showing her silver crown."

"Yes, I suppose so. They surprised me with that one."

"Well, what a nice surprise. You have a very beautiful young niece. We are going to do all we can to continue to help Rosie. She is so precious to us. I'm one of the nurses who sit with her at night. Today, I happen to be filling in for someone else. I can tell you that all of us here just adore her." The room the nurse led them to had two recliners. "Make yourselves comfortable. Please excuse me while I go let the doctor know you are here."

Dr. Bowman joined Belinda and Maxine.

"Belinda, I'm glad you were able to come," Dr. Bowman said. "I know Rosie will be glad to see you. Even though they can't talk, I believe babies sense the presence of their mother." With a more serious look on his face, Dr. Bowman said, "I need to talk to you about Rosie's health. The truth is she's a very sick little girl. She's a fighter though. To be honest, sometimes I wonder how she has endured some of the treatments she has. But, I'm afraid it's going to be a real uphill battle for her. She has had three blood transfusions already, and one of her lungs has collapsed. She's still on a respirator, not able to breathe fully on her own. That might take a while, given the condition of her lungs. Even if she makes it through all of that, I'm afraid she may have suffered significant brain damage. The reality is, she will need a lot of care, most likely round the clock care, along with special medical equipment for the rest of her life. It will be very expensive and taxing on anyone. Needless to say, she's still not stable enough for me to say she's out of the woods yet. Do you understand what I'm saying?"

"I think so. I know Rosie is sick and I have to take care of her."

"What I'm afraid of is that you may not be able to. Belinda, I would not say this if I didn't think it was in the best interest of Rosie and in your best interest. If she goes into cardiac arrest again or her lungs collapse, I don't think she will be strong enough to make it. Now, we are by no means giving up. Like I said, that little girl is a fighter. I'm just afraid she might not be able to survive another operation. I don't want to see her suffer. We are giving her all the medicine that we can to help keep her from being in pain. We'll keep praying for the best for her. Okay?"

"Yes, that's okay."

"Let's go see her," Dr. Bowman said. "The nurses have her out of her crib. She's been waiting for you."

They went into the room, where the nurse was sitting in a rocking chair, holding Rosie.

"Auntie, you ready?" said Dr. Bowman, to Maxine as he stepped aside to allow her to go into the room before him.

The nurse holding Rosie stood up. "Come on over here Mama. You can sit down right here."

Belinda sat in the rocking chair. The nurse handed Rosie to her. She cradled her tiny body in her arms. It felt strange to hold someone so fragile. It was a joy to experience holding her newborn baby, who was the purest and innocent of all of God's creatures. As she held her, she tried to think of what to say to her, but she did not know what to say to a one-month-old premature infant, struggling to fight for her life. She tried to hold her close, so Rosie could feel all the things she wanted to say but didn't know how. There was no doubt Belinda would try her best to take good care of Rosie, although deep down inside she was afraid. Just like Rosie, life for Belinda was one day at a time. She knew Michael was doing all he could to make a living for them. That's what kept her going. She believed that one day things would be better, and Rosie would be able to play with her big brother LeMarkus. She knew how much they both would depend on her to protect them from the world.

"Auntie, would you like to hold her?"

"Oh my, she's so tiny. I've never held anyone that small before," Maxine said. She took Rosie, who only weighed a little more than two pounds, into her hands. Maxine held Rosie for a few minutes and then gave her back to Belinda. After a while, Nurse Samantha came back into the room.

"It's time for her dinner," Nurse Samantha said. "Mom, you do the honors?" Belinda took the bottle of formula from Nurse Samantha and fed Rosie. When she finished, Nurse Samantha took Rosie and placed her back in her crib. Assuring Belinda that all the nurses loved Rosie, she said: "We all hold her as much as possible and give her all the love we can."

It was a week later when Nurse Samantha called from the hospital. Belinda, I was asked by Dr. Bowman to give you a call. He wants to know if you can come to the hospital.

"I don't have a way to get there right now, but I'll try."

"Okay, I'll let him know."

"What's wrong?"

"Belinda, can I call you back in a couple of minutes? Is your Aunt home with you?"

"No, I'm here alone."

"Okay, I'll call you in just a minute, all right?"

A few minutes later, the phone rang, and it was Dr. Bowman. "Belinda thanks for waiting. I'm afraid I must let you know Rosie died this morning. Her heart simply gave out. I am so sorry." He continued, "I want you to know that we truly did do everything we could have."

"Thank you for letting me know," was all she could say.

"You are welcome, Belinda. I don't want you to worry about anything. My nurses are available to provide any assistance you need. I'm going to put Nurse Samantha back on the phone," Dr. Bowman said.

"Belinda, I know this might be overwhelming for you, but at some point, I'll need to know how you want to proceed with any funeral arrangements. Do you have a minister or someone who will be helping you?"

"No ma'am, I don't."

"If you would like, we can get one of our hospital chaplains to assist you. You can even have a small memorial here in the hospital chapel."

"That will be alright, thanks."

"Give me some time, and I'll call you back after I've contacted the chaplain so that you will have the details."

"Okay, thank you, Nurse Samantha."

"Belinda, my heart goes out to you, your daughter, and the rest of your family."

When Belinda got off the phone, she called and told Roberta about Rosie and asked if she could take her to the hospital.

"I'm sorry to hear that," Roberta said. She couldn't take Belinda to the hospital right then, because she had to work, but perhaps she could take her the next day. "Let me know if there is anything I can do," she added.

When Belinda called Nurse Samantha back, she learned that Rev. Morgan, one of the volunteer hospital chaplains, agreed to do the memorial service that Saturday. She let Roberta know she didn't need any transportation until then.

When Michael came home from work, Belinda told him about Rosie. Holding her close, he expressed his sadness.

It was Maxine who drove Belinda to the hospital that Saturday morning. The funeral was at one o'clock in the afternoon, in the Chapel with Rev. Morgan. Nurse Samantha was also there. The service was a small memorial, in which Rev. Morgan said the prayer and a blessing, committing Rosie into the arms of Jesus. Belinda agreed to have Rosie cremated. An anonymous donor gave money for the cost of the funeral and an honorarium for Rev. Morgan.

When Rev. Morgan finished praying, he asked, "Would you like to hold her?"

Belinda took her baby in her arms for the last time. She was lying on a little satin pillow. Belinda knew she was holding her baby, but she looked more like a doll, only life-like. Her face looked so peaceful, like a beautiful angel resting on a cloud. Belinda held her for as long as she could. Her emotions were numb and almost as lifeless as Rosie. After a while, she handed her back to Nurse Samantha. She felt the bitter sadness of the loss of her daughter and the shameful relief of the lifted weight of not having to care for a child who was physically and developmentally handicapped. She took comfort in the fact that Rosie was in heaven now and no longer suffering. She accepted the Lord's decision to call one of his angels home.

21

Wakefield High School

WHEN BELINDA WENT back to school, it was the start of basketball season. Ms. Sampson, the girls' basketball team coach, saw that Belinda had potential and wanted to see her succeed. She saw her in the hallway one day between classes.

"Hey, Ms. Stephens, where are you headed?" Coach Sampson asked.

"To the library."

"You don't have a class this period?"

"I do, but Mr. Nelson said I could be excused to go and work on a project I need to complete. I missed it while I was out. The project the class is working on right now is optional for extra credit, so I don't have to be there."

"What do you have going on after school?"

"Nothing much."

"Okay, how about meeting with me after school in the gym? If I'm not there when you get there just wait for me. The last period of the day is when I do teacher conferences. Sometimes the meetings may go a little long."

"Okay."

After school, Belinda met in the gym with Coach Sampson as promised. Several other girls were there practicing basketball. It was already the second week of tryouts. Belinda took a seat on the bleachers. Coach Sampson was instructing to the girls on the drills she wanted them to do. Then, she left the assistant coach in charge and walked over to the bleachers.

"Hello, Belinda! Thanks for coming."

"It's alright. I didn't have anything else I needed to do."

"Good, that's just what I was hoping you would say. Have a seat." She patted the space beside her on the bleacher with her hand.

"I've been watching you for quite some time now. And what I see is a beautiful young lady who has her entire future ahead of her. Belinda, you are a beautiful, intelligent, and talented young lady. You have what it takes to do something with your life. I don't want to see you throw that away."

Belinda listened attentively to what Coach Sampson had to say.

"Have you ever played any sports before?"

"No, I haven't."

"Do you like basketball?"

"Yeah, I like it, but like I said, I never played before."

"How would you like to come out for the basketball team? Now the varsity team is pretty much set. Those girls are mostly seniors. They have been working hard and playing together for a long time. This is the final year for them to play together. But, I

146

still have some spots available on the JV team. I can't promise you anything, but if you work hard, you may be able to earn a position on the team. What do you think? Would you like to give it a try?"

Laughing nervously, Belinda said, "I would..., but I'm nowhere close to being good enough to make this team."

"Well, don't sell yourself short. Come out and let's find out."

"Okay, I'll give it my best."

Coach Sampson walked to the court where they girls were practicing layups.

"Hello everyone, gather around." Tiara was still bouncing the basketball. Coach Sampson gave Tiara a stern look and held out her hand. Tiara threw the ball to her. "Now you all know that there are still a few weeks of tryouts left. Every position is up for grabs. Many of you have played before, so you have somewhat of an advantage. The person who earns the position is the one who will get it. Am I clear?"

"Yes, Coach!" The fifteen girls responded in unison.

"Am I clear?" She asked louder.

"Yes, Coach!" They all shouted.

"That's more like it," said Coach Sampson. "We have a new player who is going to be trying out, starting tomorrow. Her name is Belinda Stephens. Make her feel welcome."

A couple of the girls spoke to Belinda and introduced themselves to her. Coach Sampson blew the whistle. "Okay, ladies, let's close out with five lapses around the gym. The last one to finish has to do ten pushups."

"Line Up!" said Coach Sampson. The girls lined-up parallel to the free throw line and with another blow on the whistle, they were off and running.

Coach Sampson turned to Belinda. "I'll see you tomorrow at 2:30 p.m. sharp. Just wear a plain white tee shirt and a blue or black pair of shorts."

"Okay, I'll see you tomorrow." Belinda left the gym. On the way out, she had to pause to let two girls pass by who were lagging behind the rest of the team. She wondered which one of them would end up doing the pushups.

When Belinda arrived the next day, half the girls were already shooting baskets. Others were standing around talking. Belinda took a seat on the bleachers. A few minutes later, Coach Sampson walked in. She blew the whistle and asked all the girls to gather around her.

"We have three more weeks of tryouts. Some of you know that you are already on the varsity team, but I have not selected everyone that going to be on JV. It's not too late for anyone. Everyone still has a shot. How well you perform here will determine whether or not you earn a spot."

Coach Sampson blew the whistle again. "Today we are going to start out with sprints. Then we are going to practice some free throw and layups."

Wearing a tee shirt, gym shorts, and sneakers, Belinda lined up with the other girls. She came in next to last in the suicide drills. Coach Sampson divided the girls up into two teams, and they scrimmaged for about an hour. Belinda was tired, but she felt good from the workout. She was excited about the possibility of earning a position on a team, but she knew her chances were slim. She had never played organized basketball before, and these girls had been playing together for years. Coach Sampson congratulated her on a good day of practice and encouraged her to come back the next day.

She attended practice every day for the next three weeks. "Belinda, keep your hands up," yelled Coach Sampson. "Don't let her make the shot." Whoosh! The ball went into the basket. Belinda ran and grabbed the ball. She threw it inbound to her teammate. When Belinda got the ball back, she stepped onto the court. She tried to go up for a layup, and somebody slapped the ball out of her hand, which resulted in an uncontested layup by the other team.

When Thursday of the fourth week came, Coach Sampson asked Belinda to stay after practice a few minutes. "Belinda, I wanted to talk with you because I am going to post the listing of the team tomorrow. I have to let you know that you did not make the team, but you showed a lot of heart. I appreciate all the hard work you did."

"It's okay I knew I didn't have much of a chance of making this team. I'm glad you gave me a chance," Belinda said disappointedly

"Belinda, do you know the real reason why you were here?"

"What do you mean? I thought I was here to play basketball."

"Well, that's part of it, yes. I couldn't stand to see someone as talented as you and with so much potential not have the opportunity to succeed in life. I have no doubt you would have made this team if you had been playing as long as these other girls. The problem is that I believe you have too much time on your hands. Part of what I was trying to do was to help keep you busy so you won't have any problems graduating." She continued, "Please don't get discouraged. I have something else in mind for you. Have you ever run track before?"

"No, I haven't done that either."

"Well, I'm the coach of the track team, and I want you to be on the junior varsity team. You're not fast enough to run with the varsity team, but you have the endurance to run cross-country. All you have to do is come to practice. As far as I'm concerned, this time you spent in basketball practice was your tryout. Here is the schedule for the track meets."

Belinda knew that it was a miracle that she was even on the basketball court. She liked the idea of running on the track team. So, she agreed. She also appreciated that Coach Sampson cared enough about her to try to find a place for her, even if it was just to keep her busy. Belinda practiced with the track team, but because of the situation at home, she never competed in a track meet.

Wakefield

The date for the high school graduation ceremony was two months away. The fact that Belinda would be graduating was becoming a reality that Michael was not ready to deal with. He began to drink more and demand to know where she was at all times. One night during an argument about her not being home, he punched her in the eye. She ran from the apartment and went to Maxine's.

"Belinda, I know how much you like being with Michael, but maybe you should go and ask Roberta if you could stay with her. I know being with a man like Michael feels good, but you have to think about your future. Staying with Roberta may be hard, but if you try hard enough, you can put up with anything for two months. When she starts in with you, just don't say anything."

Belinda left Maxine's apartment and went to Roberta's house. She asked her if she could stay there just until she graduated, and Roberta agreed.

After much anticipation, high school graduation day was finally here. Belinda wore a blue dress under her gown. Mary drove the family to the Civic Center for the graduation ceremony. She and Elena, along with LeMarkus and Belinda Uncles had come from Dalton to attend the graduation.

When they arrived at the school, Belinda met with some of her classmates. They went to line up for the march by the school administration office. Belinda was so happy. She couldn't stop smiling. She finally made it. Belinda dreamed of this day. As a high school graduate, she had accomplished a huge achievement. No one could keep her from accomplishing any of her goals of being successful in life, whatever that meant.

There were 300 students in Belinda's graduating class. When the administrator called her name, she proudly walked across the stage, shaking the hand of the Principal and other school administrators. After the ceremony, she found Elena and Mary in the crowd. They congratulated her on getting her diploma. Only two of Elena's nine children had graduated from high school Belinda, being the oldest grandchild had set the bar for the rest. While they were standing in the courtyard, Michael came walking towards them. Belinda walked over to greet him.

"I just wanted to be here to congratulate you," he said. "I wouldn't have missed it for nothing."

"Thank you. I'm glad you came." She gave Michael a quick hug. "Did you see me walk across the stage?"

"I sure did. I'm very proud of what you've done."

"I couldn't have done it without you."

"I was just along for the ride. I always knew you were going to accomplish your goal." Michael looked past Belinda at Elena and Roberta standing by the tree waiting for her. "Thank you for coming over to talk with me. You should go back and be with your family."

She wanted to ask Michael to come and join them, but she knew that would not be possible.

After another minute or two Michael said, "Well, I think I should go."

Belinda felt the fear of never seeing him again in her heart, and she thought she saw that same fear in his eyes. She watched him as he turned and walked away. She stood waiting, but she knew he wasn't going to look back. Then, she went back to where Elena and the rest of the family that was waiting for her.

22

THE FOLLOWING MONDAY, Belinda went to the Commons Shopping Center to the office of the Air Force Recruiter. She passed all the qualification tests, but it would be another two months before they could start processing any new recruits. There was already a long waiting list so there was no way of knowing how long the process would take. Belinda left the Air Force recruiter's office and walked down to the Army Recruiter's office. Sergeant David Folsom welcomed her as she entered.

"How can we help you, young lady?"

"I came to see if I could join the Army."

"Well, you came to the right place. Have a seat, and I'll see what we can do."

Belinda explained that she had been to the Air Force Recruiters office already, but they couldn't process her application. She completed the questionnaires and passed the Armed Services Vocational Aptitude Battery (ASVAB) test again. From the list of jobs that she qualified for based on her test scores, she chose the job of a military police officer.

"After reviewing her paperwork, Sgt. Folsom said, "I have some good news and bad news."

"Does that mean I'm not going to be able to enlist?"

"No, the good news is that you can enlist. The bad news is that I have to put you on the delayed entry program. I know you had your heart set on leaving right away."

"How long will I have to wait?"

"Six months. And to tell you the truth, there's no way anybody is going to be able to get you into a program any sooner than that."

"If that's what I have to do, I guess it's okay."

"Good. Actually, that's going to work out in your favor. The military has rules about going into the service with children. If you want to go in, you're going to have to find someone who can take custody of your son. That doesn't mean you can't get custody back later. If you know someone who would be willing to do that, on the delayed entry program, you will have time to get that done."

"I can ask my Grandmother."

"Okay. I'll go ahead and start processing your paperwork. When you come back in December, you have to bring a power of attorney giving her full custody. If you don't have the power of attorney when you show up, the deal is off."

"Okay, I understand."

"With your time in the Air Force Jr. Reserved Officers' Training Corps (ROTC), I can put in as a Private 2nd Class (E-2)." Sgt. Folsom smiled. "Look at that. You're already ahead of the game."

"That sounds good."

Sgt. Folsom explained the enlistment process, including the physical, drug test, and everything else she would have to do. "Now, your basic training for military police school is going to be in Anniston Alabama. We need to see where you're going after that." After checking his computer for the available duty locations, Sgt. Folsom continued, "I have you going to Ft. Meade Maryland. You will like it there. It's just outside of Baltimore."

"Baltimore, Maryland?"

"Yeah, have you ever been there?"

"No, I haven't, but I don't want to go there. Do you have something else?"

"I'm afraid that's all I got stateside. You're one of the lucky ones, who get to stay here."

"Do you have something overseas?" I didn't want to go to Baltimore." Michael was born in Baltimore and often talked about having family there. Belinda knew that no matter where she was stateside, especially Baltimore, he would find her and follow her.

"If you want to go to Germany, I'll change it. I have plenty of assignments there."

Belinda left the recruiter's office happy that she was finally going to be able to leave, even if it was six months later. She explained everything to Elena and Elena agreed to sign for custody of LeMarkus. Belinda trusted Elena to give her back custody of LeMarkus when the time came and not try to keep him because she was receiving a government check.

Belinda also knew she wasn't going to last another six months with Roberta, so she moved back to Dalton. Plus, she wanted to spend time with Elena and LeMarkus, who was now four years old, before she left. She had already missed so much time with him.

Things went well for the first few months. She was looking forward to being the first one in the family to serve in the military. Then, about three months later, the unthinkable happened. She missed her period and was pregnant again. After having gone through what she went through with Rosie, she wasn't ready for giving birth to another child. So, she decided to have an abortion. Although concerns about the health of the baby was a noble thought, the more pressing reason for the decision was because she would have been trapped in Dalton, unable to go into the Army or any place else.

Belinda called Planned Parenthood and scheduled an appointment. That next week, her friend Mark Bellamy drove her to Orlando for the procedure. She was back at home that Saturday afternoon with instructions on how to take care of herself. She didn't know if it was the amount of time she spent in the bathroom, or if Elena had seen the paperwork, but somehow Elena knew what she had done. After one of her trips to the bathroom, Elena was standing in the hallway.

"One day, that's gonna be the death of you. Mark my word," Elena said. Then Elena turned and went into her bedroom.

When December came, Belinda enlisted in the United States Army and left Dalton to go to Alabama for basic training.

Part 2

Room Two

23

Three-Room House | The Kitchen | Cambleton

BELINDA AND INEZ moved into the kitchen. The stove was in the same spot where Elena's stove once sat. Elena tacked green contact paper with a yellow floral design above the stove. Droplets of spattered grease from the frying pan, mixed with the dust, gave the contact paper a dull gray look. The contact paper was gone, and the kitchen was painted a shade of light green.

The most noticeable change inside the kitchen was the new sink with running water between the stove and the refrigerator. The door leading out to the back porch was beside the refrigerator. Just like the front porch, the back porch was now enclosed. An indoor bathroom was added to the house at the far end of the back porch.

At lunchtime, the women enjoyed a salad and some fresh fruit that Inez prepared. "You went through a lot growing up," Inez said.

"That's what people say." I really didn't know any different. All I knew is that if I was going to survive, I had to graduate from high school. Then I could leave."

"Thank God for your Grandmother."

"I do. I'm very thankful for my Grandmother. If she hadn't signed the Power of Attorney accepting custody of LeMarkus, I would not have been able to enlist in the Army. I knew I couldn't have left him with anyone else. I had money direct-deposited from my check each month to help take care of him. And I promised LeMarkus that as soon as I returned to the United States that I would come and get him. That was a promise that I was determined to keep.

I talked to him as often as I could on the phone. Every year, I took leave and went home to visit with him. My grandmother wrote letters and sent me his school pictures and report cards.

Looking back, I can see now that I was running away from everything that happened. Back then, I didn't see it that way. I just saw people's lives going around in circles. Somehow, I knew mine would do the same if I stayed. I requested to go overseas because I didn't believe there was any place in the United States where Michael would not have been able to get to me."

"It seems that he really had complete control over you. Were you afraid of him?"

"I was afraid in the end, after the time when he hit me in the eye. He didn't get physically violent until I was about to graduate from high school, and it became evident that I was going to leave. I guess he knew he wasn't going to be able to control me any longer.

Because of my age when I met Michael, it's hard to explain how all of that could happen, but he began to fill that emotional void in me from day one. I guess he could look at me and see how emotionally starved I was. Even though he wasn't there all the time, he became my world.

"You spent two years in Germany. Is that where you met your husband?"

"We met in the Army, but it wasn't in Germany. I met Charles when I returned to the United States two years later. We were in Texas. Charles was the First Sergeant of the military police company that I reported to for duty.

24

BELINDA LOOKED THROUGH the tiny window of the airplane at the city's view from above. It was a spectacular display of sparkling lights. She imagined there were a million houses below and wondered what the city looked like during the daytime. The landing was rough due to turbulence caused by the surrounding mountains. El Paso, with its pastel colors, rock landscapes, and Tony Lama boots, was much different than Florida. The only thing similar to Florida was the heat, eighty to one hundred degrees while standing in the shade, minus the humidity. Belinda felt as if she went from one foreign country to another.

The military bus transported all the soldiers from the airport to the Army base. Belinda spent the weekend at the central processing center. On Monday morning, she arrived at the 209th Military Police (MP) Company with her luggage and military orders in hand. Specialist Lowe greeted her in the lobby. "Can I help you?

"Yes, I'm Specialist Stephens. I'm here to report in for duty. Here are my orders."

Specialist Lowe examined the set of orders.

"Well, you're in the right place," Specialist Lowe said with a smile. "Let me be the first to welcome you to the 209th MP Company. You'll need to see First Sergeant Williams. Have a seat and relax for a minute."

Specialist Lowe disappeared into the office behind her desk and returned a few minutes later. "The First Sergeant will see you now." She pointed towards the office, motioning for Belinda to follow. "Right this way," she said. "You can leave your things here."

Belinda left her suitcase and gym styled shoulder bag on the floor beside the chair and walked over to the office. First Sergeant Charles Williams stood up from his desk to shake Belinda's hand. The ribbons on his uniform told the story of a decorated career soldier. Beside his desk nameplate was a studio quality portrait of him and his family.

"Specialist Stephens, welcome to the 209th," he said. "I've reviewed the set of orders you gave Specialist Lowe. I have to admit that we haven't received them yet, but that happens sometimes. You are certainly in the right place, and we are glad to have you."

He sat down and invited Belinda to have a seat. He explained the mission and duties of the 209th unit. Part of their mission was field duty, where they went into the woods to conduct training exercises for combat missions. Their other function was street patrol, where providing security on the Army base, conducting traffic stops, and investigating burglaries were part of their duties. The company rotated these duties with the 342nd Military Police Company that was located across the street. So, there were two months of field duty and two months of street duty. Currently, the 209th was getting ready to go to the field.

When Charles finished his briefing, he asked Specialist Lowe to call Sergeant Jones. While waiting for Jones to arrive, Charles introduced Belinda to the company commander, Captain Takosky.

"Captain Takosky, I'd like you to meet our newest member, Specialist Belinda Stephens. She comes to us from the 9th MP Company in Muenster, Germany."

"I'm happy to meet you," Captain Takosky said. "I know you're going to like it here. We have a great group of soldiers. I'm sure you'll fit right in. The First Sergeant here will take good care of you. He's in charge of all our men and women. I mostly just handle the paperwork. He smiled. It was clear that he respected his First Sergeant. "Seriously, if you need anything be sure and let us know."

"Yes Sir, I will," Belinda said.

When they left Captain Takosky's office, Sergeant Jones was waiting with Specialist Lowe.

"Sgt. Jones, this here is Specialist Belinda Stephens. She is going to be assigned to your squad. You need to show her around. Take her down and show her where she will be staying."

"Okay, Top," Jones answered.

Belinda grabbed her bags and followed Sgt. Jones down the hallway on the first floor of the four-story building, through a set of double doors. Along the way, Jones described the layout of the building, pointing out the dining hall and laundry room. "Twelve female soldiers share the dorms on the first floor," he said.

Belinda's assigned room was number 109. She found a folded blanket, sheets, and a pillowcase on the head of the twin bed. The bed had built-in drawers underneath. Beside the bed were an armoire closet and a nightstand.

Her new room-mate, Private First Class (PFC) Audrey Harris, greeted her. "Welcome to Hell on earth."

"Thank you, I think," Belinda said. "Looks like I have a lot to look forward to."

"It's really not that bad once you get used to it," Sgt. Jones said.

"No, there's just nothing to do here," Audrey responded.

"Well, I'll leave you two ladies alone to get acquainted. I'm sure Audrey will take good care of you. Call me if you need anything she can't provide. Otherwise, I'll see you at formation, bright and early in the morning, at 0500 hours."

Audrey's bed had a blue comforter with the lace embroidered on the bottom. There was also a blue braided rug. In the corner, a bookcase type shelf held a small stereo and a television. A heart-shaped framed picture of Audrey and a male, both dressed in a military camouflage uniform, stood out among the family photos. In the photo, Belinda saw a much happier Audrey Harris than the person standing before her today.

"Where are you from?" Audrey asked.

"I just got in from Germany last week, but I'm originally from Florida. I came over from the processing center earlier today."

"Oh, didn't you hate that place?"

"I was only there for a couple of days. Thankfully, I didn't have any problems."

"Well, I hated it. They screwed up my orders, and I ended up staying there for three whole weeks. When it came time for me to leave, I was more than ready."

"I can imagine. After being there only two days, I was ready to get to a place where I could get settled."

"Well, welcome home. I'll be the one to show you around. In a couple of hours, we'll go down for chow. It opens at 1800 hours. You might as well make use of the time and unpack your stuff. That cabinet, pointing to a wooden six-foot-tall armoire closet, with a wood grain front, is empty. So, you can put whatever you want in there. And that's your nightstand."

All Belinda wanted to do was lay down before going to dinner. She knew this would probably be one of the last days where she would have this much time to herself. So, she put the linen on the bed and rested her head on the pillow until dinner.

One Year Later | Ft. Watson, Texas

Since the women's dorm rooms were down the hall from the administrative offices on the first floor, they frequently met

Charles and the other administrative staff as they were leaving or entering the building. His office was on the side of the building overlooking the front parking lot.

One evening Belinda and some of her friends were getting ready to go out dancing at one of the local clubs. Charles was walking to his car to leave for the evening. "Hey, Y'all, I wonder what Top is doing this weekend? Lucinda asked. "Top" was the informal nickname the soldiers had for the First Sergeant.

"Why you worried about him. He does not want to be with you," Audrey said.

"How you know?" Lucinda said.

All the girls laughed. After seeing the family portrait of Charles with his wife and children on his desk, Belinda did not consider him to be available. She thought that was a bold statement for her friend Lucinda to make, joking about the First Sergeant like that, but knowing her personality, Belinda wasn't surprised.

Charles was attractive, but dating a married man was not something that interested Belinda. Not to mention the fact that his rank of First Sergeant (E-8) prohibited him from socializing with the lower enlisted personnel. Belinda and her friend's rank was only Specialist E-4.

Belinda went out on a few casual dates with Leon Wilson, one of the guys in the unit, but it was nothing serious for either of them. Wilson and Belinda arrived at the unit about the same time. They enjoyed going out to the movies, bowling, and dancing. He was a nice guy, but Belinda did not see him as the type of guy interested in raising a stepson. Belinda always considered LeMarkus in whatever she did.

A few weeks later Belinda ran into Specialist Lowe in the cafeteria.

"Can I join you? Specialist Lowe asked. Before Belinda could respond, Specialist Lowe put her tray down on the table and sat in the seat across from Belinda.

"Sure, go ahead," Belinda said.

"I see you are dating Leon."

"We went out a few times."

"Yeah, I see."

"What are you-spying on me?"

"No, I'm not spying, but some people just happen to stand out. Are you guys serious?"

"No. We're just friends, but why do you ask?"

"I was just wondering for a friend of mine."

The two women laughed. "A friend of yours, yeah-right," Belinda said. Did Leon put you up to this?

"No Girl, nobody's put me up to anything. The other day Top was at my desk asking me to type a memo. He looked out the window and saw you getting in the car with Leon. The way you all were dressed, it looked like you were getting going out on a date. Top couldn't even finish the memo. He just turned around and went back into his office and shut the door. He probably would have slammed it if he had been there by himself. Belinda, every time he sees you with someone else he gets jealous."

"Really?"

"Yeah, really."

"Why would he be jealous of me? What about his wife?"

"He's not married."

"So, who's that is in the pictures sitting on his desk?"

"That's right; you haven't been here that long. Top's wife passed away close to two years ago. She had cancer. As far as I know, he's not dated anyone since. His wife is the woman in the picture with their three children. The other female in the picture is his daughter. I believe she's away at college."

"His wife died real young. That's really sad."

"Yeah, she was sick for a long time. Top took some time off work after she died. Then, he came right back to work. Personally, I think he should have taken off a little longer than he did, but he said there was no reason for him to sit around the house doing nothing when he could be at work."

"I can't even imagine what that must have been like for him. Thanks for letting me know."

"You're welcome," Specialist Lowe said, as she left to put away her tray.

Belinda did not admit it to Specialist Lowe, but she was flattered to find out that a man as nice and as nice looking as Charles was interested in her. Still, she knew she could only admire him from a distance.

25

NEWLY-PROMOTED SERGEANT Belinda Stephens stood at parade rest in front of the squad during the morning formation. Charles addressed the company of soldiers. Most of the information was routine reminders of how they should be performing their duties. Then he made an announcement that caused everyone in the parking lot to pay attention, especially Belinda, who had been back in the United States less than a year.

"It's time to start preparing for the annual Return of Forces to Germany (Reforger) exercise. Those of you who will be going will be deploying within the next 120 days. We haven't finalized the assignments yet, so everyone needs to make sure their passports and wills are current."

Belinda wasn't the least bit excited about going back to Germany so soon. She hoped her name wasn't on the list, but if it was, at least, it would be only for a training exercise this time. After the First Sergeant finished addressing the Company he led them on a two-mile physical fitness run. When they finished their run, Charles dismissed them to prepare for their workday.

Specialist Lowe ran to catch Belinda so that they could walk into the barracks together. "I bet you never thought you'd be going back to Germany so soon."

"No, I didn't. How long will we be there? Did you hear him say?"

"I don't remember if he said, but it normally 30 days."

"A whole month out of the country-I don't know what I'm going to do with my car for that long. I just bought it, and I don't want to leave it in the parking lot with everybody knowing we're gone."

"I didn't know you had a new car."

"Yeah, it was my 21st birthday present to me."

"Why don't you talk to the First Sergeant? Remember, not too long ago; he told us that he had just purchased a new home with a two-car garage. Maybe, he will let you leave it at his house. Do you want me to talk to him?"

"I don't know about asking him to keep my car. He's the First Sergeant. You can ask him if he knows of someplace where I can leave it."

"I'll ask him. It can't hurt," Specialist Lowe said.

The next day, Charles met Belinda as he was coming into headquarters and Belinda was leaving.

"I understand the Reforger Exercise has caused a dilemma for you with your car."

"Yeah, I just bought it two months ago. Since I haven't been here that long, I don't know anybody that I can leave it with." I need to find someplace where I can store it."

"You don't have to worry. It can stay in my garage while you're gone."

"I can't ask you to do that."

"Why can't you? I have a garage, and you need a place to store your car. Consider it done. I'll give you the directions to the house. You can come out and visit one day, that way you will know where to come when it's time for you to bring the car. While you all are getting things ready to leave, that will be one less thing to worry about."

"You all, you're not going with us to Germany?"

"Nope! This time, I won't be joining you all on that little trip. I'm going let Staff Sergeant Jones handle that. I've done my share."

Two weeks later, following the directions Charles gave her, Belinda drove to the house. It sat on a corner lot with a beautiful view of the snow-capped mountains in the background. The front yard, landscaped with St. Augustine green grass and a meticulously edged sidewalk, stood out among the other rock landscape yards with cactus as the main centerpiece. A rock wall surrounded the backyard.

Charles introduced Belinda to his two boys, fifteen-year-old Charles Jr. and two-year-old Timothy. The two boys went back into the house while he and Belinda stayed outside to talk in private. They agreed that Belinda would bring the car over to the house the night before she was supposed to leave.

As planned, Belinda arrived at the housed on the eve of the deployment. After securing the car in the garage, Charles gave her a ride back to the barracks. They took the scenic route back to the military base, via the Trans Mountain Road scenic overlook. Charles parked the car so that they could talk.

"I hope I don't get into trouble for saying this, but you are a very beautiful young woman."

Belinda blushed as she thanked him. Charles shared with Belinda that he had been her secret admirer, confirming all the things Specialist Lowe had told her. Belinda let Charles know that the feelings were mutual. The couple experienced their first kiss and less than 12 hours later, Belinda was on a C-130 Cargo plane heading to Germany.

Belinda thought about Charles the entire time she was away. A month later, when she returned from Germany, Belinda and Charles began to date regularly.

While at dinner one day, Belinda asked, "What name do you like to be called? What should I call you?"

"How about Top?"

"You must be kidding. How about Charles?"

"That's fine, I guess. We just have to be careful when we are around other people."

"That's no problem, but I'm not calling you Top."

Things were tense at times, because of Charles' rank and the Army's rule against fraternization. By dating her, he was risking an eighteen-year military career. They carefully selected the restaurants where they went out to eat, so they didn't run the risk of running into too many people from the MP Company. Belinda would get dressed to go out to dinner, but when she reached Charles' house, they would spend the evening at home. Aside from not wanting to get caught fraternizing, Charles did not want to leave his children at home alone. Belinda enjoyed spending time with him and thought it was admirable how much he loved his children.

A few months after they started dating, a job became open in the Administrative Department of the military police company across the street. Charles encouraged Belinda to apply for the job. After the interviews, Belinda ranked number one on the list. Since the job was in Administrative Office of the other company, Belinda was no longer in Charles' direct chain-of-command. That solved one aspect of the fraternization issue, but it didn't solve the rank difference.

Six Months Later

One Saturday, Charles and Belinda were at the house relaxing. Since she worked in the Administrative office, she had weekends off. Charles asked Belinda, "How much are you paying for rent for that apartment?"

Belinda had moved out of the barracks so that she could have more privacy. She didn't receive a housing allowance, so the rent was a substantial portion of her paycheck. Still, she enjoyed being in her own place. "It's four hundred fifty dollars. Why do you ask?"

"I've got an idea. Why don't you move in with me and you can save some money? You're pretty much here anyway."

"I'll think about it, but it will be a while before my lease run out."

Three months later when her lease was over, Belinda moved in with Charles and his two boys, Charles Jr. and two-year-old Timothy. Shortly afterward, she kept her promise to her son, LeMarkus, who was now seven years old and sent for him. Belinda's Aunt Maxine brought LeMarkus to from Florida to Texas on the Greyhound bus.

Although Charles and Belinda were happy being together, the boys were having a tough time adjusting to the blended family. Charles Jr. resented Belinda's presence. He believed she was trying to replace his mother. LeMarkus was having a difficult time getting used to his new brothers. Belinda concluded that they could not accept each other as brothers because their parents were not married. The idea of marriage soon became the magic cure that would fix all that was wrong. It would help the boys accept that they were part of a family. It would help Belinda deal with the guilt of being a Christian living with a man out of wedlock. It would prove to Belinda that Charles really did love her as he said he did. Whenever Charles and Belinda disagreed about anything, it always ended with the fact that they were not married. After living together for three years, Charles asked Belinda to marry him.

After Belinda and Charles were married, they shared fewer activities together.

"It doesn't take much to satisfy me," Charles said. "As long as I have a good meal and a place to lay my head, that's all I need. I would be happy if you wanted to stay at home and not work, but I know you have a career. One day you're going to get tired of me and leave."

"I knew from the time we met that we were meant to be together. I will never leave you, but I don't know how to convince you of that other than to be here," Belinda said.

When Charles reached his twentieth year of military service, he retired from the Army. He purchased a tractor-trailer and became an over-the-road truck driver.

Belinda joined the Mission Valley Baptist Church, under the leadership of Rev. Donald Mosley. Rev. Mosley asked her to teach the widows and widowers Bible Study class. Some of the women couldn't read very well, but they knew what the Bible said from listening to the words of the preacher. Belinda learned more from the members of the class than she could ever teach them, which was most likely the reason Rev. Mosley gave her that responsibility. Belinda could help the women understand what the Bible said. In turn, the women could explain the application of those lessons as they had lived them out in their life experiences.

26

BELINDA RANG THE doorbell hoping Deborah, one of the women from her Bible Study class at church, would come to the door and not someone else in her family.

"Who is it?"

"It's me, Belinda. Can I come in?"

"Belinda?" Deborah opened the door. "Come on in. What are you doing out here in the middle of the night like this? It's almost one o'clock in the morning."

"I'm sorry. I didn't know where else to go."

"What's wrong? You don't have on anything but your nightgown. What happened?

"Charles hit me and threw me down on the floor. I had to leave the house to get away from him."

"Get away from him-y'all only been married two months. What can be so bad to have you all fighting like this? Where are the children at? Where's LeMarkus?"

"He's still there. Charles won't hurt him. I just couldn't stand the sight of them seeing what was happening and seeing me like that."

"Well, you need to go back and make sure."

"I will Deborah. I'm sorry I came out here like this."

"It's okay. Sit down and tell me what's going on."

Deborah led Belinda to a chair in the living room.

"For the past three years, whenever we argued, it was about the fact that we were not married. Now that we are married, we argue about not doing things together." I was asking him about why we couldn't go out anymore. He started complaining about LeMarkus. Since school's out, LeMarkus and Tim are home all day while I'm at work. They argue almost every day. It's always, my Mama this or your Daddy that. Both of them are just fighting for attention. I thought now that we are married, they have no choice but to accept each other as brothers. This is the first time LeMarkus has lived with me since I left him with my Grandmother three years ago. I told Charles he should try to spend some time getting to know LeMarkus instead of always wanting to punish him for misbehaving. Instead of trying to understand LeMarkus, Charles said he didn't have time to spend with Tim, his own son, so how can he spend time with LeMarkus. He was too tired from working on his truck to worry about taking care of someone who didn't appreciate it. So, I told him if he doesn't have time for LeMarkus, he didn't have time for me. That's when he hit me. The kids heard us fighting and came out of the bedroom. They saw me lying on the living room floor in just my nightgown. I didn't want them to see me like that, so I got up and ran out of the house. Then, I drove over here."

"I'm sorry to hear that all of this is happening so soon. You know what they say. The way things are in the beginning is normally how they are going to be."

"I know. In the beginning, we did do some things together. We went places, not that many, but we did go out to dinner sometimes. With Charles being the First Sergeant, we had to be careful. He didn't want to jeopardize his career, and neither did I. When I got a new job as the Administrative Specialist in the 342nd MP Company, they told me it was because of my administrative skills. Now, I think Charles orchestrated the assignment to get me out of his chain of command. After my transfer, being together in public was no longer a problem, but Charles said he didn't want to have to leave the children with a babysitter. We would make plans to go out, and when I arrived at the house, Charles talked me into to staying home to watch a movie on television. I liked the fact that he was the type of father who wanted to take care of his children, so I agreed. I didn't mind staying at the house because I was with him. All I wanted was for us to spend time together. I didn't think we wouldn't ever do anything outside of the house again."

"You guys don't ever go anywhere?"

"Not without it involving work. Every now and then, Charles might go to a "Hail and Farewell," going away party for one of the guys at work. But, other than that we don't do anything anymore. We couldn't even go on a trip for a honeymoon. I would have been happy with just being away for a weekend."

"Well, you're married now. The two of you need to try and work things out. How about talking with Rev. Mosley, do you think Charles will listen to him?"

"I don't know. He might. Charles hardly goes to church, but he did go through the marriage counseling sessions. We couldn't get married if he didn't. A lot of good it did though."

Tomorrow, you should call Rev. Mosley and talk with him. See if he can give y'all some counseling. Now, go back home and try to get along. Plus, you need to check on LeMarkus. I'm sure he's probably afraid and worrying about where his Mama went. Being a man, Charles is probably asleep anyway and you out here like this. Here, let me get you a robe to put on. You can bring it back to me later." Deborah handed Belinda one of her robes. "Just don't say anything else to him tonight. If he's sleep, just let him sleep. You can sleep in the living room, so you don't wake him."

Charles was asleep when Belinda got back home. She took LeMarkus out of bed. By the time the noise awakened Charles, she was leaving out the front door with LeMarkus. Belinda rented a motel room for the night. The next day she met with Rev. Mosley. He prayed with her and gave her some scriptures to read concerning marriage and the submission of the husband and wife to each other. The next day, she found an apartment in the same rental complex where she lived before moving in with Charles. When Belinda went back to the house to get her belongings, Charles apologized and tried to convince her to stay, but it was no use. The one thing she would not accept was physical abuse.

LeMarkus was happy. For the first time, he had his mother all to himself in their own place. It was a cozy two-bedroom, one bath apartment. Four months later, at Christmas time, Charles came to visit and brought presents from him and the boys. He apologized to her again and promised not to ever hit her again. Charles asked Belinda if she and LeMarkus would come back for Christmas dinner. At dinner, he asked if she would come back home for good. She agreed, and she and LeMarkus moved back home.

Charles and Belinda decided to have a child together. Seven months later, she was pregnant with their son, LeDarius. He was born in April of 1988. Belinda's term of service in the Army expired that same month. She did not reenlist, fearing that the next set of orders would send her away and separate the family. In June, Charles Jr. graduated from high school and enlisted in the Army.

The following summer when school was out, Belinda, and the boys went to Florida for summer vacation. She proposed to Charles the idea of them staying in Florida if she got a job to cover their expenses while he took care of the household expenses in Texas. Since he was driving a tractor-trailer cross-country, it didn't matter what state he stopped in to spend time at home. He agreed. With her experience as a military police officer, Belinda was a perfect candidate for the Wakefield Police Department. That next August of 1989, Belinda became a police cadet at the police academy, and the children enrolled in school in Florida. They moved in with Belinda's grandmother Elena until Belinda could find an apartment. They stayed with Elena until Belinda graduated from the police academy. Soon, Belinda was able to purchase a home for them in Wakefield. The following year, Charles loaded all their furniture from the house in Texas into his trailer and joined his family in Florida.

27

1990 | Wakefield, Florida

AT WORK, WHILE patrolling the neighborhood, Belinda worked hard to keep from thinking about her Grandmother, Elena. The last time Belinda saw Elena was two days ago. She was lying in a hospital bed. Attempting to stay focused, Belinda drove around looking for a traffic violator to pull over. Belinda looked for anything she could find, a red light, rolling traffic stop. At this point, an expired tag would be good. That would give Officer Ramirez something to put on her evaluation report once he observed how well Belinda handled the stop. Pickings were slim though. So far, the night's activity was slow. The later it got, the fewer cars there were on the street. With less traffic at night, it was easier to get from point A to B. During the day shift, traveling was almost impossible. If it wasn't the rush hour traffic, it was the conscientious person with a case of blue and white fever, afraid of getting caught speeding in front of a police car, was sure to slow you down. So, the night shift was preferable, at least when it came to getting around the city. It was a beautiful night, one where you didn't feel like being at work. The temperature was just right, with a light breeze. There were plenty of stars in the sky and a crescent moon. Thankfully, there was no full moon to bring out all the "crazies."

Belinda was in phase four of the sixteen-week Field Training program. She finished the first twelve weeks of training without any problems. Now, she was back riding again with Officer Ramirez, the same training officer she started with during phase one. Officer Ramirez had several years of experience as a field training officer. He trained over a dozen new recruits. Her training officers taught her everything Belinda needed to know as a new rookie officer. Now it was time for her to show how good of a student she had been. Besides, Belinda knew the real training didn't start until she was alone in the car, with no one watching over her shoulder to keep her from messing up.

Officer Ramirez wore blue jeans and a blue collared pull-over shirt. His badge hung down around his neck to identify him as an officer. On one side of his hip, strapped onto a black leather belt was an off-duty holster, which held his Glock 40 caliber semi-automatic handgun. The Motorola hand-held radio was encased on the other side. By design, Belinda was the only one in uniform so that the people would approach her first. Up on the block, the old timers knew the difference between the rookie officer in training and the plain clothed veteran officer. Most of the time they walked right past her and went to Officer Ramirez anyway.

Unable to shake the thoughts about her Grandmother, Belinda told Officer Ramirez, "It's possible I could get a call from the hospital while we're on duty. My Grandmother is sick. She has cancer. The doctor told us she does not have much longer. Last week we had to call an ambulance for her. They rushed her to the hospital and revived her heart. Her doctor told us the family needed to consider what to do if her heart stopped again. He said she has less than six months to live, so they assigned a hospice nurse to her. Two days ago, she was in the hospital again."

"I'm sorry to hear that," Officer Ramirez said. "Anything you need, just let us know. I wouldn't worry about having to take time off in a situation like this. If you want, I can let the Sergeant know, or you can tell him. I'm sure he will understand."

"Thanks. Right now, there's nothing I can do so I don't need any time off. Plus, I didn't want to miss too much time from training and have to make it up later."

"I wouldn't worry about that either. You're doing fine. I can't imagine how missing a few days will make any difference in where you are right now. Didn't you once tell me that you lived with your Grandmother?"

"Yeah, we did when we first moved back to Florida. Now we have our own home. It was my grandmother who raised me. Even though I know my mother, Roberta, my Grandmother Elena is really the only mother I know."

"Did you know she was sick when you moved back to Florida?"

"No, I just sensed I needed to come back home. First, I came here on vacation. Then, my husband and I agreed that if I could take care of the expenses here, while he took care of things back in Texas, the kids and I could stay. Fortunately, things worked out, and I was able to get this job."

"This has got to be hard for you," Ramirez said.

"Yeah. It is."

Belinda drove through the back alleys behind the businesses on Main Street. She shined her spotlight on the doors and areas surrounding the buildings checking to make sure no vagrants were loitering. The stats for business burglaries had spiked this month.

Twenty minutes later, dispatch called to them on the radio. "Dispatch to Thirty-three ninety-one."

"Go ahead to thirty-three ninety-one."

"Thirty-three ninety-one, do you have Officer Williams with you tonight?"

"That's 10-4."

"I have an emergency phone call for her," the dispatcher said. "She needs to contact the emergency room nurse at Wakefield Memorial Hospital as soon as possible. I have a number for you. Prepare to copy."

Before the dispatcher could provide the number, Belinda spoke up. "That's alright. I have the number."

"Dispatch we have the number," Officer Ramirez responded. "We are on our way to the station."

"10-4, on your way to the station," answered the dispatcher.

"It's my grandmother. It's funny how I just finished telling you about her."

Belinda's personal vehicle was in the employee lot at the rear of Police Headquarters.

"Just pull over behind your car. Go ahead and go. Don't worry about anything else," Officer Ramirez said. I'll let the Sarge know what's happening."

"Thank you for understanding." Belinda threw her police gear in the trunk of her personal vehicle. Before pulling out of the parking space, she used her cell phone to call the hospital. She explained who she was and why she was calling to the person who answered. The lady connected her to the Emergency Room nurse's station.

"Hello, this is Cheri, Wakefield Emergency room, how can I help you?"

"Hi, my name is Belinda Williams. I got a message to call here."

"Yes, Mrs. Williams. One of your relatives, I believe a Mary Willington, asked that you be contacted. It's about your Grandmother, Elena Stephens. She's here in the hospital."

"Yes Ma'am, Thank you. I'm on the way. Would you let my Aunt Mary know?"

"I'll let her know. Drive carefully."

Twenty-five minutes later Belinda pulled into the parking lot of the Wakefield Memorial Hospital. She took off her gun belt and uniform shirt and put them in the trunk of her car. Belinda found an old tee shirt in the trunk she received from participating a March of Dimes walk and slipped it over her white

V-neck undershirt. The emergency room was full of people. A father was complaining about having to wait for several hours and wanted to know when a doctor would see his son. Belinda checked in with the receptionist, who checked the patient's list and escorted her from the emergency room to Elena's room. They had moved Elena from intensive care to a private room.

When Belinda arrived in the room, her eyes met with her Aunts' Mary and Maxine. The look in their eyes confirmed the seriousness of Elena's condition. Under the circumstances, the staff permitted all the family present to stay in the room with Elena. They had as much privacy as possible.

Mary was sitting in the chair beside the bed. Maxine was standing up beside Mary. Roberta, Belinda's birth mother, was on the other side of the bed. There was an IV in Elena's right hand with tubes were running to the bag on the IV pole. A large tube, connected to a machine at the head of the bed, was inside her mouth. An oxygen tube was inside of her nose. The monitors displayed graphs and beeped of the rhythm of her heart rate, blood pressure, and other vital signs. The look of Elena lying in the hospital bed was almost too much for Belinda to bear, but she was determined to be strong for Elena's sake and the rest of the family.

The steady beeps from the machine continued, along with spikes in the graph as the blood pressure and number of heart beats per minute were displayed on the monitor.

Johnny was sitting on the ledge in front of the window. He was the first to speak. "Belinda, I'm so glad you made it." He walked over and hugged Belinda.

"They told us they would get the message to you. Someone, I don't know who it was, did call back, and say that you were on the way," Mary said.

Belinda stood next to the bed, gently rubbing Elena's hand. She felt the sharpness of the bones in her fingers and raised veins in the back of her hand. "How is she? What happened?"

"Well, we were at home, and she had just finished eating," Mary explained. She had a good day up until that point. I turned the TV channel on to the Jefferson's, and she was watching TV. You know she likes to watch Louise and old George Jefferson go at it. Then, all of a sudden, I heard her take a deep breath like she was having a hard time breathing. I looked over at her, and it looked like she had stopped breathing. I called, "Mama!" After I called her name a second time and she didn't answer, I called 911. The ambulance got there right away. They used them paddle things on her chest and got her heart started again. Then they put that IV in her arm and rushed her to the hospital. Doris was there at the house with me when it happened. Before we left the house, I hurried up and called Johnny and told him to meet us at the hospital. Then we rushed over here."

Johnny said, "I called Maxine, and I guess Maxine tried to call Leroy. Well, you know, Chris was with Maxine, because that's where he's staying right now."

Mary continued, "When we got here they had already worked on her and hooked her up to all these machines. She seems to be doing a little better now. The doctor was in here just before you got here. He looked at her but didn't say much. He just said they were monitoring her closely. He asked if all the family was here. We told him most of us were here and you were on the way. Then he said he'd be back later to check on her progress."

"That's the way it stands right now, Belinda. She's in the hands of the good Lord," Johnny said.

It was close to an hour before the doctor returned to the room. He listened to her heart with his stethoscope and opened her eyelids to shine the light into her eyes as he examined her. Then he wrote some notes on her chart.

When he finished, he asked Belinda if he could speak with her. They walked into the hallway just outside the room.

"Hi, I'm Doctor Dixon."

"Hello, Doctor, I'm Belinda Williams."

"Mrs. Stephens, who is she to you?"

"That's my Grandmother."

"Earlier, I spoke with your family members, Mary and Maxine. Who are they?

"Those are my Aunts. Roberta is my Mother."

"I explained your Grandmother's condition to them. As you know, she has cancer, in addition to her heart condition. The cancer has spread throughout her body. She's been fighting for a long time now. Some of the problems she's' having is due to the cancer. There are also other problems complicated by other issues, such as diabetes and her high blood pressure. She is in a coma now. The machine you see her hooked up to is what's helping her to breathe."

"Okay."

"When I spoke to your family, they told me that someone else was on the way. I presume it was you. I got a sense that they were all waiting until you got here." When I saw you in the room, there was a sense of calmness that seemed to be present, and I watched all eyes fall on you. Right then, I knew you were the one that I was supposed to talk to."

Unsure of how to respond, Belinda continued to listen as the doctor spoke.

"The truth is that the breathing machine your Grandmother is hooked up to is not just helping her, it is what's keeping her right now. She has been through a lot."

Belinda nodded in agreement.

"I understand this is the second time in the past two days she has been revived."

"Yes, it is. She was just here on Wednesday."

"I know this is a big decision for the family, but, I need to know how long you all want to keep her hooked up to the machine or whether we unhook the machine and let her breathe on her own. Basically, it's out of our hands now. There is nothing more medically that we can do for her now. If it's decided to take her off the machine, I can't tell you how much time she has. That's up to someone higher than you and me. It could be hours. It could be weeks. But, off the machine, we will know if it's her or if it's just the machine that's keeping her alive. Do you have any questions?"

"No, I think I understand."

"Would you speak to the family and explain the situation to them?"

"I will."

"Okay, good. I'll come back after you all have had a chance to discuss it to see what you've decided. I know this is difficult. Thank you."

28

Wakefield Memorial Hospital

WHEN DOCTOR DIXON left Belinda went back into the room and stood by her grandmother's bedside where the rest of the family was gathered. She asked if she could speak to them to tell them what the doctor said.

They agreed to go to the family waiting area down the hall to a group of peach colored vinyl couches and chairs. Roberta flipped through the magazines on the small wooden magazine table between the two chairs. Mary and Maxine's nerves would not allow them to sit down. Belinda told them what the doctor said earlier. When Belinda finished talking, Mary looked at her with sadness in her eyes.

"Belinda, what do you think?" Mary asked. I feel kind of lost right now.

Belinda told Mary, "We all do, but before we decide anything I think somebody needs to call Uncle Calvin and Aunt Willie Mae."

"I think Johnny tried to call Calvin earlier, but he either didn't get an answer, or he wasn't home from work yet," Chris said.

"Yeah Belinda, I tried to call. Janice, his wife, answered the phone. She said he should have been on his way home. I told her I would call her back," Johnny said.

"What about Leroy, anybody heard from him?

"No, nobody has seen Leroy. He stopped by the house one day last week, but we hadn't seen him since Mama's been back in the hospital, Mary said."

"Okay, I'll go and see if I can find a phone and call Calvin."

The rest of the family went back to Elena's room. Belinda walked down the aisle to the nurse's desk. Then, Belinda realized she didn't have her address book that had all the phone numbers she needed. So, she went outside to the car. The address book was inside her duffle bag. Remembering that she also had a pair of tennis shoes in her duffle bag, Belinda took off the uniform boots and put on her tennis shoes. Although she still had on the uniform pants, she felt much more comfortable. She thought, without the boots, people might not notice the pants were part of a police uniform.

When Belinda went back inside the hospital, she met Dr. Dixon as he was coming down the aisle from the other direction. "Belinda told Dr. Dixon she had explained the situation to the family, but they had not reached a decision yet. She also needed to call her Aunt and Uncle who lived out of town to let them know what was going on."

"Of course, I understand," Dr. Dixon said. He pointed to an office in the back of one of the nurses' desk. "If you need to use a phone, there is one in there. If there's anything else you need; Nurse Marilyn will be here to assist you."

The nurse looked up from her computer screen when she heard her name. She smiled and nodded in agreement to what the doctor said. "Let us know. We'll be happy to help you," she said.

Belinda thanked Dr. Dixon for helping her. Then she went into the little office. Following the instructions for an outside line, Belinda dialed the number for her Uncle.

Calvin answered the phone.

"Hi Uncle Calvin, it's Belinda."

"Hello Belinda, what's going on?"

"I guess you know Mama is back in the hospital."

"Yeah, I got the message from Janice. She said Johnny or Maxine called earlier. She couldn't remember which one." How is she? What are the doctors saying?'

"That's the reason why I am calling. The doctor explained how cancer had advanced and spread through her body, and her heart was failing. He said she is in a coma now and that the breathing machine is the only thing keeping her alive. He wants the family to decide whether or not to take her off the machine."

"Belinda, you are there, and you know what's happening. What does everyone else feel we should do?

"They haven't said yet, but I think they are all thinking the same thing. It's just that nobody wants to be the one to say it."

"I trust your judgment. Do what needs to be done. I support whatever you decide."

"All I know is that Mama always said if it ever got to the point where she could not take care of herself, and somebody had to be feeding her and giving her baths, she didn't want to live like that. She repeated it before she went back to the hospital last week. According to the doctor, she's already gone. The machine is the only thing that's keeping her alive. The only way we will know for sure is to unplug the machine."

"Then it looks like it's settled then, said Calvin. Keep me posted. I'm going to see what flights are available so I can start making plans to come down. Is everybody else there?"

"Everybody, except Leroy and Willie Mae."

"Do you know how to reach them?"

"I have an old number for Aunt Willie Mae. I am going to try it when I finish talking with you. Leroy is probably out in the streets somewhere. If he doesn't make it here within the next couple of hours, then, I'll make some calls to have somebody go and see if they can find him."

"Alright, I'm going to go so you can try and call Willie Mae. I'll talk to you later."

"Okay Calvin, I'll talk to you later."

Belinda dialed the number she had for Willie Mae.

"Hello," Willie Mae answered.

"Hello Auntie Willie Mae, this is Belinda."

"Hello, Baby, how you doing?"

"Not so good right now. I'm calling to let you know about Mama. They rushed her back to the hospital tonight. She is having problems with her heart. She is in a coma right now." This is the second time she had been here in the past two days. They rushed her to the hospital last Wednesday, but she was able to go home."

"You say she is in a coma. So, she is not aware of what is going on."

"No, but I believe she knows we are here. Obviously, she can't respond. Everybody is here except for Leroy and Calvin."

"What does the doctor have to say?"

"That's the other part of the reason why I'm calling. The doctor wants the family to decide whether or not to take her off the breathing machine. I told him that I would speak to the family to see what everybody felt."

'Belinda, I can't make that decision. You and Mary are there and know what's going on better than I do. I imagine whatever they decide will be the right thing."

"I know Aunt Willie Mae. I just didn't want something to happen and you to feel hurt because nobody told you what was going on."

"I appreciate it, Baby. I know you will do what is best."

"Okay Auntie Willie Mae, I'll call you back later to let you know what's going on." Right now, all we know to do is to just keep praying. I know you're not here, but I know you will be praying also."

"Okay Baby, I'll talk to you later."

Belinda hung up the phone and left the room. "Were you able to dial out? Did you find everything you needed?" Nurse Marilyn asked.

"Yes, I made the calls I needed to make, Thank you."

Belinda walked back to the room where the family was gathered. Belinda called them together again in the waiting area. Leroy was now present with the family.

"Hi, Leroy! I'm glad you're here."

"Yeah Belinda, I made it. I didn't know what was going on or I would have been here sooner. I was down there at the Back-Alley Club on Wood Street. I had just got home last night when Big Mack came by and told me you all were trying to get in touch with me. I couldn't get a way up here until now."

"Leroy, you know you could have called, and somebody would have come to pick you up," Mary said.

Belinda knew Leroy didn't want to admit it, but he was probably too intoxicated to come to the hospital last night. She figured everybody else was thinking the same thing, but no one said it.

Belinda told them about the conversations she had with Calvin and Willie Mae. No one spoke for a few seconds. They understood Calvin and Willie Mae agreed with whatever decision made by those who were present.

Johnny broke the silence. 'You know the Bible says, man is appointed once to die" And once you die to the old nature if you got Jesus in your life, you don't have to worry about the sting of old man death no more."

Maxine said, "We know Mama got Jesus in her life." She's been serving him for a long time. She didn't always go to church, but she knew the Lord."

"We all knew it would come to this one day. Mama always said she didn't want to be down where she couldn't take care of herself," Mary said, somberly.

"Yeah Mary, I know she said that, but if she has a chance-," Doris said, defiantly.

"Roberta, what do you think?" Doris asked.

"I don't have nothing to say right now."

Everyone once again all looked at Belinda.

"We all know what Mama has been through and everything the doctors have told us about what they have done for her," Mary said.

"You're right," Belinda said. We know what Mama's wishes are. She told them to all of us, more than once. I think we should go ahead and let the doctor know they can disconnect the machine. Let her breathe on her own. "

Mary nodded, and said, "Okay Belinda."

Chris, Leroy, and Maxine agreed.

"Okay Linda, that's what we will do. The good Lord will decide," Johnny said.

"If anyone is not in agreement, here is your chance to say something before I talk with the doctor."

When Doctor Dixon returned, Belinda told him the family had decided to allow Elena to breathe on her own. They all gathered back at her bedside. Dr. Dixon called in a couple of nurses to assist him. He disconnected the ventilator machine. Then he carefully removed the tubes from her mouth. After a few gasps of air, Elena started to breathe on her own. Her breathing was difficult at first. Each breath sounded more labored than the one before. She'd relax and then took deep breaths again until her breathing finally evened out.

Everyone was in the room, but at the same time, they were somewhere off in another place, trying to make sense of the moment. Johnny and Chris fought to hold back tears. For Mary and Maxine, the pain of their impending loss was too much to bear. At times, they sobbed openly.

Maxine rubbed Elena's head and kissed her cheek. "Mama we are all here," she said.

Johnny asked everyone to gather around the bed for prayer. They prayed for Elena that God would heal her if it were his will, that God would comfort her and keep her. They prayed for themselves; that they would have the strength to make it through the night. For some of them, it would be the hardest day of their lives.

As time passed, they continued to pray, both individually and together, as they sat at her bedside. Mostly, they sat in silence. Every now and then somebody would laugh and smile with a big old grin while remembering something funny Elena once said or did. Maxine told childhood stories that some of them had never heard. The laughter seemed to help the pain. Each of them talked about the love their mother had for them. They did all they could to stand strong. Before her recent illness at the age of seventy-two, Elena had never once stepped foot inside of a hospital.

The nurse periodically inserted morphine into Elena's IV. "This will help keep her as comfortable as possible," the nurse said.

Five hours seemed like five days. They sat at her bedside, watching and praying as Elena Franklin Stephens took her last breath. The Matriarch of the Stephen's family went home to be with the Lord.

29

THE FOLLOWING YEAR during Elena's birth month, Belinda gave birth to Patricia, her and Charles' second child together. Belinda remembered Elena's words, "When the Lord takes one away he always sends another." LeMarkus and Tim were teenagers in high school. With Patricia's birth, three-year-old LeDarius was no longer the baby in the family.

The pressures of operating a business and keeping up with the financial responsibilities caused Charles to be away from home for extended periods of time. Belinda was a rookie officer with no seniority, so she worked the midnight shift. Having a fourth child, crazy work schedules, and difficulty making the truck payment left Charles with no choice but to sell his truck and became a stay at home dad to take care of Patricia. Then, almost two years to the date and with Belinda's blessings, Charles purchased another truck and went back on the road.

Charles and Belinda focused their attention on taking care of the children and work. There was no time for them to spend time together as a couple, even if they wanted to. They attended school plays to watch the children perform, volunteered in the concession stand at little league practice and spent Thanksgiving and Christmas with Belinda's family. Their relationship evolved around the children and work. Belinda became accustomed to going places alone unless the children went with her. That was alright with Charles, but Belinda soon felt as if she was still single but married.

1993 | Wakefield

"Charles let's go out and do something this tonight."

"I would like to go, but I can't. I have too much work to do on that truck. If that truck doesn't move, we don't make any money."

"I know, but just this once, let's get a babysitter and go to the movies. It's been a while since we've done anything together. I can call Wanda to see if she can watch the kids for us."

"It's Friday night. Wanda's a young woman. She's probably busy tonight."

"What are you saying, Charles? Wanda is actually a year older than me. Just forget it; I don't want to go anywhere."

"You are always taking what I say and trying to make it into something else."

"What else can I make that into Charles? It's clear. You don't see me as a young woman with needs, but you can recognize those needs in my friends who are the same age as me or even older.

"As hard as I work, I can't please you, no matter what I do, it's never enough."

"Charles, I just would like to do something with you sometimes like other couples." Out of all these years, we've never taken a trip together, just the two of us. Everywhere I go, I'm always alone, but I'm supposed to be married."

"I would like to go someplace sometimes, but I'm too tired. I've been working all day and all night in that truck."

Charles went into the kitchen and grabbed a cold beer. He didn't drink beer while he was working, but when he wasn't working beer was the only thing he drank. He sat on the sofa to watch TV. Soon, he was fast asleep. Belinda stayed in the bedroom. She cried until the tears no longer fell and she was asleep.

Belinda tried to express her feelings. At times, she still felt unappreciated by Charles. One day she became so angry she threw a glass, breaking it against the wall. She'd be fine for several months until she couldn't hold the anger and disappointment inside any longer. Then the least expected thing would cause her to explode and display uncontrollable emotions. No matter what, Charles remained unmoved.

Three Years Later

LeMarkus became rebellious and was associating with a group of boys who seemed to always be in trouble with the law.

He skipped school and was in danger of not graduating from high school. Tim became more distant and withdrawn. Belinda attributed the changes to their going through a teenage phase until she couldn't ignore the problems any longer. She pleaded with Charles to spend more time with the boys but work always got in the way. She appreciated Charles being a good provider for the family but felt that being a good dad and husband was more than just paying the bills.

Problems with LeMarkus deteriorated. He would stay out of the house overnight. Belinda asked Charles to talk with LeMarkus about his behavior, but Charles said he was only his stepfather and didn't want to interfere. Charles couldn't seem to understand how much LeMarkus needed him. Charles was the only father LeMarkus had. For the most part, Charles left it up to Belinda to handle the situation. The next couple of years Belinda and all of the energy of the family focused on LeMarkus. Eventually, LeMarkus left home permanently. The following year, Tim, who was two years younger than LeMarkus, graduated from high school and left home to go to college. Now Charles and Belinda were alone with their two younger children, seven-year-old LeDarius and four-year-old Patricia.

With LeMarkus and Tim gone, LeDarius appeared to be depressed because he missed his big brothers. Belinda was concerned about LeDarius and sought the help of a family therapist. Some sessions were with the entire family, while others attended by just her and Charles. Belinda attended the counseling sessions until it didn't make sense anymore. If she wasn't going to follow through with making the necessary changes to make things better, which to her counselors meant leaving Charles, there was no reason to spend money on counseling. That time, she actually filed for a divorce but later withdrew the divorce orders, vowing to do whatever she could to make things better in their relationship.

Belinda sought help from several therapists throughout their marriage. She tried male counselors, female counselors, Christian, and non-Christian. Charles never made it past the third visit. The result was always the same. The time Belinda spent in counseling alone; she worked on the events of her past, involving her father. When she believed their relationship would never change, Charles would promise to try to do better. For a few months, he did. They would spend time together as a couple. Charles would even go to church with Belinda. However, the changes never lasted more than a few months. Whenever the subject of a divorce surfaced, it was one Belinda could not make. She refused to give up hope. She felt as if God was asking her if she had truly done all that she could do regarding her ability to meet Charles' needs and be a good wife to him.

One evening Belinda came home from work and joined Charles, while he was sitting on the back patio. The children were still at school. Belinda was feeling depleted, depressed, and hopeless. "Why don't you love me? She asked.

"What do you mean? I do love you."

"Then why don't you ever want to spend any time with me?"

"Belinda, do we have to go through this again. Can't I have any peace?"

"Yeah Charles, you can have your peace. I just wanted you to know how I felt. I don't know the words to say to make you understand how I feel. Maybe, I can show you." She pulled her Glock 9 mm. handgun out of the holster and pointed it to her head. Her finger rested on the trigger guard. "Charles, this is how much I hurt. I feel like I can't go on anymore. Don't worry, I'm not going to pull the trigger or do anything to hurt myself. I just don't know any other way to get across to you how much pain I'm in."

"This is what I've done to you?" Charles asked. His voice was sad.

"I'm not blaming you. I just don't know what else to do." Belinda lowered the gun and put it back in the holster, then went inside the house." She spent the rest of the evening in bed.

Belinda knew she needed to seek help. The next day, Belinda made an appointment with their family therapist. She discussed how she was feeling and what she had done. She assured him she was not a danger to herself and would not use her weapon to harm herself or anyone else.

30

Ten Years Later | Wakefield, Florida

ALL BELINDA COULD SEE was darkness. Barely able to breathe, she frantically gasped for air. She tried to scream, but nothing would come out, not loud enough for anyone to hear anyway. With the first attempt, her voice only shrieked. Now, all that could escape was a whimper. The grip around her throat was too tight. Still, Belinda kept trying to yell. It was like a game to him. For several minutes that seemed like an eternity, his grip would tighten. Belinda thought for sure she was going to die. Then, the grip would loosen. She gasped again, taking in as deep a breath as possible. She tried not to panic by controlling her breathing, taking in long, slow, and deep breaths. Breathe in deep- five seconds-hold it. Then exhale. Again-one second, two seconds, three seconds, four seconds, and five seconds. Then breathe. Silently, in the dark, Belinda prayed unto Jesus. "Jesus, help me," Belinda pleaded. She believed if she called on the name of the Lord, she would be released. But, even as she prayed his grip tightened. Belinda knew she wasn't getting free, so she relaxed her body, quit struggling, and let go. It was pitch black. She started falling. It was such a long way down. She felt as if she was falling the entire length of several twenty-foot skyscrapers. They just kept coming one after another. She fell continuously without stopping. Then, just as she was about to hit bottom, suddenly, her body jerked, and she was free.

Belinda sprang up in the bed, surveyed the room, looking from left to right. The television in the armoire in front of the bed was playing. The Early Edition News was starting. Belinda heard the news anchorman giving the highlights. As much as she could see from the light from the television, everything was intact, and there was no danger. Charles was in bed next to her. Normally, he would have been asleep and not known anything about what was happening, but this time he was awake. He was lying on his side propped up on his right elbow, watching her.

"Did you see me while I was sleeping?" Belinda asked in a tone that indicated the question was loaded with more than what it sounded like on the surface.

"Yeah, I did, Charles said."

"Did it look like anything was happening to me?"

"Looked like you were having trouble breathing."

"Wow! You saw that. I was having trouble," I'm glad that finally, someone can see how much I struggle in my sleep. "Why didn't you wake me?"

"Well...I..." He stuttered a bit. "You woke up." Charles blurted those words out as if the redeeming response popped into his head just in the nick of time.

"The next time you see me struggling like that, wake me up-Please!"

"Yeah. Okay. But, what was happening?"

"I couldn't breathe again. It felt like something was choking me. This time it was worse. I just can't sleep on my back. I've never been able to. The nightmares have always been there. I remember when I was younger, one day my Grandmother, Aunt Mary and Roberta were sitting in the living room talking. I was sitting on the sofa beside Mary, and I fell asleep. I could still hear them talking and the voices on the television, but I was paralyzed and couldn't move. I tried calling out to them for help, but nobody could hear me. I was screaming. The more I struggled to get free, the worse it got. I remember begging them to all hold hands and call on Jesus. When they held hands and mentioned Jesus' name, I was released. I opened my eyes, and they were all watching television, unaware that anything was happening to me.

There have been other times when I've been awake and became paralyzed from my waist down. One day I fell on the bed because I couldn't stand. Then, after a few minutes, the feelings returned to my legs, and I could stand again. I have no idea why this happens to me."

"I'm sorry Sweetheart. Next time I'll try to wake you and by the way, Good Morning."

"Yeah, Good Morning!"

Charles went into his walk-in closet to get dressed. Belinda rolled over on her side. She considered trying to go back to sleep, but when she glanced at the clock; she saw that it was too close to the time she was supposed to get up. She reached for her Bible from the headboard of the bed. After reading a few verses from the Book of Psalms, she got out of bed to get ready for the work. By the time Belinda got downstairs, LeDarius and Patricia had already left for school. Charles, already downstairs, had brewed a fresh pot of coffee. He was sitting at the table reading the morning newspaper.

With car keys in hand, Belinda was heading towards the front door when she heard Charles call her name.

"Belinda, I might be late for the game tonight, but I'll be there," he said. "I've got to make a delivery in Brooksville. Depending on how fast I can get my truck unloaded will determine how soon I can get back. I tried to tell the dispatcher I wouldn't be working anymore on Fridays, but the newspaper printing plant ordered a special load of sale advertisements flyers to be included in the Wakefield Herald this weekend. If you see LeDarius, can you remind him?"

"If," Belinda emphasized, "I see LeDarius, I'll tell him. I have training at the Department today. Afterwards, I'll be working the game." Belinda thought about giving the extra-duty detail away, but she decided she might as well watch the game and get paid too. "I hope you make it back in time. I'll see you when you get there."

Wakefield Police Department

Several people were already seated in the conference room on the second floor of the Wakefield Police Department when Belinda arrived. She took the vacant seat at the end of the table, next to Lt. Richman. A few moments later Chief Robinson arrived carrying his coffee cup in one hand and his notepad in the other one. At 5 ft. 5, he was shorter than many of the officers in the department. Smelling the fresh coffee, Belinda wished she could have stopped for coffee but arrival with less than five minutes to spare didn't allow time for coffee.

"Good morning everyone," Chief Robinson said "This morning, I think I'll start at the opposite end of the room. Belinda, what do you have for us?" As a newly promoted lieutenant, Belinda oversaw the Southside midnight shift.

"Good morning Chief. Last night our guys arrested two black male juveniles for burglary. They caught them breaking into the J-Mart Convenient Store on Central Avenue. The officers were patrolling on bicycles when they saw two bikes lying in the alleyway behind the store. As they got closer, they heard the glass breaking from a cinder block that was thrown in the store. Then the alarm went off. The officers had the store secured. The juveniles came out when we threatened to release the dog inside."

"Good job! Who made the collar?"

"Officers Fountain and Jacobi."

"Make sure you make a note of that in their file. That's good solid police work."

"I already have Chief. I'll be sure to pass on your remarks to them."

"Anything else?"

"I gave the good news first. We still have someone out there doing car burglaries. Last week we had a total of eight cars broken into. There were no prints and no witnesses. One lady said she remembered her dog barking about two o'clock in the morning but didn't think anything of it. The next morning, she discovered her cell phone and some loose change was missing from the center console."

"Okay, that's something. Let's see if anybody has been using the phone?" If so, find out who they are calling. That will lead us back to our bad guy."

Detective Sergeant Camilla spoke up. "Chief, I can add something to that, if I may."

"Sure, Frank, what have you got?"

"Last night we arrested Daryl Clayton for dealing in stolen property. He had enough cell phones that he could have opened his own kiosk in the mall. One of them was our victim's phone from that burglary. However, according to Clayton, he's not the one doing the burglaries. He just traded some guy named Tony for the merchandise." We talked with him for about an hour before he lawyered up."

"How many burglaries have we had in the city so far this month?"

"So far we have had 28 car burglaries and 19 house burglaries."

"We're just a little over halfway through the month with a total of 47 burglaries so far. What are we doing about this problem?

"Chief, I propose we put a few more guys from the tactical squad out and just flood the area," Sgt. Carmella said.

"Do we know when and where most of these are taking place?"

"I have not done an analysis yet, no Sir."

"Okay, next week, come prepared with that information. Get with our crime analyst and let's put it up on the map. Also, go ahead and get with Belinda about putting some extra men out in sector eight. Let's catch these guys. They're killing us in the crime stats."

"Belinda, what else do you have before we move on?"

"Our guys also made 35 citizen contacts in the areas where the burglaries occurred. They also wrote 123 traffic tickets, made five felony arrests, and made seven misdemeanor arrests. That's all I have Chief."

"Thanks, Belinda. Good job! Who's next?"

Belinda caught a glance at Lt. Mike Brunnell, who gave her a quick wink as Lt. Brady began to make his report. Mike knew, as well as Belinda, that no matter what she said or did one of the golden-haired boys would have something to say to try to make themselves look more important. Belinda also knew that as long as she came prepared, there was nothing anyone could say to draw criticism.

By the time the staff meeting was over, it was close to 10:30. Belinda went to the office to check her email, sign-off on whatever memos that needed her signature. Mike walked past the office and saw her sitting there.

"Hey Belinda, what are you doing for lunch? Rich and I are going to the Bright Morning Café. You're welcome to come along. We'll be leaving in just a few minutes."

"Sounds good, but I have to finish up a couple of things here. I'll try to meet you there. If I don't see you at the restaurant, I'll see you later at training."

"All right, I done already told you, girl, that it's alright to let some of that stuff wait but suit yourself. I know you." Laughing, Mike said, "I'll see you at training."

"Thanks, Mike, I'll see you later."

The training class ended early that afternoon. Belinda debated whether to go all the way home before her extra-duty detail started. It was only four thirty. She wanted to get there a few moments early to check in with the school's contact person, but it was not necessary to be two hours early.

Belinda considered going to visit with her mother since Roberta lived a few blocks from the school. Belinda had not seen Roberta in several weeks. Several of Belinda's friends told her that they had seen her mother. They all talked about how Roberta was still complaining about Belinda. They tried to talk to Roberta to get her to see things differently but felt they couldn't get through to her. Belinda imagined how the conversation would go if she went to visit with Roberta. They would both say hello to each other, how's the weather, and then say good-bye. She found it difficult to have a real conversation with her mother. Sometimes, it was hard to convince herself it was worth the try.

The phone rang, interrupting her thoughts.

"Hello, this is Lt. Williams, can I help you?"

"Mom, Good! I'm glad I caught you."

"Hello, Pat, What's wrong?

"I left my black socks at home. Could you get a pair for me and bring them to me in the band room?"

"You're lucky you caught me. I was just trying to figure out whether I wanted to go all the way home just to turn around and come back. How did you forget your socks?"

"LeDarius was yelling for me to come on downstairs so we wouldn't be late. I forgot to take them out of the dryer. By the time I remembered them it was too late to turn around."

"Okay, I'll go back to get them."

"Thanks, Mom! Is Dad still coming to the game?"

"He might be a little late, but he said he would be there. He had to go to Brooksville today."

"Okay!"

"See you in a bit."

31

Blazer High School | Wakefield

BLAZER HIGH SCHOOL was one of the few historical African-American schools in the community that wasn't torn down. Now, it was one of the most sought-after schools in the district because of its student's academic achievements. The football team was competing for a position in the playoffs. A large crowd was expected. Most of the parking spaces in the front parking lot were full. The volunteers were helping pedestrians cross the street from where their cars were parked at the gate's entrance. Recognizing Belinda's white unmarked patrol car, one of the volunteers stopped oncoming traffic so Belinda could turn into the parking lot. She glanced at the dashboard clock - 5:40 p.m. "Good, I still have twenty minutes," She thought. Officer Matthew's marked patrol vehicle, #125 was already in the parking lot. Belinda met Officer Matthews by the ticket booth. He was talking with Deidra Swanson, who is an alumna, and long-time supporter of the school. Her blue polo shirt with the Blazer school logo was perfectly framed by the gold-painted ticket booth forming the school colors of blue and gold. The painted "Blazer" flames covered the bottom portion of the booth, symbolically making it look like it was on fire.

"Hey, you just missed your daughter. She was just up here looking for you," Deidra said.

"Okay, thanks. I got something she needs."

"How old is she now? I remember when you were pregnant with her."

"She's fourteen and in the ninth grade."

"Man, I'm getting old."

"Time doesn't stand still," Belinda said.

"No, it sure doesn't.

"Don't you have a son too that's on the football team?"

"Yeah, LeDarius, he's a senior."

"How are your other boys, Tim and LeMarkus?"

"They are fine. LeMarkus is doing well. He should be here tonight. Tim, he's enrolled in a Master's Program at Tampa University."

"I'm glad to hear they are doing well and now, I know for sure I'm getting old," Deidra said.

"Lieutenant, Mr. Davis was here earlier to meet with us," Officer Matthews said. I told him you were on the way. I think he had our checks to give you. Here is the assignment sheet he left with me to give to you. He said he'd catch up with you on the field."

Colton Davis had been the Athletic Director for the past ten years. He and Belinda had a good working relationship.

"If it's alright with you, I'll take the front entrance," Matthews said.

"Yeah, that's fine."

"I'm going to go meet with my daughter, Pat in the band room. I'll be right back. Call me if the other guys get here before I get back."

"Okay, Lieutenant."

The other officers were arriving as Belinda was returning to the front gate. She gave them their assignments while she remained a floater.

No one was waiting in line at the gate to buy tickets when the officers left. Deidra took the opportunity to speak privately with Belinda.

"Belinda, I didn't want to say this while the officers were standing here, but I saw your mother, Roberta, a few days ago."

"Oh yeah?"

"I was standing in line behind her at the grocery store. She was talking to the cashier. From the sounds of the conversation, I would say they knew each, but she didn't know who I was. Belinda, she was saying some awful things about you, and she apparently didn't care who was listening. I don't know for sure, but I think she might have been drinking too. I did smell alcohol."

"I'm sorry to hear that," Belinda said.

"Belinda, I know you. We go back a long way. I don't know what has happened between you and your mother, but I know you haven't done the things she was accusing you of doing. And I also know some of the things you've done to try and help her, but that's not the story she's telling around town. I think you should try to talk to her."

"Deidra, you're not the only one I've heard this from. I don't know what to say. It's been like this for a long time. Now other people are starting to see things for what they are. But, thanks for letting me know. The only thing I've done was to try and help my mother when I could."

"How is Charles? Is he going to make it tonight?"

"He's fine. This morning he said he might be running a little late, but Charles is not going to miss seeing his daughter playing in the band or his son playing football. For the last twenty years I couldn't get him to walk out of the house with me past the front yard, but for his children, he would go to the end of the earth if they wanted him to."

"That's a man for you. Don't be too hard on him," Deidra said.

"I guess."

Hearing adults talking and the playful laughter of small children, Belinda turned around. Two children were briskly walking several feet ahead of their parents towards the ticket booth.

"Looks like you have some customers. I'll catch up with you later."

"Okay, take care of yourself."

It was the middle of the first quarter when Charles arrived. He met Belinda beside the gate at the entrance to the bleachers. He was wearing a pair of jeans, a blue polo shirt with the Blazer's logo and LeDarius' name and number"23" screen printed on the back. He was also wearing his favorite black Ivy cap that he wore if he wasn't wearing a baseball cap.

"Hi, I got here as fast as I could," Charles said. What's the score?"

"Nobody's scored yet. The game just started, so you haven't missed much."

"Good. Has LeDarius been in the game yet?"

"He's been in once, but again, it just started."

"Look at him, it's hard to believe he was once so small that I could almost hold him in my hand," Charles said.

"He only weighed four pounds, and you were afraid to hold him."

"Yeah but look at him now."

Charles reached out his arm to hug Belinda. Instinctively, she adjusted the radio mic on her shoulder to keep it from pressing it accidentally. Charles pulled back. "Oh, I'm sorry. I forgot I shouldn't kiss you while you're in uniform."

"No, it's not that. I was just trying to keep from broadcasting it to everyone, that's all."

Officer Matthews called Belinda on the radio. "I.D. 1530 to Lt. Williams"

"Go ahead to Lt. Williams," Belinda responded.

"Lieutenant, this is Officer Matthews. I have Mr. Davis over here by the front entrance."

"10-4, I'll be right there."

Belinda looked at Charles.

"I heard it. You have to go. I understand."

"I'll find you later."

A sea of blue and gold covered the fan's bleachers. The colors were on everything, including the seat cushions, the band uniform, cheerleaders' uniforms, tee shirts, hats, and jackets. Everyone was dressed in something to show off the school pride with the school colors and the Blazer logo. At the base of the bleachers, Charles stood to the side to allow a mother and her two-year-old daughter to go in front of him. He smiled at the toddler, noticing that she had the blazer flames painted on the side of her cheek.

Charles sat in the stands with some of the other parents who were also members of their church. As soon as he sat down, LeDarius made a huge tackle that opened a hole for Dwight Hightower, the team's star running back. That play positioned Hightower to score the first touchdown of the game. The crowd exploded with a cheer for the team. Ten moments later, LeMarkus arrived and sat beside Charles. He was wearing a gray button-down dress shirt with blue jeans and dress shoes.

"Hey, you made it," Charles asked.

"My little brother's playing in a big game like this one; I wasn't going to miss this for nothing. I came straight from work."

"I'm glad you came, I know LeDarius will be happy."

"Where's Mom?"

"She's around. She's here working the game tonight. A little while ago she was over by the concession stand, but she had to leave to go meet with someone," Charles said.

"I saw Pat when I came in just now. The band passed by me as I was trying to get to the bleachers. Has anybody heard from Tim?"

"Tim won't be here tonight. He said he was taking the last class for his Degree. It must be a hard class because he said he couldn't come to the game because he has to study."

"That's understandable," LeMarkus said. I can only imagine what he's going through."

Once again, the crowd erupted in cheers after the Blazers scored another touchdown. In the end, the final score of the game was 21 to 7, in favor of the Blazers. The team was headed to the playoffs for the first time in over 15 years. Everyone was so happy. People were shaking hands with people they didn't know, congratulating each other with high fives, and slapping each other on the back.

Charles and LeMarkus joined the other family members waiting for the players in front of the locker room. Belinda dismissed the officers from the detail, except for two of them held behind to provide security for the remaining parents and employees. Then, Belinda joined them Charles and LeMarkus. When LeDarius came out of the locker room, Charles was leaning against the post, next to the steps.

"Hey! Dad, you made it." LeDarius' face was beaming.

"Yeah son, that was a good game."

LeDarius spoke to Belinda. Then his eyes landed on LeMarkus, and his face lit up even brighter. "Wow, LeMarkus, where did you come from?"

"What you mean, where did I come from. I told you Lil Bro, I'm gonna be there with you all the way. Great game, Darius" LeMarkus said, hitting LeDarius on the head with the game program.

"Thanks, man. It really means a lot to me seeing you here."

LeDarius turned his attention back to Charles. "Dad, I'm going to go with the team. I'll get a ride home, so you don't have to wait for me."

"Okay, go celebrate with your team-mates. You deserve it."

"Thanks, dad! Bye, everybody!" LeDarius ran to catch up with a couple of the guys on the team.

Charles, LeMarkus, Belinda and the other parents walked towards the front exit gate. Pat ran from behind to catch them. "Hey Dad, Y'all wait up," she yelled.

"Well, Hello, I was wondering where you were," Charles said. "When I didn't see you, I thought maybe you were out waiting by the car."

"No, I saw Y'all when you first left the bleachers, but I had to wait until the band was dismissed. Hey Mom!"

"Hi Pat," Belinda said.

"Wait! Dad, did you see LeDarius tackle that guy?" Pat asked, excitedly.

"Yeah, that was a good hit. He really played a good game tonight."

Pat moved to the other side of the sidewalk, next to LeMarkus and gave him a sisterly punch to the arm.

"Ouch, hey, watch out," LeMarkus said.

"Oh, did I hit you? Sorry Bro," she said as she laughed. "LeMarkus, man, I'm glad you were able to get off work and come see LeDarius."

"Yeah, me too, our little brother's going to the playoffs. I'm happy for him.

Two Weeks Later

The big game in the playoffs exceeded the excitement expected. The entire city came out to support the team. People who had not been to a football game in fifteen years since the last time the school competed in the playoffs, bought tickets to the game. Students and faculty of other high schools whose team did not make the playoffs were there. All the bleachers on both sides of the field were full.

The Blazers played a team that had been in the playoffs three out of the last five years. Two years prior, that team was the state runner-up in the state championships. The Blazers kept them from scoring for the first quarter, but they scored two touchdowns right before half-time. Despite their best efforts, the Blazers lost the game by a score of 37 to 6. The team was heartbroken, but they came away with a resolve to do better next year and the belief that it was possible. Everyone in Wakefield celebrated their accomplishments.

After graduation, LeDarius enrolled in the local junior college and moved into an apartment near the school.

32

One Year Later | Wakefield Police Department

BELINDA WAS SITTING at her desk at Police Headquarters finishing the end of shift activity report. For a weekend on the midnight shift, there wasn't much activity to report compared to the number of incidents that would typically happen on the weekend. In fact, the night would have been deemed uneventful if it wasn't for the burglary arrest on Remington Street in sector eight.

Straining to stay awake, Belinda rubbed her eyes. The twelve-hour shifts were long, and this was the third night, which always seems the longest. Belinda couldn't keep from yawning. She leaned back in her seat, stretching before typing the next sentence. Under the heading "Significant Events," Belinda wrote:

An intoxicated Hispanic male was arrested for burglary of an occupied dwelling. He gained entry to the house by breaking a glass pane of the rear french doors. The homeowner was asleep on the sofa. She woke up to the frightening sound of breaking glass. However, she had the presence of mind to grab the portable phone from the end table and run into a back bedroom to call the police. When officers arrived, they found and arrested the male, who was still inside the house. The occupant was found hiding in the closet unharmed.

Thinking about the incident, Belinda knew things could have turned out a lot differently, especially for the homeowner, if not for the quick response of K-9 officer Marc Freeman. The burglary was dispatched at 4:05 a.m. Belinda knew that Officer Freeman had already gone home because Belinda heard him sign off-duty a few minutes prior to the call. Other officers might have turned off their radio as soon as they signed off-duty. But Officer Freeman heard the call dispatched, apparently as soon as he was pulling into his driveway. Belinda heard Freeman tell Dispatch he was turning around to respond to the burglary from his residence. Because he lived in the city limits, he was only a few streets away from the address of the house burglary. Freeman arrived within a few short minutes, along with his K-9 partner, Andrew. From reading Freeman's report sent over the report writing module, Belinda learned the suspect gave up when he when heard the dog barking. Fortunate for him, Freeman did not have to release the dog. With the burglar being transported to jail by one of the officers driving a sedan, Freeman and his partner, Andrew were able to sign-off duty again.

Reflecting on the night, Belinda thought it ended pretty good for Freeman and the rest of the squad. Belinda knew all too well how things could change in an instant. One minute, all is right with the world, and the next is like someone suddenly opened the gates of Hades and threw away the key. Two weeks ago, they had one of those nights. Just when things were quiet, out of nowhere, Freeman was involved in the two vehicle pursuits. During the last one, he wrecked his patrol car. Both pursuits were still under review as to whether they were justified. As much as Belinda always wanted to go to bat for her officers, she couldn't support Freeman on the last one. Making matters worse, their diminished fleet of spare vehicles was now even smaller. Freeman had a reputation of being someone who would chase down his own mother if she broke the law. He seemed determined to live up to that reputation. Despite his attitude and reputation, it was his keen instincts, often referred to as the sixth sense, which made him one of the best officers on the shift.

Belinda shut down her computer and ejected the laptop from the docking station. Then Belinda stood up from the desk, but upon hearing the next radio transmission, she wasn't able to take the next step to leave the office.

"Dispatch, I'm in pursuit, helping a State Trooper who's in pursuit! We're heading northbound on East Avenue off Deer Field Road, 40 miles per hour, no traffic. It's a green 4-door Chevrolet Impala, looks like the driver's a black male." The roar of the police car's engine and the siren wailing in the background drowned out the pursuing officer's call identifier.

"No. This can't be Freeman. Not again," Belinda thought.

A second officer came on the radio. Belinda recognized his voice as being that of K9-2, Officer Benson.

"K9-2 to Dispatch, I'm with him."

"10-4, K9-2," answered the dispatcher.

"We just made a left turn on 8th Street. Now we're northbound," advised the pursuing officer. The siren was not as loud this time, and Officer Freeman's voice was clear.

"We are still northbound, picking up speed. Fifty miles per hour, still no traffic," advised Benson.

"Dispatch, I'm gonna go north, up ahead of them and set up Tire Spikes on County Line Road," said Officer Murphy, who was now a third officer involved in the pursuit.

"10-4, setting up Tire Spikes on County Line Road."

Belinda radioed Officer Freeman, "PD One to K9-1, what are you chasing him for?" There was no response. PD One to K9-1, Belinda repeated. The heavy thud sounds like two blunt metal objects suddenly colliding told Belinda that another officer's radio trying to transmit at the same time stepped on her transmission. She waited a while before trying to transmit again.

"Dispatch, we just made a right turn on Oakland – eastbound," Freeman said.

"Maybe there's a problem with my radio battery," Belinda thought. She had the same battery she started her shift 12 hours prior. Two fully-charged batteries were in the multi-radio battery charger. Belinda quickly exchanged her radio battery with a fresh battery from the battery charger. A series of numbers flashed on the radio display panel, as it went through a brief self-function check. When the numbers stopped flashing, the display panel read WTX WPD 1, but the radio was silent. The radio was silent for a moment and then broken by Officer Freeman.

"Dispatch, we're now heading northbound on Creekside Road. Eighty miles per hour. No traffic. He's on the side of the road... on the shoulder. He's slowing down. Slowing down," shouted Freeman. There was a moment of silence. "Looks like he's gonna bail," said Freeman. Then after 15 to 20 more seconds of silence, Freeman yelled, "I see the car door opening." Without letting up on the radio mic, he added, "Now, he's taking off again."

The dispatcher repeated, "Be advised the suspect is taking off again, still in the vehicle."

"We're continuing northbound, fifty miles per hour. Entering Martin County," said Freeman.

"Now, this is getting out of hand," thought Belinda. The officers were getting close to crossing the county line and approaching a major highway. Although it was early, there would be more traffic entering the highway as people were starting to drive to work. "Officer Freeman break it off," Belinda said.

"10-9, Lieutenant," Freeman replied, "Would you repeat last?"

Using a more deliberate tone, she repeated, "Discontinue the pursuit. Dispatch, notify Martin County and Salem County of the description of the vehicle and direction of travel."

The dispatcher replied, "10-4, Notify Martin and Salem County."

Officer Freeman spoke again. "Okay, Lieutenant." The tone of his voice had dropped as if he was just benched in a championship game where he was the one scoring all the points. He continued, "Dispatch, be advised per PD One, I am discontinuing the pursuit of a driver, signal zero, who just pulled a handgun on a trooper. The vehicle is a green, 4-door, Chevrolet Impala, Florida license tag WKM127, last seen heading north on Creekside Road."

Belinda's stomach tightened into a ball of knots. She felt as if every ounce of energy drained from her body. Keying the mic again, she said, "Okay, I did not hear that part, K9-1, disregard last. Get back in the pursuit. Belinda repeated, "Get back in the pursuit!"

Within minutes they were back in the pursuit. Officer Benson spoke up on the radio. "Dispatch, I'm still with him. The driver just took a few turns that landed him right back in the City. Right now, he's turning westbound onto Jefferson Avenue."

"Turning westbound onto Jefferson," echoed the dispatcher.

"He just tried to turn onto to 11th Street, and lost control of the vehicle and hit a tree," said Benson.

"Southbound! Southbound!" yelled Freeman. "Black male, blue shirt, blue jeans."

Freeman was now chasing the suspect on foot. Freeman' breathing into the microphone sounded as if he was almost out of breath.

"He's somewhere in between these houses, between 11th and 15th street," said Freeman.

Belinda stood from her desk, grabbed her keys and jacket to respond to the crash scene. On the way out of the building, she passed Officer Hutchins, one of the veteran officers working as the front desk officer. "I didn't hear it," Belinda said.

"You got to listen" yelled back Hutchins.

When Belinda arrived at the crash scene, she saw the front end of the green Chevrolet lodged into a small tree on the corner of 11th street and Jefferson Avenue. There was a white wooden house which sat back from the corner. Belinda pulled her vehicle up next to Sgt. Walden's vehicle. He was directing officers to establish a perimeter. Three deputies from the Martin County Sheriff Office came to assist. They took up a position on the perimeter. By now, there were about a dozen patrol units on scene and others arriving. The officers were positioned to tighten up the perimeter. Martin County's helicopter was already up in the air, volunteering to assist with the search. Belinda authorized the tasks conducted in the efforts made to identify and locate the suspect.

While they were conducting the sweep of the area, the dispatcher advised the name of the driver of the pursuit vehicle was Walter Derrick Brown, a 28-year-old black male. The computer records showed a previous address of 1112 15th Street, a few streets away from where he crashed the vehicle. The records also showed he had a brother who lived in the area. Belinda sent officers to the brother's address.

The officers reported over the radio that an uncooperative female at the house refused to give any information. They later reported that the family allowed them to check the residence and the suspect was not there.

While things had momentarily settled down, Belinda telephoned Captain Miller to notify him of the incident. There was no answer, so Belinda left a message on his cell phone. She also took an opportunity to speak with Sgt. Walden.

"I didn't hear the part about the gun," Belinda said.

"Yeah, I heard you," he replied. "I couldn't get on the radio either. I tried to answer you to let you know I was listening, but I kept getting bumped off." Before they could talk further, they heard the K-9 Supervisor calling the dispatcher.

"K-9 Supervisor to Dispatch"

"Dispatch to K-9 Supervisor, go ahead."

"We're getting ready to start the sweep."

The dispatcher repeated, "K-9, starting the sweep, zero, six forty-five."

"We're walking south on 18th Street, Checking 1821."
"Negative."

"Hey, check underneath those cars in the yard," one of the officers called out.

"Over here!" yelled one of the officers. The canine was barking at someone hiding underneath a Buick Century parked in the front yard of 1825 18th Street. 1821-1825 18th Street was a duplex with 1825 on the west side.

"Come out! Or you're gonna get bit. Come Out! Commanded the K-9 officer.

The officer could see the suspect's legs under the vehicle, but the man did not move. The dog was barking frantically. The dog grabbed the suspect's leg with his teeth, dug into his flesh, attempting to pull the suspect from underneath the vehicle. The man let out a painful cry.

"OUST!" K-9 Officer Benson yelled. The dog immediately loosened the grip on the man's leg. His body was far enough out from underneath the vehicle that the officers were able to grab his leg and arm. They pulled him out from underneath the vehicle.

"Get your hands behind your back!" Officer Benson commanded.

He pushed the suspect over on his stomach and placed a pair of handcuffs on his wrists. With the help of another officer, they raised him up into a seated position on the ground. With one on each side, they took his arms and helped him stand up. The pain from the dog bite caused the suspect to bend his leg a little, but he took a couple of hops on one leg to quickly straighten up again, while the officers held him steady. After a quick search of the suspect for weapons, Benson yelled, "He's clean." Then they walked him towards the street.

The other officers exploded with cheers. It sounded like their team had come from behind to win the World Series with a walk-off home run to win the game. Smiling from ear to ear, officers jumped up and down, hugged each other, and gave each other high fives. Complimentary "good job" was reciprocated followed by a pat on the back or a hug.

"We got him Lieutenant!" said Officer Lewis, with a big smile on his face.

"Yeah, we got him!" Belinda said, smiling back at him.

"Officer Lewis, I didn't hear the part about the handgun."

"He was by himself," Lewis responded.

Once again, those words rang in her ears. A group of officers parted to make room so the officers escorting the suspect could get through the crowd. They placed him in the back seat of a patrol car to transport him to Police Headquarters. Belinda saw Officer Freeman and approached him.

"Good Job Marc," Belinda said, congratulating him on a job well done. Then Belinda told him she was sorry for calling off the pursuit in the beginning. "I didn't hear the part about the gun."

"That's okay, Lieutenant. We got him. That's all that matters." said Freeman.

Sgt. Walden approached Belinda. "Lt., we searched this entire area, and no gun was found. He must have ditched it somewhere along the way. Belinda sent a couple of officers back over the pursuit route to see if they could locate it."

While he was still speaking, Florida Highway Patrol (FHP) Trooper Goddard arrived.

"I just want to thank you and all of your men for your help. I'm glad we got him."

"Trooper, no thanks is necessary," Belinda said. "I just want to tell you that I'm sorry about calling off the pursuit at first. I didn't know the suspect was armed."

'Lieutenant, I don't care about none of that. The main thing is that he's in jail. Again, thank you."

"Trooper, I'll see you at the station. The suspect is being transported to our Criminal Investigation Division."

'Good, my supervisor and another Trooper are on the way. We'd like to talk with him."

Belinda gave the okay for everyone to clear the scene and report to Police Headquarters. She had driven only about a mile down the road when she heard Officer Scoggins on the radio.

"We got it. Please be advised Officer Shellenburger just found the handgun. It was lying in the dirt, in the 4300 block of Creekside, said Officer Scoggins. Sarge, what do you want us to do with it?"

"Don't touch it," said Sgt. Walden. I'll get the Crime Scene unit to respond to the scene to collect it as evidence. "

Upon hearing those words, Belinda thought, "It was the perfect ending to a bad start. No one was hurt, the gun had been located, and the bad guy was on his way to jail."

33

BACK IN THE REPORT writing room, Belinda was signing overtime slips when her cell phone rang.

"Hello Lieutenant, this is Captain Miller. Are you finished out there?"

"Yeah, we are finished. I've signed all of the paperwork, and I'm getting ready to go home."

"I know you signed overtime slips for the guys, but make sure you complete one for yourself too. Then come see me in my office."

"Okay, I'll be right there."

On the wall behind Miller's desk was a picture of him on the tennis courts, standing beside his seventeen-year-old son. On the other wall was a picture of John Wayne.

"Lieutenant, did you all find the gun?" He asked as he directed her to the chair in front of his desk.

"Yeah, Officer Shellenberger found it along the pursuit route. Everybody thought this guy was going to bail on foot when he slowed down and opened the car door, but that must have been when he ditched the gun."

"Good, I'm glad you found it. That's all we needed was another handgun lying on the street for some kid to find."

"I called you earlier to brief you. I didn't get an answer, so I left you a message. It was pretty early, and I wasn't sure if you would be up yet."

"Actually, I was already up, getting ready to come to work."

"You get up early."

Miller leaned back in the chair, propped his feet on top of his desk and crossed his legs.

"Lieutenant, how did this happen?"

"What do you mean?"

"I didn't call you back earlier, because I've been here all morning answering complaints about you and this incident, but mostly about you."

"What about me?" Belinda asked.

"The guys don't want to work for you. It's not just the guys on the shift. I've heard complaints from others also, who are not on the shift. I don't know what the problem is. Perhaps, people are jealous," he said. "You have a lot of good qualities about you, many of which I wish I had. You are a good person. But, I don't know what to do. I've been in this office listening to complaint after complaint. Why none of this hasn't come up before now, I don't know. But this right here is a problem. I'm so glad that trooper wasn't hurt. This agency we would have been negligent. We would have had to answer to that trooper's family if something would have happened to him. Thank God, he's okay."

"I'm glad he wasn't hurt too," Belinda said. "As soon as I heard there was a gun involved, I told the officers to get back in the pursuit. There wasn't hardly any time delay."

"Why didn't you hear it?" Captain Miller asked.

"I was changing radio batteries. I thought perhaps my radio wasn't transmitting so I changed the battery."

"So, you changed the battery in the middle of a pursuit you were supposed to be listening to."

"Yeah, I did. I could hear them on my radio, but I wasn't sure if they were hearing me, I see now how stupid that was."

"Okay, but why did you call it off?"

"The pursuit had left our jurisdiction and it was getting crazy. Plus, I know I probably shouldn't have considered this, but Officer Freeman was just involved in two other pursuits last week. Captain, you know at least one of those was not within policy. I tried to ask him why he was chasing the vehicle and what the offense was, but I got no response."

"So, you made a decision without knowing all of the facts."

"I guess I did, but I made the decision based on what I knew. Then, when I knew more of what was happening, I corrected it."

"Lieutenant, go home and get some rest. I don't know what I'm going to do. When do you come back to work?"

"This is the beginning of our three-day weekend. We come back to work on Monday."

"Good. You got three days to clear your head. I'll talk to you later."

Belinda woke up about 2 o'clock in the afternoon. She was satisfied to have gotten a good four hours of sleep. She walked into the living room and turned on the television then the phone rang. It was Capt. Miller.

"Hello Lieutenant, how's it going?"

"Okay, I guess. I just woke up."

"Hey, I was just calling to let you know Lieutenant Brady is going to take over your shift for a while. You're being placed on Administrative Leave. You are not being punished or restricted in any way. I talked with the Chief. We just want you to take some time off and rest. When you come in on Monday, see Edith if I'm not here. She's got some paperwork for you to sign. You're going to be off for a week. You come back to duty on the 18th."

"So, I'm going to be off for a week, but I'm not being punished," Belinda said, trying to process in her mind what she had just heard.

"That's right. This is not a punishment. There is no investigation. You don't have to stay at home or check-in. You're not turning in your badge or gun, or nothing like that. You can come and go as you please. What happened out there last night was pretty serious. I want to give you some time and the guys some time."

"Okay, Captain. What else can I say?"

A few hours later Charles arrived home. Belinda waited until he had a chance to relax. He sat down on the sofa with a drink.

"Can we talk? I have something I need to talk to you about," Belinda said.

"Sure, what is it?"

Charles took a chair from the dining room table where she was sitting and positioned it opposite her chair.

"This morning I called off a pursuit by mistake, and I've been placed on administrative leave," she said. Belinda's mouth was dry, and the words were hard for her to get out. She took a drink from a glass of water and then continued. "The driver was armed with a handgun. I didn't hear that information because I was changing my radio battery. When I could hear what was going on again, I thought the pursuit was getting out of hand, so I called it off. When I found out about the gun, I told them to get back in it. They did and eventually caught the guy. Even though he was arrested, everyone was mad, because I called it off in the first place."

"You made a mistake," that's all. Everybody makes mistakes." Charles held Belinda close to him.

"Yeah, I made a mistake, and I've been placed on administrative leave. Other people make mistakes, and they get promoted," Belinda said.

"Be strong. We will get through this," Charles said.

As instructed on Monday morning, Belinda went to Captain Miller's office to meet with Edith, the Patrol Bureau administrative assistant. Edith had her back to the door. She was placing papers in the officer's mailboxes located on the shelf behind her desk. Upon hearing Belinda, she turned around.

"Good Morning Lieutenant. The Captain is not in yet, but you're welcome to have a seat."

Belinda returned the greeting. No sooner than she sat down, Miller arrived.

"Good morning Edith, Lieutenant," Miller said. He walked between Edith's desk and the chair where Belinda was sitting and went into his office. "Come on in Lieutenant Williams."

He invited Belinda to have a seat, motioning towards the empty chair in front of his desk. Then he called out to Edith. "Bring me that paperwork I left with you on Friday."

Edith handed Miller the written memorandum. He briefly looked at the memo. Then he gave it to Belinda. The memorandum was dated the same date as the pursuit. It read,

"You are placed on administrative leave and will remain on administrative leave until Friday, November 18, 2006. During this time, your duty hours will be Monday through Friday from 0800 to 1600 hours at your residence. Please be available by phone between 0800 and 1200 hours each workday in case Capt. Miller needs to be in touch with you. Otherwise, you are not restricted in any manner."

It was signed by Chief Gregory G. Robinson. After reading the memo, Belinda took the pen from the cup holder on the desk and signed her name on the line marked, "Officer Receiving Memorandum." She had issued many memos like this during her career. This was the first time she would be on the receiving end.

"Lieutenant Brady volunteered to give up his North District Commander duties and go to the midnight shift to help out," Capt. Miller said. "This shows he's not just a great guy but a team player who is willing to do whatever he can for this department. As you know, the North District has a lot of community meetings that he has to attend. But he is willing to rearrange his schedule and do both jobs for a while until we can get this worked out."

"I guess I should thank him," Belinda said. "It's not like he's not getting paid," she thought.

"Captain, I would like to go back and speak with the officers on my shift. Am I allowed to do that?" Belinda's oversaw the midnight Alfa shift.

"Certainly, as a matter of fact, I think that is a great idea. I'm sure it would mean a lot to them."

"Do you have any other questions?" Miller asked.

"No, not at this time."

"Okay then, we will see you in a week. The only thing I ask is that you just keep a phone with you, in case we need to get in touch with you about something."

"Sure, Captain"

"Thanks"

Belinda left the office.

Leaving the department, Belinda was not sure of where to go or who to talk to. It was mid-morning, too early for lunch and too late for breakfast. She decided to stop by the local coffee shop thinking it might help take her mind off what was happening. After all, she didn't have to stay at home, just be available by phone.

When Belinda entered the restaurant, a waitress approached her. "Go ahead and sit wherever you like. Can I get anything for you to drink?

"Sure, a cup of coffee, cream, and sugar." Belinda smiled politely.

The sign hanging at the front of the restaurant listed the daily lunch specials. The restaurant was more crowded than Belinda expected for it not to be lunchtime. A women's book club held their monthly breakfasts at the restaurant, and this was their morning to meet.

Belinda took a few sips of her coffee. She was looking at the menu when her cell phone rang.

"Belinda, hello, this is Johnathan Graves."

"Hello, Rev. Graves."

"I was thinking about you, and I just wanted to call to see how you were doing?"

"I'm doing fine. Thanks for asking."

"Hey, Lieutenant, I was wondering if we could get together, maybe for lunch sometime. I got some free time coming up in the next week. I thought perhaps we could spend some time together."

"Sure, when?"

"How about Thursday, Simply Salads, on East Avenue?"

"That sounds good, I'll see you Thursday."

The phone rang again. It was Charles.

"Hello, Sweetheart."

"Hello, how are you?"

"Oh, I'm fine. The question is, how are you? You must have been really tired last night."

"Yeah, I was. I know I fell asleep on the couch."

"I didn't want to wake you. I just called to check on you to see how you were doing."

"I'm okay. I got served this morning with admin leave papers."

"Oh yeah."

"Yeah, since I can go anywhere and do anything, I decided to get some breakfast, but now I don't feel too much like eating. Hey, guess who I just got a call from."

"Who"?

"Rev. Graves, the department chaplain."

"Oh yeah, what did he want?"

"He said he just happened to be thinking about me and invited me out to lunch on Thursday."

"That's nice, isn't it? I mean, you should enjoy that."

"If I thought it was his idea I would. Do you know how long we have been talking about getting together and he hasn't had time ever since we walked together on the prayer walk through the City. Now, all of a sudden, I'm placed on administrative leave, and he just happens to be thinking about me. I could be wrong, but I think someone may have suggested that he call. Anyway, I told him I would meet with him on Thursday. Even if it wasn't his idea, it would be good to talk to him. I just don't know if I should trust this or not. He and Captain Miller are pretty close. Even if Miller didn't tell him what was going on, he or someone probably suggested to him that he call me."

"Well, I'm sure you will decide on whether or not you're going to meet with him. I have to go now. I think they are loading my truck now. I should be home late tonight. I'm on my way to Miami."

"All right, I'll see you when you get back."

"I love you."

"I love you too. Goodbye."

Wakefield Police Department

On Tuesday evening Belinda walked into the squad room and sat at the table beside Lt. Brady and Sergeant Walden. The officers entered the room through the door at the rear of the room. Officer Benson and Belinda's eyes met when he came into the room. Before taking his seat, Benson, like the other officers, cleared his weapon in the gun barrel. Then he looked at the wanted posters on the wall to see if there were any new faces posted since the last time they worked. Belinda waited until Lt. Brady finished giving out the BOLO information. Then Belinda addressed the squad.

"Hello everyone, I just wanted to come here tonight and talk with you a little bit about what happened last week. I want to thank Lt. Brady for giving me a few minutes and for carrying on in my absence. There's not much I can say except that I apologize to you, especially Marc, Benson, and Lewis, about what happened. I hope you know that I would never intentionally do anything to cause any harm to any of you or any other law enforcement officer. I understand how some of you might still be upset and not want to have much conversation right now. That's okay. I didn't call the pursuit off because I didn't want to help a fellow officer. I didn't hear the part about the person having a handgun. Without knowing that information, it sounded like the pursuit was getting out of hand. I know I have to earn your trust again. I can't change what happened, but I hope we will be able to work past this. You guys do great work. So, in the meantime, keep doing what you're doing. Keep looking out for each other."

"Lieutenant, Thanks for coming in here and saying what you did," Officer Shellenberger said. "I appreciate it, and I know others here do also. That means a lot."

L.T., I already told you that night, I'm just glad we got him. That's all that matters. See you when you get back," Officer Freeman said.

Officer Benson never looked at Belinda while she was talking. A few other officers kept their head down, staring at their notebooks the entire time. Belinda repeated her comments at all three shift briefings, North, Central, and South. She was satisfied she had done what she felt was necessary and what she felt in her heart was the right thing to do. She could not control how any of them would respond.

On Thursday, as planned Belinda met with Chaplain Graves for lunch. She told him about her current work status. It was nice to have someone who could listen to how she felt. He denied that anyone had suggested for him to contact her. Although she didn't entirely believe him, she was sure he thought he was doing a good thing. It was unfortunate, but she knew that some people would stop at nothing to get what they wanted. They will use whomever they thought they could use, including the department chaplain. With that in mind, Belinda never trusted that anything she said to Chaplain Graves was in complete confidence or that his counsel was given necessarily with her best interest in mind.

The week of administrative leave was scheduled to end that Friday morning. Belinda met Captain Miller in his office.

"Lt. Williams, you're going to work day shift until I can sort this out. Lt. Brady is going to continue to handle your shift for a while. You'll eventually be reassigned, but I have to find a place for you. Until then just report for duty here in the administrative office. I've got some stuff I need some help with."

Miller picked up a stack of papers and handed them to Belinda. "Here is the paperwork for the budget. I can use some help with this, and I know this is one of your strong points. I want you to complete it. Feel free to go to any of the Sergeants and ask for whatever you need."

34

Roberta's House | Wakefield

ROBERTA HAD JUST finished tearing up the last photo when she heard the knock at the door.

"It's open," Roberta yelled. "Come on in."

"Hello," Tonya said. She sang the word out of her mouth with her bright and cheery voice to announce her entrance. Roberta was in the kitchen sitting at the table. There was a half-full bottle of Regal wine in the middle of the table. Roberta refilled her glass.

"Hey, what are you up to today?"

"Nothing much. I was just sitting here thinking about things," Roberta said.

"I was headed over to City Fashions and stopped by to see if you wanted to go with me." Tonya couldn't help but notice the bottle of wine. Several pictures of Belinda that had been torn into small pieces were lying on the floor. Other pictures of Belinda taken with other family members had the portion showing Belinda torn away from the photo.

"What's all this?" Tonya asked. She held one of the photos.

"What?"

"All of this, that's what." Why are these pictures of Belinda all torn like this?"

"Those pictures are not pictures of anything important. That's what Belinda is to me right now, nothing. As far as I am concerned, she doesn't exist anymore. That's why I destroyed these pictures."

"Why, what did she do to you, after all of the things she has done for you? How can you say that?"

"Easy. You don't know what they done, her and Charles...and Belinda just don't give a darn. I don't know why everyone else just pretends like they don't know. You all act like she has done something so great when they just left me here by myself. Today, they took all of their stuff out of the storage she left my stuff there."

"Mother, I'm sure if they left your stuff in storage they are not going to just leave them there without helping you get them later."

"Well, that's what you say. I don't have the money to pay for the storage. She knows that. Even if I had to get new furniture there are other things in there I can't replace. And look at this place. It needs painting, and the carpet needs cleaning."

"Yeah, look at this house. Anyone would be glad to live in a house like this. You got a three bedroom, two baths, and a nice dining room. Look at this, and it has a nice yard, and this is a nice neighborhood."

"Well, you don't know what I know. Belinda is not the person you think she is. She has always done things to disrespect me, and I'm not having it anymore."

"Mother, you should be ashamed of yourself, with all of the times Belinda has helped you pay your bills, your car payment, and your house payment. It's not Belinda's fault you lost your house. She and Charles let you stay in this house, and they are trying to help you start a business. You call that disrespecting you."

"She was supposed to do those things. I'm the mother." Plus, if you knew the kinds of things she's done, you wouldn't want to have anything to do with her either."

"You forget. I was there. I was young, but I knew what was going on. You blame Belinda. You should blame yourself."

"Blame me. For what?"

"Mom, you know. Some of the same things that happened to Belinda happened to me too. She got away. I'm glad she left, and I'm proud of her for what she has done with her life."

"Well, you, Belinda, and the rest of the world can just go you know where." Roberta used several explicit adjectives Tonya hadn't heard her say in a while. "I haven't forgotten all of the things you did either."

"I can't stay here and listen to this. I'm leaving." Tonya stood and headed towards the door.

Roberta followed her. "Go ahead. I don't care," Roberta said, slamming the door after Tonya walked out.

35

Wakefield

LEMARKUS STOPPED by the house one afternoon to visit with Belinda. "Mom, Grandma called me on my cell phone, but I haven't spoken to her yet."

Belinda could tell he was upset by the expression on his face. "You should call her."

"I will, but it's hard to talk to her anymore. When I go over to her house, everything starts out okay, but then she starts to accuse you of doing all kinds of things to hurt her. I try to tell that you haven't done anything but try to help her, but she won't accept it."

"What does she think I did to her?"

LeMarkus sighed. "I don't know Mom. At first, I wouldn't say anything, because I like to go over there just to check on her to see how she was doing. Then it was the same thing repeatedly. She would say, Well LeMarkus, there are some things that you need to know. I asked her what things and she wouldn't say anything. She would just bad mouth you like you were doing things to try and hurt her. I told her you have never said anything bad about anybody in this family. All I hear is her saying bad things about you. Then, she started calling Darlene and telling Darlene stuff. And what really got me, is that day when I went to see her, and she said, "LeMarkus let's go take a ride." We went over to one of her friend's house. Then her friend started saying stuff that wasn't even true. I just couldn't take it anymore. I didn't want to say anything."

"Son, I know. Don't let it worry you. Everything is going to be okay."

That next Friday, Belinda went to Roberta's house after she dropped Pat off at the movie theatre. Several cars parked along the street caused Belinda to find a space farther down the street from the house and walk back. People were sitting on the front porch of the house she parked in front of. Belinda asked them if it was alright for her to park there for a few moments. Belinda was about to walk away when she heard one of the women on the porch called her by name.

"You don't remember me, do you?" Terri said.

"You look familiar, but I can't recall your name right now."

"I'm the one who came over to your house when my sister was selling Avon. You hosted a party for her."

"Oh yeah! Terri!"

"Small world, isn't it?"

"Yeah, it's a small world. I heard Roberta talking about somebody named Terri stayed next door to her, but I didn't know it was you. Good to see you."

"Speaking of your mother, here she is right here. You know these other two people too." LeMarkus and his girlfriend Darlene came from inside the house and joined Terri and Roberta on the porch.

"I was on my way to your house, but I see I don't have to walk as far as I thought I did. Everybody is right here."

"You might as well join us," Terri said. LeMarkus and Darlene just got here a few minutes ago."

"Yeah, we couldn't find a place to park up by the house, which worked out alright, because we wouldn't have seen Grandma down here," LeMarkus said. He and Darlene joined Belinda on the sidewalk in front of the house.

"You just missed your niece Brandee," Roberta said. "She should be back in a few minutes. She went to get some pizza. Her birthday is tomorrow, and she mentioned having some pizza at the house. So, I asked her to go get it."

Darlene looked away in reaction to what Roberta's comments. LeMarkus turned to Belinda, "Mom, you just had a birthday, didn't you?"

"That was last week LeMarkus," Belinda responded.

"I didn't know, Happy Belated Birthday," Roberta said.

"You can't remember your own daughter's birthday," LeMarkus said.

"Lately, I've forgotten a lot of things. Apparently, I didn't remember Tonya's birthday either."

"How could you forget your own children's birthdays, but remember somebody else's birthday?" Belinda asked.

Roberta took a drink from the cup she was holding. A bottle of rum was on the table beside her.

"Well, I just stopped by to talk to you, but I'll come back later when you're at home," Belinda said.

"Hey Mom, wait, where's Pat? She didn't come with you?"

"No, I dropped her off at the movie theater before I came over here."

"What are you going to do until the movies let out? If you want, Darlene and I can go and get Pat. Then you can get her from our house. Why don't you stay here and talk to Grandma?

Belinda addressed Roberta. "I don't want to take you away from visiting your friend. Plus, I didn't call and tell you that I was coming." Belinda wanted to talk with Roberta in private, not with everyone else listening.

"It's okay Belinda. You're not interrupting anything. We're not doing anything but sitting here," Terri said. "Look here go Brandee. She done made it back, and she's got her mother, Tonya with her." "Hello Auntie, I didn't know you were coming over here too?"

"I just happened to stop by. I didn't know all of you were over here." Belinda hoped Brandee bringing the pizza would be enough of a distraction, so she and Roberta could talk civilly to each other. She knew she needed to clear the air with her mother and not put it off any longer. Hopefully, it would not be a disaster like the last time she tried to talk to her. That ended in them screaming at each other. So, Belinda wasn't sure of what to expect.

Brandee gave the pizza box to Roberta.

"It looks like I'm just in time," Belinda said.

"Auntie, that's not a whole pizza. It's just a few slices that I had leftover at the house. I promised Grandma that I was going to bring her some pizza back," said Brandee."

Roberta stood holding the pizza box. She looked at Belinda and said, "I heard you wanted to talk to me."

"Yes, I did," Belinda said. Can we go next door to your house?" They were still outside beside Brandee's car.

"What do you want?" Roberta asked. "We don't need to go anywhere. If you got something to say to me, you could say it right here."

"I just want to know what is wrong. Why are you upset with me?

"I'm not upset with you, and I don't have anything I need to talk about."

"Why can't you talk to me?" Belinda sighed. "All of my life, you never talk to me." Roberta took a few steps, attempting to move away from Belinda, but Belinda moved to block her path. "I'm not leaving until you talk to me. You talk at me, you talk about me, but you never talk to me. My whole life is upside down. I need to get past this. I need for you to talk to me." Belinda snatched the pizza box out of Roberta's hand and threw it on the ground.

Roberta, holding on to the box, fell forward when Belinda grabbed it. Then she Belinda pushed her back, causing Roberta to stumble before catching her balance to keep from falling.

"Get away from me!" Roberta shouted. "The problem is that you hate me. That's what's wrong!"

"What are you talking about?"

"I ain't got nothing else to say. There's nothing to talk about." Roberta kept walking backward as Belinda was walking towards her.

"Yes, there is. Why can't you talk to me?"

All the commotion caused other neighbors to come outside to see what was going on.

"Roberta, you need to talk to your daughter," Terri said. "I know it hurt, but if it is like she says, you both need to talk. I had to talk some things out with my mother."

"Grandma talk to her," LeMarkus said. "All she is asking is for you to talk to her, you talk to everybody else, all these winos walking up and down the street, those white folks you work for, me, and everybody else. Talk to your daughter."

Roberta walked down the street to her car parked in her driveway in an attempt to get away from Belinda. Roberta got into the car, but the traffic on the street blocking the driveway, prevented her from leaving. She blew the horn and yelled for the cars to move to no avail. Belinda arrived in time to reach inside the car and snatch the car keys out of Roberta's hand. Then, Belinda threw the keys across the street into the tall grass of the vacant wooded lot. Roberta jumped out of the car and hurried towards the house. Belinda pleaded for Roberta to stop and talk to her.

"I can't talk to you. I'm afraid of you."

"What do you mean you're afraid of me?" I don't understand that at all. I'm upset now, but before now, I've never yelled at you nor did anything to try and hurt you. Belinda followed Roberta to the front door of the house.

Roberta yelled, "What are you going to do, shoot me? Don't hurt me."

"What am I going to shoot you with my finger?' Belinda said. She tried to keep the door from closing, but Roberta had already locked it. Belinda went to the garage door, but it was also locked. Standing outside the door, Belinda could hear Roberta talking to someone inside the house. It was just as well that I couldn't get in, Belinda thought.

"I tried," Belinda said to LeMarkus and others standing around. "She does not want to talk to me. I gave it my best shot."

Belinda thought about the car keys she had thrown in the bushes. Maybe she still had a chance of making Roberta talk to her. Belinda figured there should be a house key on the key ring as well. If she found those keys, she might be able to get inside the house. Belinda walked across the street to look in the bushes for the keys. Terri gave her a flashlight because it was getting dark.

"Don't worry about the keys. Mom, I'll find them," LeMarkus said. He joined Belinda in the search. While they were looking for the keys, a Wakefield police officer arrived. He parked in front of the house and approached Belinda.

"Hi Lieutenant, we got a call that there were some people involved in a fight," seventeen-year veteran officer, Berryman said.

"Everything is okay," Belinda said. "This is kind of embarrassing.

"You don't have anything to be embarrassed about. What's going on?"

"I was involved in a dispute with my mother. I guess it got a little too loud for the neighbors, but you don't have to worry. I'm getting ready to leave. You might want to go and talk with my mother. I'm assuming she's the one who called."

While Berryman was inside the house, LeMarkus found the keys and gave them to Belinda. She thought about what would happen if she did use the keys to get inside the house and decided that nothing good could come of it.

Berryman returned a few minutes later. "I spoke with Roberta. She did not say anything to indicate that there was a problem here." Then, he called his supervisor. He reported there was no problem and that he would be clearing the scene without writing a report.

"I'm not trying to tell you how to do your job, but I would suggest you write a report," Belinda said. "As a matter of fact, I'm requesting that you document this. That way, no one can say anything that could come back to bite you later."

"You're probably right," Berryman said. Then he requested the dispatcher give him a case number for a dispute. Belinda gave the set of keys to Berryman and asked him to give them to Roberta. Then Belinda walked back down the street to where she parked her car.

Belinda was amazed that her mother was afraid of her. She could see that Roberta wasn't just saying those things, but she acted like someone who was actually afraid. Belinda knew she could not make Roberta talk to her but thought Roberta would at least listen.

36

WHEN BELINDA REACHED her car, her friend Francis was there. Wearing a long blue denim skirt that reached her ankles and Nike tennis shoes; she was leaning against Belinda's car. Francis always credited God for everything that happened, whether it was good or bad. According to Francis, even the bad things would be for her benefit in the end. Francis and Belinda became friends through their children, who shared some of the same extra-curricular activities. They attended the same church and worked on several neighborhood projects together. Francis got to know the rest of the family when Elena was sick. Francis would come to the house to pray for Elena and help in whatever way she could.

"Hey Francis, what brings you over to this side of town?"

"I would say that I was just in the neighborhood, but that wouldn't be true. A mutual friend of ours called me and said you might be able to use a friend. They didn't say what was going on, so I just got in the car and came on."

"How long have you been here?"

"Long enough to see you and your mother out in the front yard."

"I'm sorry that you had to see that."

"That's okay. You should know that your mother also called me from inside the house. You don't know this, but I've been talking with her for some time now about releasing the hurt between you two. She's ready to talk to you now. I told her I would hang around to make sure you were willing to talk to her."

"What does she think I was trying to do? She's the one who's not willing to talk with me."

"Belinda, she couldn't talk to you by herself. I promised her that I would sit down with the two of you, that is if you are still willing to do so. You both need this. Come on. Let's go talk to your mother."

Belinda walked back to the house with Francis. Brandee and Tonya drove past them as they were arriving. LeMarkus, Darlene, and Terri were still outside. Most of the other people in the neighborhood had gone back inside their homes. Officer Berryman's patrol car was in front of the house. He was finishing his report. Roberta was still inside. Berryman met Belinda and Francis when they arrived.

"Hello Officer," Francis said. "What's happening here is between a mother and a daughter. We don't need the police. Besides, Roberta is afraid, because she feels like Belinda has the upper hand with the police being on her side. She called me and asked me to come over to be here, so she and her daughter can talk."

"Francis, he is here because someone called the police. He's just doing his job," Belinda said.

"That's fine Belinda, but now, he doesn't need to be here anymore."

"Berryman, everything is alright. I respect you guys too much to create a problem for you to have to come back here."

"It sounds like the two of you talking would do some good. I just suggest that both people be fair and honest. Belinda, you need to lay down the ground rules."

"Belinda cannot set the ground rules in this instance, because it involves her," Francis interjected.

"Francis is right in this case," Belinda said. But, no matter who set forth the rules, they will be the same anyway. Trust me. There won't be any fits of rage or violence on my part."

"Okay, but you know how to reach me if you need me." Then Berryman got in his car and left.

"Mom, go ahead. Don't worry about having to get Pat from the movies. I'll make sure I'm there when the movie ends, so I can get her and take her to my house. Then, you can come get her from there," LeMarkus said.

Roberta invited Francis and Belinda into the house. Belinda sat down on the sofa facing the door. Francis sat in a chair between Belinda and Francis.

"It's apparent there are some problems between the two of you," Francis said. The devil would love to get in there and make a mockery out of both of you, but, the devil is a lie. Both of you have a ministry, something that the Lord has for you both to do. But the devil is trying to keep that from happening. So, I'm here to help, because you need to talk through this thing and not let the enemy get the victory."

Belinda spoke first. "I just wanted Roberta to talk to me. I know she's upset about something, but I don't know what it is. All my life, she's always talked at me, about me, around me, but never talked to me."

"Belinda, you know that your mother loves you, don't you?"

"Do I? What has she ever done to show me that she loves me?"

"Roberta, your daughter just asked you a question," Francis said.

"Everything," Roberta said.

"Like What?"

"Well, when I used to come over to your house and cook for you. All the time that I spent at the gift shop trying to help you start a business and the flowers I sent. All of that was for you. I always put you on top shelf. But, I knew that you hated me."

"I don't know why you think that, but I appreciate you talking to me. This is the first time in my life that I feel like you're talking to me."

"It's because of the letter. That's why."

"What letter."

"The letter you wrote to Michael when you were staying with me. It came back to me because the address was wrong. In the letter, you said you hated me and resented me for being your mother. You said you wished somebody else was your mother."

"I don't remember the letter, but I was seventeen years old and going through a lot of things. Why didn't you ever talk to me about it? When I first came back to Florida, I tried to talk to you, but you wouldn't talk to me. So, I just stopped trying.

"Belinda and Roberta, it's time for you all to be honest with each other. See, the devil has been playing with both of you long enough. And if you don't use this opportunity, he's going to keep on doing that. It is especially critical for you, Belinda, because of your work for the Lord."

"Francis, I don't know what you mean. As far as being honest, this is the first time we have actually talked. I can't be any more honest than I am right now," Belinda said. "The only thing that happened recently was I wasn't able to help her as much with her bills as I promised her. I did the best I could. But I guess you want me to go back to the beginning."

Belinda looked at Roberta. "As you know, Mama was the one who raised me. People always told me I was with Mama because I was born in Mama's house and that's where I stayed. I figured you left me there because you were too young and wasn't able to take care of a child. I really don't know why, because I never heard that from you. Based on what they told me, I assumed that was the reason. I grew up feeling like I didn't have anyone there for me. I knew who you were, but you came back to visit your mother, not me. I know Mama always told you what was going on. Whenever I wanted to do something she would call you, like the time when I wanted to join the Girl Scouts. You said I couldn't because it cost too much money and they would always be going places Mama couldn't afford to take me. Some people were willing to help Mama pay for everything, but you still said no."

Belinda continued. "When I was ten, we moved to Dalton. I remember the day Mary took me to the grocery store, and we saw Michael. She said, "That's your daddy over there." I was thirteen. I always wanted to meet my father, but if we didn't run into him at the grocery store, I still wouldn't know who he was. Still, to this day, you've never told me whether or not he is my father. Is he? If he's not, that's okay. I just need to know the truth."

"You ought to know. You got all the papers," Roberta said.

"How could I know? What papers?"

"Roberta, she's waiting for you to answer," Francis said.

"Yeah, he's your Daddy."

"Wow, thank you. I'm glad you were able to tell me that, but I still don't understand why-."

"Because of the letter and other things."

"What things?"

"You were having a relationship with your Daddy. That's what things. You were old enough to know better. You should have known better. I just recently heard it for the first time that he molested you."

"Well, yea he did. You think it was my fault. I was a child. Anytime an adult has sex with a child, it's never the child's fault."

"Well, did you tell anybody?"

"Yes, I did. And if the statute of limitations had not run out, he would be in jail right now. I can't tell you how many counselors I've been to and how many people have prayed with me to be free of this. I've had nightmares and suffered in ways I didn't understand."

"Why didn't you say something? I asked you if there was something wrong."

"You don't just say stuff like this. Besides, you wouldn't talk to me when I tried to tell you. The last time I tried to mention Michael to you, your response was "What's that got to do with me?" So, I never said anything else to you. The problem is it wasn't about you. It was about what was happening to me."

"I guess I didn't understand," Roberta said.

"When I returned to Florida, I tried to talk to you again. The last time I tried to talk to you, the same thing happened. Remember? You were staying in the house across from the store. We were sitting on the porch. I told you that I left Florida with the intention of never returning. I had forgiven you and didn't blame you for what happened to me when I was young. Instead of saying anything to me, you started crying and ran inside the house. So, I never got the courage to try and talk to you again."

"Do you remember the flowers that I sent to you after that? I know you got them," Roberta said. "They were in the big blue vase. They were beautiful. It cost me all that I had to get them. I sent you the flowers to show you that I loved you."

"I'm sorry, but I don't remember. All I remember is that you never said anything to me."

"Roberta, sometimes people need for you to verbally respond to them," Francis said. You can buy things like you said, you bought the flowers, but that doesn't replace actually talking to a person. They don't always receive the gifts in the way that you meant it. The gifts are nice, but they may not be as important to that person."

"Well, okay, but Belinda, I have always loved you. I have always been proud of you, and all your accomplishments. Even, if you hadn't achieved all of what you have, I have loved you. You were always number one. You have always been top shelf. So, I'm sorry I have not been a good mother. I heard one time that both Tonya and you were plotting to kill me. I hope you can forgive me."

"Nobody was plotting to kill you. I guess you are talking about when I came home on leave from the Army and Tonya had a gun hidden in a shoebox underneath her bed. I told her to get rid of it. I don't know what happened after I went back to Germany. Anyway, thank you for saying how you feel and I do forgive you. I hope you forgive me too."

"I forgive you," Roberta said.

"Well, I think this is a good start," Francis said. I believe that you both should continue these talks; because this is just the beginning. The two of you need to forgive each other for past hurts. I believe you both love each other. I believe you are both hurting. But, you got to forgive each other from the heart. It's not just what comes from the lips. I'm going to ask both of you if you can keep from talking to other people, especially other family members, who really have nothing to do with y'all's relationship and who the devil could use to cause confusion. There is a lot of information out there, and many people are talking who don't know what they are talking about. The enemy will use those who are close to you to keep things from getting better."

Francis continued, "And Belinda, your son LeMarkus said a lot of things to your mother tonight that other people listening shouldn't have been able to hear. Some of it was not his place to even be saying, and I don't know that he has all his facts straight. So, would you please talk to him?"

"I will talk with him and his sister and brothers because they need to know the truth. LeMarkus would not have anything to say if people hadn't been telling him stuff they don't know anything about. I've never talked with LeMarkus about any of this.

"Now, I'm afraid it's getting late, and I hate to say it, but there are some things that I must do on tomorrow. So, I need to go home and get some rest. But, before we leave, we need to pray," Francis said.

The three of them held hands while Francis prayed a prayer for forgiveness and reconciliation. They hugged each other, said, "I love you," and then said, "good night."

Francis offered to assist again if needed. She told Belinda and Roberta they should seek the help of a counselor.

Belinda left Roberta's house and drove to LeMarkus' house to get Pat. LeMarkus answered the door and came outside.

"Everything turned out okay," Belinda said.

"Mom, I'm sorry about some of the things I said, but I got tired of Grandma and the rest of them saying all of the things they were saying. And then, when Auntie Tonya came around, that just made it worst. You were busy talking to Grandma, so you didn't hear the things Auntie Tonya was saying. I had to correct her on some of the things she was saying. Tonya started talking about "LeMarkus; your mama is working in the church. She knows better and shouldn't be acting like that." Then, I just told her, "Like you knew better when you did the things you shouldn't have done. She didn't know I knew about all of that."

"Well, we all did things when we were young. Go tell Pat to come outside so we can go home."

It was 2:00 AM when they got home. Charles was asleep, and there was no reason to wake him. The next day she told him about what happened.

A few days later when things were calmer, Belinda met with LeMarkus, Tim, LeDarius, and Pat. She told them about the abuse she experienced. "Now, you all know what happened. You've heard it from me," Belinda said. "I know people have said things and will probably continue to say things to you, but they are only repeating what they've heard others say. You don't have to try and correct them. Just know that you know the truth."

"It's okay Mom. Thanks for telling us," LeDarius said.

"I'm sorry to have had to have to tell you these things. I guess it was all going to come out one day. Your Daddy, he already knows everything I told you. I told him before we were married, so he's always known."

37

Wakefield Police Department

WHILE WALKING THROUGH the rear parking lot of police headquarters, Belinda heard someone calling her name.

"Hey, Belinda! Wait up. How you doing?

It was Lieutenant Bainbridge.

"I'm okay, I guess." She heard herself giving that answer, but she knew that she was far from okay.

"What's going on? I just got back from vacation. I couldn't believe what I heard. Is it true that they put you on administrative leave?"

"Yeah, that's true. I couldn't believe it either, but everything is gonna be alright."

"What happened? What are they telling you?"

"That morning after the pursuit, I went home. About 2: o'clock that afternoon, I got a call from Captain Miller. He told me Lieutenant Brady was going to take over my shift for a while and I was being placed on administrative leave. He kept stressing that I wasn't being punished or restricted in any way. According to him, he talked with Chief Robinson, and they just wanted me to take some time off and rest. I was supposed to go back to work a week later, but that didn't happen. Instead, Miller placed me on administrative duty. It's funny. I've served a few of those before, but never thought I'd be getting one myself."

"I know it doesn't make you feel any better, but nobody ever thought they would do this to you. Are they telling you anything else?"

"Just that I was on administrative duty, and that I wasn't being punished."

"Let me know what they consider punishment. Technically, that may be true, because you haven't suffered monetarily, and you haven't lost any time in grade, but don't let them fool you. They may not be calling it that, but they are trying to punish you. I wouldn't trust them if I were you. Call me if you need anything. Alright?"

"Yeah, thanks."

Four Weeks Later

Belinda made an appointment to speak with Chief Robinson.

"Belinda, Hi! Come on in. What can I do for you?"

"Chief I asked to speak with you because I would like to go back to my shift. I'm not doing anything. I'm ready to move on and put this all behind me."

"Belinda, I would like to see you get past this too. This was a pretty serious incident. It is being looked into. I know that Captain Miller is doing everything he can to try and get an assignment for you. Unfortunately, we have a lieutenant who is out on bereavement leave right now. Any changes that we make will not just affect you, but it will affect everybody. Lieutenant McPherson had done nothing wrong. This is a difficult time for him right now. I don't want to make any decisions that are going to affect him while he is out."

"Chief, I been doing nothing. If I can't go back to my shift why can't I go to some other shift?"

"I've got 200 hundred officers to consider not just you. I can't put you back on the shift right now. I have a responsibility to them also. There are twenty-seven guys on the shift and one of you. My decision had to be one made for the greater good of the majority.

It was hard for Belinda to hear the words Chief Robinson spoke. Her eyes filled with tears. She prided herself on being the kind of officer who could focus without being overly emotional. She couldn't keep a tear from escaping and landing on her cheek. She'd never felt more humiliated or abandoned in her entire professional career.

"I can see how difficult this is for you. McPherson will be back soon, and we can get this worked out. Look, you are a good officer. You do good work. Just keep your head up and keep coming to work every day."

38

Wakefield Police Department

CAPTAIN MILLER WAS in his office talking to Attorney Dobbins. Miller and Attorney Dobbins had been friends for several years. Before starting his private practice, Dobbins was an Assistant State Prosecutor. Belinda stuck her head in the door.

"Hey Captain, Excuse the interruption, but I was wondering if there was any decision on my assignment."

"As a matter of fact, there has been. I was just talking to the Chief about you today. You're going to be transferred to South District Commander."

When Belinda left Miller's office, she went to speak with Chief Robinson.

"Hello Belinda, what can I do for you? Gail, the Chief's secretary, asked.

"Is the Chief available?"

"Hang on. I think he's got somebody in his office, but he should be finished in a minute."

"Okay, I'll just come back."

"No, hold on. Just wait a minute."

Gail opened the door and stuck her head in. Chief Robinson was speaking with Captain Dale Tomlinson of the Criminal Investigation Division.

"Chief, Belinda is out here, and she needs to speak to you. Do you have a minute?"

"Yeah Gail, tell her to come in."

"Dale, do the best you can. Let me know how things turn out."

Captain Tomlinson excused himself. "Okay Chief, thanks. I'll let you know how things turn out." He greeted Belinda as he left the office.

Belinda took a seat at the small round table in front of his desk.

"What can I do for you?"

"Chief, I came to find out about my assignment. When am I going to be assigned to a shift?"

"Well, you asked at a good time. I just got off the phone with Capt. Miller, not even twenty minutes ago. We were discussing your assignment. You're going to be assigned to the South District. I want you to know that this is a lot of responsibility. The South District is the largest District in the City. There is a wide range of demographics with a lot of neighborhood meetings to attend. Most of the people are very nice. If you answer their questions, they will be happy. You are there on behalf of me. Whatever needs to be done, you will be responsible for getting it taken care of. I know you can handle it. If I didn't have confidence in you, I wouldn't put you there. How does that sound to you?"

"The South District is fine Chief. I just want to get back to work."

"Go see Captain Miller. He should have everything worked out. As a matter of fact, let me get him on the phone."

Chief Robinson dialed Miller's number.

"Ed."

"Hello, Chief."

"Ed, can you come into my office for a minute. I've got Belinda here. We were discussing her assignment."

A few minutes later, Miller appeared.

"Hey Ed, I was just telling Belinda that we were discussing her assignment today. She's going to be assigned to the South District. How soon do you think that change will be made?"

"Well Chief, the problem is that more than just Lieutenant Williams is involved in these assignments. I've got Lt. McPherson, who as you know, just returned from bereavement leave. I didn't want to make any changes while he was gone. And I wanted to give him time to get settled again after he got back. Having said that, I'll get right on it and contact McPherson tomorrow. I don't see why it should take any longer than two weeks at the most."

"Okay, Good, then it is settled."

"Thank you, Chief," Belinda said."

When Belinda came to work the next Monday, Miller called her into his office.

"Hello, Lieutenant. Have a seat. I've talked to McPherson. He is going to the North District. I've assigned you to the South District. Get with McPherson, and he will explain to you what meetings he's got on his calendar. The two of you can work out a schedule. I've got a lot to do, and the timing is not perfect for me to try and do this, but that's okay."

"Is there something wrong Captain?"

"No, there is nothing wrong. You're starting to fight, and that's good. Am I happy about you going to the Chief? No, I'm not. I told you I was taking care of it and you couldn't wait. But, that's okay. It's being done now. You'll do a good job. Go see McPherson."

"Captain, it's been two months."

"I know, but the guy's brother just died. I was trying to give him some time."

Belinda met McPherson for lunch at the Bright Morning Café to discuss the change of assignments.

"Man, that's a bunch of bull," McPherson said. "With everything that Miller has done. You know they say he was responsible for getting the old Chief fired. How can he try and do anything to you? They have never done that to anybody before. I spoke to Miller a couple of times while I was on leave. He never said anything to me about changing assignments. I'll work wherever they send me, you know that. Hey, be careful with him. If you need anything, you let me know."

The transfer to the South District was a smooth transition. Belinda was responsible for two sworn employees. One was the Crime Prevention Officer, and the other one was the Volunteer Program Coordinator. She was also the liaison between the police department and several neighborhood organizations. She kept them informed about the crime in their neighborhoods and what the department was doing about it. The South District, being the largest, in any given month there could be as many as twenty meetings to attend. Belinda found herself running from place to place, with just enough time to get from one meeting to the next. There was hardly time enough to prepare in between. A lot of late night hours were spent reading reports and getting ready for the following day's meeting, but it didn't matter. It felt good to be back at work again.

39

Six Months Year Later

BELINDA WAS COMING OUT of the back of the police headquarters building when she saw Lt. Dewayne Nichols, walking across the parking lot towards his car.

"Hey Belinda, how's it going? How's the new job coming?"

"Hi Danny, everything is going well. Thanks for asking.

"I just wanted you to know that I had a meeting with the Chief the other day and he was saying how pleased he was with the job you are doing in the South District."

"He actually said that? What does he think that I don't know how to talk to people?"

"Well, you know how it is. Sometimes we have to prove ourselves a little bit more than others."

"Yeah, I know, the story of my life."

"Hey, where are you heading now?"

"I was going to the awards ceremony. I really don't want to, but I guess it wouldn't look right if I weren't there, considering that's where everyone else is going to be."

"I know you're right. I was just getting ready to head that way myself." You want to ride with me?

No, thanks, I'd better drive. I'll probably have to leave and go pick up my daughter, Patricia, from school before the ceremony ends.

The awards ceremony was inside the auditorium of the Blue Falcon Performing Arts Hall. Belinda took her seat among the other officers.

The ceremony opened with a prayer given by Chaplain Graves followed by the pledge of allegiance. Chief Robinson spoke first, welcoming everyone to the ceremony. Then he presented the mayor, who acknowledged the other commissioners in the room.

Among the categories presented was the officer of the year, meritorious service medals, lifesaving medals, and the unit commendation medals.

Chief Robinson started with the unit commendations. "On the night of November 11, 2006, a group of brave men and women heard a state trooper chasing a gunman, who had just pointed a gun at the trooper. These officers assisted the trooper by joining in the chase. The pursuit ended when the suspect hit a tree and continue to flee on foot. The man was located hiding underneath a vehicle and subsequently arrested. Because of their actions, a would-be cop killer was taken off the street."

As expected, Belinda had to leave before the ceremony was over to go and get Pat from school.

The next day when Belinda went to work, she had virtually no energy. The office looked unfamiliar. It was as if she had never been there before and she could not come up with a reason why she should be there then. There was nothing on her calendar and if there had been it didn't matter. Belinda drove around for a couple of hours. Hearing Lt. Dewayne Nichols on the radio, she met with him on the downtown walking beat. Dewayne was a friend and opened minded enough to listen objectively to what she had to say. He was a tall African-American, who reminded many people of T.D. Jakes. His mere presence put the fear of God in the criminals on the street, but he was the kindest and most compassionate officer that you would ever want for to a victim.

"Hey Belinda, what's going on?"

"DeWayne, I've decided this is my last day working here."

"We've had this conversation before. Are you sure?"

"Like you said, I've been considering this for some time. I'm sure."

"Let me ask you this. What is it that you still would want to do here?

"There is nothing that I want to do. I'm not trying to be a police chief. I have no interest in being a patrol bureau commander, and that's the next step for me. I know I don't know everything, but I believe I have learned everything that I'm supposed to learn here. It's time for me to move on.

"I told you the last time that if you wanted to leave, make sure you leave on your terms and not anybody else's."

"I know, and that's part of the reason why I stuck it out during that whole administrative leave incident. I've been thinking about leaving for a long time, but I kept getting promoted. Plus,

I really don't have any desire to work for a department or a city that would treat someone like that. No wonder somebody's always suing us. For two months, I walked around this city like I had some kind of plague. I felt like I did when I was in high school. That Captain in Martin County called off the pursuit of that guy who shot and killed that guy in the middle of the intersection. Nothing happened to him. We caught the guy, and they treated me like a criminal. All they did was focus on the mistake I made."

"I can see you're upset. Tell me this. Are you feeling like doing anything to hurt yourself or anything like that?"

"No DeWayne, I'm not suicidal. I'm upset, but I'm not homicidal either. You don't have to worry about me going off on nobody. I'm just tired, and I feel like I'm walking in quicksand and can't take another step."

"Okay, then do me a favor before you make any final decision."

"What's that?"

"Go talk to someone. I can get the number to the Employee Assistance Program (EAP) office for you if you don't have it. Give them a call. It won't hurt."

"Sure. I'll call them. I should have the number."

Two Days Later

"Hello Mrs. Stephens, my name is Dr. Bernard Lewis."

"Hello, Dr. Lewis."

"I see here that you're with the police department."

"Yes."

"I looked at becoming a police officer when I was younger, but I opted to go into the service instead. I've always admired what you all do. What is it that brings you here today?"

"I'm here because I'm about to make a decision that if one of my officers came to me and told me that they were considering doing what I'm about to do, I would tell them to go and get their head examined. I'm considering retiring from the city. I want to make sure that my decision has nothing to do with some events that happened in my childhood."

"How soon are you looking at leaving your job?"

"I'm 46, and I have 18 years of service. The retirement age is 50 years or 25 years of service. So, I'm short four years."

"So, what we have to do is see how we can get you through these next four years."

"Yeah, I guess."

Dr. Lewis obtained more background information from Belinda. "The way this works is that we are a referral agency. I have a couple of names of people who have experience in treating persons who have gone through what you have. I will give you both their names. One is a male, and one is a female. I don't know if you have any preference for either."

Belinda took the paper from Dr. Lewis with names of the referrals written on it.

"In the meantime, I suggest you go and see a medical doctor, your family doctor if you have one. He can make a diagnosis and prescribe some medication that will help you. You may be able to take some time off from work. Most likely it will be short term. But, it will give you a little while and then you can work on a plan for what you want to do."

Belinda made an appointment for the next day to go see her private doctor. She explained what was happening. He prescribed some anti-depression medication and wrote her a script to be off work for two months.

"You're depressed. It's probably been coming on for a couple of years," her doctor said. I'm giving you two months off work." Take some time off. Then, go back to work. Don't make any major decisions right now. Come back to see me in two months."

The next week Belinda went to an appointment with Dr. Susan Schneider, one of the counselors on the list of referrals. Dr. Schneider met with Belinda every two weeks and extended her leave from work for another two months.

Belinda felt weak and was unable to eat. Whenever she tried to sleep, her mind would not shut off. The thoughts and images emerged like a kaleidoscope of images of people and things in her life, but the pictures were not fully developed. When she did drift off to sleep, she was awakened by something choking her. She once felt so sick that she went to the emergency room, but they told her there was nothing wrong and to go home to get some rest.

When Belinda was awake, she felt sad. She constantly cried, seemingly for no reason. It was as if someone turned on the faucet to her tear and refused to shut it off. These were different from the tears she cried when she felt neglected by Charles. These were tears of cleansing. She cried for feeling abandoned by her mother and father. She cried the tears that came too late when she was giving birth to LeMarkus. She cried for her daughter's death and the loss of her aborted child. She cried the tears she never cried when her grandfather died and the ones that never fell when her grandmother died. She cried the tears that could not fall whenever she was hurting and couldn't let anyone know. And when the tears stopped falling, she began to feel. Then, she began to act.

Belinda's sadness turned to anger, which she now recognized for what it was. She discussed one of the incidents on one of her visits with Dr. Schneider.

"Belinda, how much land did you say there was at your house?" Dr. Schneider asked.

"It's a little over five acres."

"So, there are lots of trees."

"Yes."

"It's good that you are experiencing and recognizing your emotions, but I would suggest that you not throw and break the things you worked hard to pay for. When you feel angry, you can go outside and cut down a few trees or cut some grass."

"Her suggestion made Belinda laugh."

"Besides, breaking things-that doesn't become you. That doesn't even sound like you."

Belinda agreed. Since, she acknowledged her anger and learned to control it, instead of feeling victimized, she was able to control the feeling of rage.

The time was approaching for Belinda to go back to work. She contemplated taking a leave of absence for a year and discussed her options with Charles.

"Why do that?" Charles said. "You might as well just go ahead and quit instead of going through all of that. We'll be fine."

Two Months Later

Belinda received a letter in the mail from Chief Robinson requesting to meet with her about her position.

"Belinda thanks for coming in to meet with me. I asked to meet in person with everyone affected by the changes we need to make because of the budget. This is one part of this job that I have to admit, I do not enjoy. You're here because I had to eliminate the South District Commander position, but you don't have to worry. You are being reassigned back to patrol as a shift commander. Just so you know, there will be some other changes made. I also have to temporarily demote one lieutenant back to sergeant. Two sergeants will go back to being patrolmen. All of this is temporary. When we can make promotions again, they will get their rank back."

"Thanks for letting me know Chief."

"Like I said, I wanted to let you know in person. That way there would be no misunderstanding because of rumors that might be flying around. If you could come back on Wednesday, I'll have the transfer letter ready for you."

Belinda went back to meet with Chief Robinson that Wednesday, as scheduled. He handed Belinda the memorandum authorizing her transfer. Then, Belinda gave him her letter of resignation.

"Belinda, are you sure about this? What are you going to do?"

"Yes Chief, I'm sure."

"Well okay, if you've made up your mind. I know that you will be successful in whatever you choose to do. People leave this department under many different circumstances. I want you to know that you are always welcome to come back."

"Thanks, Chief!"

"No, I need to thank you, Belinda, and so does the lieutenant and other officers that I was going to have to demote. With you leaving, I no longer have to do that. You have just created enough money in the budget to save their jobs. I will be sure to let them know that. If you ever need anything, let me know."

Part 3

Room Three

40

CONTINUING TO THE right from the kitchen was the third
and final room in the house, the rear bedroom. A curtain tacked
over the doorpost marked the entrance to the room since there
was no room door. Inez pulled back the curtain so Belinda could
see inside the bedroom.

"This is the room where I mostly sleep," said Inez.

The bed was nicely decorated with a purple accented
bedspread, color coordinated to match the curtains and the rugs
on the floor.

While growing up, this was the room where all the children
slept. Two beds lay side by side, with just enough room to walk
between them. The boys slept on one bed and the girls on the
other. They alternated with one lying at the head and one at the
foot of the bed.

At night, small house mice, huge wood rats, and every size in
between scampered across the floor. At times, one might run
across the bed. Those in the ceiling sounded like they were
playing a game of soccer with cheese.

It wasn't uncommon to find a rat snake hiding in the wall,
curled up among the newspaper. Belinda recalled being terrified
of the rodents. One night, she screamed at the top of her lungs

when one of those big wood rats fell from a hole in the ceiling and landed at the foot of her bed. Everyone in the house woke up. Elena and Bobby came running to find out what was wrong. When they realized that it was only a rat, Elena told Belinda not to be afraid and to go back to sleep.

"Go back to sleep, just like that," Belinda thought. "How can she just go back to sleep after all she'd been through?"

"You have been through a lot," Inez said. "I'm glad you were able to get help through counseling."

"Yeah, I was fortunate. I remember one of the things Susan told me was that I needed to come to terms with my orphanage. It's funny. I never looked at myself as an orphan, but that's what I was. Regardless of the reason, both my mother and father left me. I had always prided myself on going through all that stuff I went through and coming out on the other side unscathed. I think I did pretty good, but Susan helped me see that I had developed a lot of coping skills. I basically left Florida to go in the Army and never stopped running until I couldn't run anymore. When I left the Wakefield Police Department, that was only the first step of many towards reconciling my past.

"It's getting late," Inez said. "It doesn't make sense for you to try and drive in the middle of the night without any rest. Why don't you stay here tonight and start out fresh in the morning?"

"You've been more than nice. I don't want to intrude any more than I have already."

"I insist," Inez said.

41

September 2008

CHARLES WAS OUTSIDE in the driveway. He had just finished checking the oil in the car when LeMarkus arrived. "Hey LeMarkus, I'm glad you stopped by. I need you to help me check out the brake lights on this car. I finally get a chance to check things out on this car. Your Ma, she stays gone so much that the car doesn't stand still long enough for me to ever get a chance to work on it."

"Okay, Dad, what you need for me to do?"

"I just need for you to get inside and tap on the brakes when I tell you. I'll stand behind it to make sure all of the lights are working."

Belinda came outside to find out how long Charles was going to be working on the car. It was still early, but she had tickets to the Steve Harvey, *Tear Your Mouth Out* show in Tampa for that evening. Surprised to see LeMarkus, she said, "Hey LeMarkus when did you get here?"

"Hey, Mom. I just got here a few minutes ago. I was coming in the house to see you. I was just out here trying to help Dad check the brake lights."

"Don't take too long. He needs to stop soon so he can get ready."

"Get ready for what? Where are you guys going?"

"We got tickets to go see Steve Harvey tonight."

"Well alright then. Dad, you better hurry up. You don't want to be late for that."

"I'm not going," Charles said.

"What do you mean, you're not going?" Belinda asked. "I've already bought the tickets. You promised me that you would go."

"I changed my mind. I don't want to go."

"That's what you always do. What am I supposed to do with these tickets? I bought them because you said you would go with me. I thought I finally found something you and I could enjoy together since you don't want to do anything else."

"Dad, you sure you don't want to go to that? Man, that's Steve Harvey. I wish somebody would have bought me tickets to go see Steve Harvey."

"Steve who? No, I'm not going anywhere. I got too many things to do," Charles said.

"What do you have to do that can't wait?" Belinda asked. "You know what? That's okay. Just forget it." Belinda threw the pair of tickets on the ground. "LeMarkus, if you want these tickets, you can have them. I'm sure you can find somebody to go with you."

"What?" LeMarkus said. Holding the tickets, he couldn't stop smiling. "This must be my lucky day- a pair of Steve Harvey tickets. Wow! Dad, you're sure you don't want to go? This is Steve, the comedian from the TV show and the Steve Harvey radio show that comes on in the mornings. Dad, you don't want to miss this. I can't take these." LeMarkus extended his hand out to Charles, gesturing for him to take the tickets.

Charles took the tickets from LeMarkus and laid them on the hood of the car. Belinda went back inside the house, slamming the door behind her.

Thirty minutes later, Charles came into the bedroom. Holding a suit that he took from his closet, he asked Belinda, "Which tie do you think I should wear with this suit?"

"Belinda was torn between being mad and still wanting Charles to go with her, rubbed the tears from her eyes with her thumb and index finger. "The green one," she said.

"You better finished getting dressed," Charles said. We don't want to be late."

"Is LeMarkus still here?"

"No, he left right after you came in the house." Charles pulled Belinda close. For a moment, it looked as if things could be the way she imagined.

Belinda wore a sage green dress to compliment Charles's suit. They arrived at the Mahaffey Theater within an hour. Even though most people referred to the show as being in Tampa, the theater was actually located in St. Petersburg. The dinner before the show was buffet style, which included an entre of steak, roast beef, or chicken and all the sides. A cash bar was available for anyone who wanted an adult beverage.

From the time Steve Harvey was introduced as the original King of Comedy and appeared on stage wearing a white suit and white hat, the crowd roared with excitement. After giving thanks to God, Steve told his first joke. Belinda had never seen Charles laugh so hard. He didn't stop laughing until the show was over. As much as Belinda enjoyed the show, the look on Charles' face and knowing that he had a good time was even more enjoyable. "The fact that they were together made everything that she went through to get there that evening worthwhile," she thought, "but it shouldn't be this hard."

42

WHILE ON THE WAY home, Belinda stopped at the grocery store. She called Charles to ask what he wanted for dinner. Charles happened to be on his way home too, so he met her in the grocery store parking lot. Instead of cooking, they decided to order a pizza.

"Hey, I just got a call from LeDarius," Charles said. "LeDarius said his girlfriend Nichole is home cooking dinner for us. She wanted to surprise us."

"She is home cooking dinner where?"

"At our house."

"Okay. This is just amazing," Belinda said, searching for some word to describe what she was feeling.

"I know what you're thinking, but she just wants to fit in. He feels like when they are at her parent's house, they make him feel like he is part of the family. Nichole doesn't feel that way here."

"Well, I'm sorry she doesn't feel that way. The fact of the matter is that she is a guest. And if she wants to fit in she shouldn't do things like come into my kitchen messing with things when I'm not home. First, there was the incident upstairs. Now, she's cooking in my kitchen."

"I know. They should have checked with us first to see what we were planning, but they didn't. LeDarius and Nichole just wanted to do something nice to surprise you."

"Yeah? Well, they succeeded. We are out picking up dinner, and somebody is home cooking. That's just great."

"The only thing to do is to go home and have both," Charles said. "We'll just take the pizza home and put it on the table along with whatever she's fixing. If you feel you can't do that then maybe you should just go somewhere else."

Belinda looked at Charles with disbelief about what he just said.

"Go somewhere?"

"Yeah, if you don't think you can sit across the table from her and not get upset; rather than causing some big scene, you shouldn't come."

"I'm tired of people telling me that I should just go away. That's my house, but you want me to be nice to someone who keeps going into areas of it where they don't belong. Okay, I'll go somewhere. Charles, you can go back home and enjoy your dinner."

"Why do you have to say it like that? Why do you always have to twist whatever I say?"

Belinda got into her car and started the ignition. Charles stood in the parking lot as he watched her drive off. When Belinda came to the crossroads, she decided to go north onto Interstate 75. The tears she had been suppressing ran down her face. "Why do I always have to suppress my true feelings, so others can feel better?" Don't my feelings matter?" She thought. "Where am I supposed to go? I've been pushed out of work, - just go somewhere." At church, and now at home. There is only one place for me to go if I'm gonna keep going at all. Otherwise, what's the use?"

Belinda continued to drive north on Interstate 75. She didn't stop driving until she reached the Georgia state line.

43

Douglas Georgia

BELINDA STOPPED AT the first convenient store to buy gas and a map of the state of Georgia. Surprisingly, Douglas was only 200 more miles. It was 4:00 am when she arrived in Douglas. The streets were almost deserted. The address listed on the computer under directory assistance for Michael Dawson was 213 Maddison Street. Six single-family, one car garage homes built in the early seventies lined the short dead-end street, which backed up to an industrial park.

A patrol officer noticed the unfamiliar car in the neighborhood and asked Belinda if she needed any help. She explained to him that she was there on a personal matter, looking for a relative she hadn't seen in years. The officer immediately recognized Michael's name. He let Belinda know that the neighborhood was quiet for the most part and Michael Dawson was a model citizen. On the other hand, his son Michael Jr. from Miami was a different story. The officer remembered that Michael Jr. came to visit and was nothing but trouble from day one. It wasn't long before they arrested Michael Jr. on drug charges and sent him back to Florida.

"Thanks for your help," Belinda said, "It helps to know where I'm going."

It was only a few hours before morning daylight. Rather than get a hotel room, she just decided to take a nap in her car. The Save-Market parking lot seemed like the safest place underneath the parking lot cameras. After a while, she went inside the store and purchased what she would need for the day, clean underwear, toothbrush, toothpaste, deodorant, and a comb. Then, she called Charles to let him know where she was. There was no answer, so she left a message on his cell phone.

Later that day, when Belinda went to the house, no one was home. She visited the little corner store and ate at one of the neighborhood restaurants.

"You're not from around here are you?" The waitress said.

"No Ma'am I came to visit some relatives. Do you know a Michael Dawson?"

"Yeah, he comes in here all the time. You related to him?"

"Yes, he's my father."

"Well, we're very fond of your father here. He comes in here almost every day."

Belinda drove back to the house. A car was in the driveway that wasn't there previously. She took a deep breath and said a prayer asking God to give her the strength. Then she knocked on the door.

An older Michael, who looked more like his father Dawson Sr., opened the door. "Hey! Man, what a surprise! Come on in."

Michael turned and yelled to a woman inside the house. "Baby, look who's here," he said. "There's somebody here you need to meet."

A short brown-skinned woman, in her early fifties, hurried to join Michael and Belinda in the living room. "Annie, this is Belinda, my daughter," he said. "Belinda, this is my wife, Annie."

"Well, I finally get to meet you," Annie said. I've heard a lot about you. All your Daddy has ever talked about is his other daughter. He is so excited to see you."

They exchanged pleasantries. Then Annie said she had some things to go get from the store. She wrote a list of items to purchase and then left Michael alone with Belinda.

"There is somebody else I want you to meet too," Michael said. You have a younger brother named Nathan.

"Oh yeah, how old is he?"

"He's twenty. He's out right now, but he should be in here soon."

"Okay."

"Would you like to go for a ride, so we can talk?"

"Sure!"

Belinda drove Michael to the drug store. It was in the shopping strip mall at the corner of the street. She parked in an area where there were only a few cars near one of the landscaped islands. They got out and stood underneath the tree.

"Well, I knew the day would come sooner or later when you would come At least, I hoped it would. I always wanted to know how you were doing. To make sure you were alright. I kept up with you as much as I could. Are you still a police officer?"

"How did you know I was a police officer?"

"Oh, I don't know, somebody told me. I don't remember who right now. So, how's the family? How many children do you have now?"

"I have four. I don't mean to be rude, but to discuss my family is not really the reason why I came to see you."

"I always wondered about you. I see now that you did very well, but then, I always knew you would. This is a nice car you have. I always wanted a Cadillac."

"Thanks!"

"I know you want to talk about things. I also wanted to have the opportunity to let you know how sorry I was and to apologize for what happened."

"I want to know why you did what you did."

"That's not an easy answer. All I can say is that I love you. There is something special about you. I couldn't help it. I knew you were my daughter, but that was a time in my life when I needed someone. I'm not saying that it was right, but I actually fell in love with you and wanted to spend the rest of my life with you. Although, I know that would not have been completely fair to you."

"What you did to me was wrong?"

"I know. I don't know what else I can say other than to say I'm sorry. What you are looking for is answers I can't give you. I know you want to know why. All I can tell you is that I love you."

"Were there others? Have you done this to anyone else?"

"No, I have not."

"Are you sure? What about Regina?"

"Yes, I'm sure."

"Why me then? Why did you pick me to ruin my life?"

"I'm sorry. I don't mean to ruin your life. I know it was selfish. You were the most amazing thing that could happen to me. I could just sit and talk to you for hours. You have a calming effect on people that you don't even realize. When my life was spinning out of control, you brought a sense of balance."

"What do you mean?" Belinda asked.

"I don't know. I had just come back home. Dad had been sick. That's really why I was in town, to take him to his doctor appointments. Then he died later that year. I was going through this thing with my wife. The world was caving in on me. The only thing that brought any joy was you."

"So, you abused me, because I brought you joy. I needed you. I needed a father. All my life I wished you would show up. I needed someone who would be there for me, and I trusted you. I needed for the world to make sense to me and you let me down. You took advantage of me. You don't love me. You never did."

"You're wrong. I do love you. I'm so sorry. I hope you forgive me for what I did. Whatever I can do to make it up to you, I'll do that."

"Will you admit what you did?"

"Of course, I will. I've always told you that I would tell whomever you asked me to about what happened. If I have to go back to jail, then I would just do that."

"Would you be willing to go to counseling?"

"Sure, I told you-anything."

"How are you going to do that? Are you going to come to Florida?"

"We'll figure it out. I will do what it takes to make things right with you. I will always love you. Any type of relationship I can have with you, I will be fine with. If you want things like they were before or if you want to just talk on the phone from time to time, that's okay too."

"What do you mean, if I want things like they were before? I was just a kid, and you used me. You set me up from the very first day. And now you are suggesting that I would want to be with you."

"I know you can't understand it. You won't be satisfied until you get answers, but you're asking questions that I'm not sure there will ever be an answer that exists to satisfy you. I don't know why things happened between us. For me, you were my world, and you always will be."

"I can't believe I'm hearing this," Belinda said. "I have to go." She ran to the next row of parking spaces away from Michael and slumped down on the ground. She wiped the tears from her face with her hand. She heard part of an apology that she always wanted to hear. The other words she heard were those from that didn't make sense from an obviously sick man. "How could he suggest such a thing, if he wasn't mentally ill? Belinda thought.

Belinda needed to talk to the one person who she believed did love her. She needed to feel grounded again. She needed to hear Charles' voice. She dialed his number on her cell phone. The phone rang and went straight to voicemail. She called again. Once again, there was no answer. Belinda cried and pleaded for Charles to please pick up the phone. "Charles, I need to talk to you. Please answer. I don't know what to do. I needed help. Please call me." The phone rang just as she hung up.

"Mom, where are you? Are you alright? Pat asked.

"Yeah, I'm okay. I just need to talk to your Daddy. Where is he?"

"He's outside. I'll go get him."

Belinda could hear Pat's footsteps and the door opening as she went outside to get Charles.

"Dad, Mom's on the phone. She needs to talk to you."

"I'm busy right now," Charles said.

"But, it's Mom. It sounds like she's been crying."

"I told you I was busy."

"Mom-, Pat said."

"It's okay Pat. I heard him. Don't worry about it. I'll be okay. Just tell him that I should be home tomorrow."

"Are you sure you're okay?"

"Yeah, I'm sure. I love you."

"I love you too, mom."

When Belinda hung up the phone, Michael moved closer and offered her a comforting embrace. Belinda pushed him away.

"I suppose I deserve that. I wish I could change things, but I can't," Michael said.

"Let's go," Belinda said. She drove Michael back to his house. Michael's son Nathan was standing in the front yard when they arrived. Michael introduced Nathan to Belinda.

"You're from Florida?" Nathan asked.

"Yeah, she lives not too far from your other sister, who lives in Tampa. The one in Tampa wants to get all of you guys together. She's always asking me if I had heard from you," Michael said.

"How many children do you have?" Belinda asked.

"There are twenty in all. You have twin brothers in Baltimore. You, Junior, and Regina are in Florida. The rest are scattered about."

"That's really amazing," Belinda said. "It's getting late. I have to go.

"I'm glad you came. I wish I could meet the family one day."

"I don't think that's ever going to be possible. Goodbye."

44

Wakefield, Florida

BELINDA PULLED INTO the driveway and parked. The hood on the semi-truck was open. Belinda spoke to Charles when she got out of the car. He continued to check the air pressure in the tires on the truck. The familiarity of being back at home felt good. So, she ignored the fact that he didn't speak to her. Apparently, he was more upset with her than she thought. After thirty years of suffering, she knew she had a major breakthrough in her healing after seeing Michael. She wanted to tell Charles all about it, but she knew he wasn't interested.

When she walked into the house, their golden retriever, Lucky met her at the door wagging his tail. He followed her into the bedroom. Belinda began to put away her belongings. Patricia ran downstairs to meet her.

"Mom, you're home," she said, giving her a big hug. "I missed you!"

"I missed you too. I told you I would be back sometime this evening."

"I know, but I was worried because I didn't know what might happen."

"Everything is alright. I'm home now."

"Come; Let me show you what I did."

"What did you do?"

"Let me show you my room."

"Oh, wow! Let me go and see this." Belinda went upstairs with Pat. The furniture was polished. Pat had vacuumed the floor and put everything in its place. "This is really nice. Thank you for doing this. I bet you sleep a lot better at night with everything nice and clean," Belinda said.

"I slept good before."

"Okay, well I hope this will last a while."

Pat smiled and said, "We'll see."

Belinda went back to the bedroom downstairs. She had just driven over fourteen hours straight, and she was exhausted. Placing her purse on the dresser, Belinda fell across the bed. All she wanted was to feel the comfort of her head on her pillow. She had been lying down for a few moments when Charles came into the bedroom.

"Where have you been?" he asked?

"I've been where I told you I was. I was in Georgia."

"Belinda, I'm tired. I can't take this anymore. If you want somebody else, I think I should just go ahead and leave, and I'll get out your way. Apparently, what I do is not good enough for you. So, why don't I just get the hell out the way and let you get who you want."

"What you talking about? I told you I was in Georgia with my father. I tried to call you, but you would not answer the phone."

"What were you doing in Georgia? I thought you were just going to go somewhere for a little while. Then when you felt better or whatever, you were going to come on home."

"So, you thought I should just forget about my feelings and just come and pretend everything was alright."

"Yeah, I thought you were coming home. Everybody was here wondering what happened. LeDarius wanted to know if there was something he did to make you mad, the reason why you didn't come home. Nichole was just trying to be nice. She tries so hard to fit in over here. Apparently, when LeDarius goes over to their house, they make him feel like he's part of the family. If it's late, they let him sleep in one of the extra bedrooms. They just embrace him. She just wants to feel welcome here."

"You really don't get it. Charles, I have actually been fighting for my life. Everybody has been telling me to go somewhere. Everything that happens is always my fault. My mother blames me. The guys at the police department blame me. In the Army, they don't blame the guy who's fraternizing with the woman. They always blame the woman and send her away or transfer her to a different unit. And, you blame me." Belinda stood facing Charles. "Well instead of going away for good and ending it all, I decided to go and confront the person, who caused my life to be turned upside down in the first place. For almost 30 years I didn't know what I would do if I saw my father. I didn't know if I would shoot him, yell at him or what. I tried calling you. I needed you, but you were so mad at me that you couldn't even answer the phone. Pat called me and said she got the message and tried to give you the phone, but you wouldn't take it. It breaks my heart to know that she heard me crying on the phone. If something doesn't fit within what you think is right, then, it doesn't matter what anyone else is going through."

"Belinda, I'm sorry, but you left, and you don't tell anyone where you are going? I had no idea you were going to Georgia. I thought you would have gone over to your Aunt's house for a little while or to the movies or something."

"I didn't know I was going to Georgia either, but I'm glad I went. It may have been irrational, but I finally faced my demons from the past. Now, I'm tired. I've been driving all day. Can't I just lie down and get some rest?"

"Sure, I'm glad you made it back safely."

Two Months Later

Michael called Belinda a few times. She questioned him about when he was coming to Florida or talk with her therapist on the phone as he promised. It was evident that he had no intentions of coming to Florida or admitting what he had done to anyone other than her. At her next appointment with her therapist, Belinda celebrated the progress she made by confronting Michael. Her counselor helped her see that Michael was incapable of loving her the way a father should, and she could not trust what he said. She also learned Michael had sexually abused at least two of his other daughters.

Belinda's counselor also helped her see what Charles had done for her, despite his distancing her, not treating her with the respect she deserved by treating her like a child. Charles had helped provide her life with love and stability. Strangely, the two men in her life had reversed their roles. Her father, Michael, treated her like a lover. Her husband, Charles, treated her as his daughter, although he wouldn't admit it. Belinda was growing stronger as a person, but her relationship with Charles was strained.

One Year Later

After Pat graduated from high school, she went away to college. For almost a year, Belinda Charles, and Lucky were together alone in a house that was built for a family. Belinda was active outside the house with her church, friends, and a new job at a police department in a neighboring county. Charles watched sports on TV, ate breakfast, lunch, and dinner, and slept on the sofa in the living room. Since there was nothing in common between them, there was no conversation between them.

"Charles, I don't know what I'm doing here."

"What do you mean, this is your home."

"Charles, you know what I mean."

"I told you it doesn't take much for me. I'm fine, but I know that you need more."

"I don't need much either, but we are supposed to be married, and there is nothing that we do or have together, except for our children. Somehow, they all turned out to be loving, kind, and amazing adults, in spite of us. Now that they are on their own, where does that leave us? This is what I was afraid of. With the way we're living, it really doesn't matter if I'm here or not."

"You're always complaining about me not doing anything, I guess the problem is our ages."

"It's not your age. Plenty of people just as old as you are, some older, are actively enjoying their lives and not sitting around watching it pass by. It's not just about doing things either. We should be able to enjoy each other's company. You would rather play a game of solitaire on the computer than play a game of cards with me. I'm not a plant or an animal that all you have to do is feed or provide for and watch it grow. I'm a person, who requires some form of intimacy."

"I should have married an older more settled woman. Me and my first wife, we had our set of friends and places where we did things together socially."

"We could have had that too, Charles. People always invited us to go places, but you refused. I always ended up going alone."

"Yeah, Bainbridge and his wife were nice."

"If you didn't plan on sharing your life with me, then, why did you marry me?

"Let me ask you this, how was it in the beginning?"

"Seriously, in the beginning? So, you knew what I needed all this time, and you refused to share that part of yourself with me. I gave you the benefit of the doubt. I thought you just didn't feel comfortable being with me around other people or just didn't know how. You did it on purpose?"

"I needed someone to be a mother to my children, to help raise them."

"So, you're telling me that this has been nothing more than a modern-day color purple. I can't do this anymore. I've tried to do everything I could to love you, but I'm dying here. I appreciate everything that you've done for me, but I'm not the same person you met twenty-seven years ago. I've grown. I admit that back then, in some ways, I was still a child in an adult's body, but by the grace of God, I've been set free. I never thought I would have to admit it, but I've spent all this time trying to do what only God can do. I will never give up on what God will do for us. In the meantime, I have to go."

The Next Day | Cambleton

When Belinda woke up the next morning, Inez was sitting at the kitchen table drinking a cup of coffee.

"Good morning!" Inez said. "How did you sleep?"

"I slept very well, thanks. As a matter of fact, as far as I can remember this is the first time I was able to sleep through the night on my back without feeling like I was drowning, or someone was choking me. I almost couldn't believe it. And this morning when I got out of bed, I heard God calling my name."

Belinda hugged and thanked Inez again for her hospitality. As she drove away, Israel Houghton was singing about the freedom that God gives, as a healer who makes all things new and how it was time to move forward.

EPILOGUE

People say that I'm different. Sometimes, they tell me that I'm more approachable than I was before. They can talk to me now and feel like they are connecting, when before it seemed as if I was always distant. I'm not sure I always know what they mean, but I am different. I remember when one of my sons took an eye exam at school and we discovered he needed glasses. I felt so bad as a mother. He made it all the way to high school, and we had no idea he couldn't see. One day when we walked into a department store, he said, "wow, I can see those signs up on the back wall. I never knew those were there." I could only imagine what his life must have been like not being able to see what others saw. In some ways, he didn't miss anything because he didn't know there was anything to miss. On the other hand, he must have sensed something was wrong when people talked about things for which he had no frame of reference. For me, allowing my true self to emerge was like my son getting his new glasses. Some people call it coming out of the fog. All I know is that I woke up one day and the world was different, and I was set free from forty years of bondage. It wasn't easy, and it didn't happen overnight, but it was worth it. It happened one step at a time. I can honestly say that it is only now that I am truly alive.

I realized that some people are not accustomed to me and my new-found freedom. They don't always know how to respond to the new me. That's alright. One of the reasons why is because they don't understand what happened to me. They never knew I was bound. I did an excellent job of hiding it. In some cases, people may be dealing with their own issues that they may not be ready to face. So, now I realize that I'm the one who must be understanding, patient, and kind.

My husband, a Vietnam veteran is a good provider, who shows love the way many men of his generation do. Some things he regards as love, I see as controlling and oppressive. I hope he can learn to love the person who's no longer hidden inside of me and afraid to see past the boundaries. My father and husband are two men that I once thought could fill a void in my life that only God, my real father, could fill. God's love is unconditional, and it lasts forever.

Acknowledgments

I have so many people to thank, who have encouraged me in the writing of this book that I am tempted to omit this section for fear of forgetting to include someone's name. However, the more I think about it, there is no way that I cannot express the gratitude that I have for everyone who played a part in my completion of this project, especially when it has taken ten years to complete. First, I give thanks and all credit to God, because none of this would be possible without Him.

I want to thank my husband, Booker T. Jackson and my children, Alicia, Brian, Jason, and Demetrius. There is no way I can tell my story and not include you. I also want to thank my mother Earnestine, the other eight siblings from that little three-room house, and my sister Kimberly for being who you are.

I will never forget the day in 2009 when I met Cheri Cowell in the cafeteria of Asbury Theological Seminary. Thank you, Cheri, for introducing me to the Florida Christian Writer's Conference that helped nurture the idea that I could possibly write a book. I also say, "thank you" to Jerry Jenkins, Cecil Murphy, and other seasoned authors, who will not remember me from the other hundreds of people you have encouraged at various writers' conferences. I took in and hung on to every word of advice you gave.

Thank you to authors C. Kevin Thompson, Barbara Hattemer, Jeannette Watt, Joe Stinson, Mark Hancock, and Russell Jarvis who participated in our initial writer's group in 2009. I finally finished.

To Dr. Tapiwa Mucherera, my other professors, and fellow classmates at Asbury Theological Seminary, who prayed for me and poured into my life to help me find the Healer and the healing that I needed.

A heartfelt thanks to my friends Anita D. Williams, Wendy Webb, and others who listened to me endlessly when I needed to talk. You let me know that true friendship is not about what you've done, but who you are as a person.

Thank you to my police families and my Christian Methodist Episcopal (CME) church family. Your support is invaluable. To Dr. Charles Roesel, Pastor Emeritus, First Baptist Church Leesburg, Florida, thank you for your faithfulness. It truly is a God thing.

To Edward Poetry and the members of the Charles Houston Community Writers, you gave me the final kick to help cross the finish line. You also helped me see that this is not the end, but the beginning.

Finally, to everyone whose name is not listed individually, but you helped nudge me, supported me, or read and helped edit a draft copy of the manuscript, I am truly grateful for what you have done.

Multiplied Blessings,
Alfreda

Helpful Resources

National Sexual Assault Hotline: National hotline, that serves people affected by sexual violence. Hotline: 800. 656.HOPE https://www.rainn.org.

National Sexual Violence Resource Center: This site offers a wide variety of information relating to sexual violence including a large legal resource library. https://www.nsvrc.org.

National Domestic Violence Hotline: Advocates provide local direct service resources and crisis intervention.
Hotline: 800. 799.SAFE
http://www.thehotline.org.

Survivors of Incest Anonymous: Provides information on incest survivor support groups and empowers individuals to become survivors and thrivers.
http://www.siawso.org.

National Alliance on Mental Illness Provides information and referral services, not counseling. Helpline: 888. 950.NAMI - https://www.nami.org.

Alfreda S. Jackson lives in both Florida and Northern Virginia. *Old Enough To Know Better* is her debut novel, based on the true life story of the author. She welcomes readers to visit her website, www.alfreda-jackson.com.